HEART OF

Hope

Women of Tenacity Series, Book 2

by
USA Today Bestselling Author
SHANNA HATFIELD

Heart of Hope
Women of Tenacity, Book 2
Originally titled Country Boy vs. City Girl

Copyright © 2011 by Shanna Hatfield

ISBN: 9798611379219

For permission requests, please contact the author, with a subject line of "permission request" at the e-mail address below or through her website.
shanna@shannahatfield.com
shannahatfield.com

To those who learn
the fine art
of meeting in the middle.

Books by Shanna Hatfield

FICTION

CONTEMPORARY

Holiday Brides
Valentine Bride
Summer Bride
Easter Bride

Rodeo Romance
The Christmas Cowboy
Wrestlin' Christmas
Capturing Christmas
Barreling Through Christmas
Chasing Christmas
Racing Christmas
Keeping Christmas

Grass Valley Cowboys
The Cowboy's Christmas Plan
The Cowboy's Spring Romance
The Cowboy's Summer Love
The Cowboy's Autumn Fall
The Cowboy's New Heart
The Cowboy's Last Goodbye

Friendly Beasts of Faraday
Scent of Cedar
Tidings of Joy
Boughs of Holly
Wings of An Angel

Silverton Sweethearts
The Coffee Girl
The Christmas Crusade
Untangling Christmas

Women of Tenacity
Heart of Clay
Heart of Hope
Heart of Love

HISTORICAL

Pendleton Petticoats

Dacey	*Lacey*
Aundy	*Bertie*
Caterina	*Millie*
Ilsa	*Dally*
Marnie	*Quinn*
	Evie

Baker City Brides
Tad's Treasure
Crumpets and Cowpies
Thimbles and Thistles
Corsets and Cuffs
Bobbins and Boots
Lightning and Lawmen
Dumplings and Dynamite

Hearts of the War
Garden of Her Heart
Home of Her Heart
Dream of Her Heart

Gifts of Christmas
Gift of Grace
Gift of Hope
Gift of Faith

Hardman Holidays
The Christmas Bargain
The Christmas Token
The Christmas Calamity
The Christmas Vow
The Christmas Quandary
The Christmas Confection
The Christmas Melody
The Christmas Ring

Prologue

Josh Carver glanced around the spacious living room of his hosts' apartment and inwardly groaned.

Phil and Amelia Granger were good friends and clients, but he detested their parties. The guest list generally included haughty socialites, snide women in full man-hunting gear, pretentious executives, and conceited ladder-climbers.

So far, the group milling around the room proved even worse than his already low expectations.

Josh silently observed Byron Jenkins, a particularly obnoxious investment banker who handled the Granger's accounts, as he attempted to palm a young woman. Unlike most of the women in attendance, this one was dressed in a surprisingly tasteful dark blue gown.

The girl skillfully sidestepped Byron's groping hands as she worked her way toward the kitchen, no doubt seeking a means of escape.

From his position next to the buffet table, Josh couldn't see her face. As he studied her, he contemplated if she was someone new to the usual crowd. Distracted by the woman, he absently picked up an appetizer and popped it in his mouth.

Josh nearly choked on the nasty tidbit when she turned around. Soft, inviting lips and appealing curves made him want to meet her.

Quickly swallowing the appetizer that held all the flavor of sawdust, he popped a mint into his mouth, hoping to dislodge the bad taste Amelia's hors d'oeuvres left behind.

When Byron draped his arm around the woman's shoulders, Josh felt an inexplicable need to rescue her. He'd been clawed, petted, and pawed at enough of these parties to know what a nightmare it could be.

She shrugged off Byron's arm and spun around, bumping into Josh's chest as he approached them. He gazed down at her, drawn to the honest, natural appearance of her face, framed by shoulder-length brown hair.

Refusing to look at the detestable banker, he smiled at the woman. "My apologies, Mr. Jenkins, but I'm in dire need of this lady's immediate assistance."

Byron glared at him, but took a step back.

Josh held out his arm to the woman and inclined his head toward the kitchen. "Shall we?"

"Yes, thank you." Without any hesitation, she took his proffered arm and walked with him inside the kitchen.

She pointed to a small patio door, so he escorted her outside into the fading evening light, away from the noise and annoyances of the party. Quietly closing the door behind them, he leaned against the balcony railing, appreciating the view of the Portland skyline from the high-rise terrace.

Pleased to escape the party with such a lovely companion, Josh stuck out his hand and offered a friendly smile. "I'm Josh Carver."

She grasped his large hand in her small one, sending currents zinging up his arm, and gazed at him with the warmest brown eyes he'd ever seen. It was like dipping into a pool of molten chocolate. And Josh was quite partial to all things chocolate.

"Thank you, Mr. Carver, for coming to my rescue. I'm Jenna Keaton."

Josh liked the strength and confidence in her voice. She sounded and acted like a no-nonsense kind of person.

"I'm glad to be of service, Miss Keaton. I'm not in the habit of stretching the truth, but I did sincerely hope you'd help me escape the party, at least for a moment or two. What brings you to Phil and Amelia's this evening?" he asked, genuinely interested in knowing more about the lovely girl.

She took a step away from him and appeared to gather her thoughts before she spoke. "Phil and Amelia are my aunt and uncle. I just moved here a few days ago to start a new job on Monday and they insisted I join them for the party this evening. Aunt Amelia said it would be a great opportunity to meet people. However, if Mr. Jenkins is any indication, I don't think I'm in a hurry to make too many acquaintances. That man has the mind of a guttersnipe and the hands of an octopus."

Jenna's smile, full of humor and warmth, did funny things to Josh's ability to concentrate on anything but her when she looked at him.

"Phil and Amelia mean well," Josh hurried to offer his reassurance. At more than one of their parties, he'd been unwillingly paired with women he had no interest in dating and could only imagine who Amelia would try to set Jenna up with. "I think they miss having their kids around now that they've all flown the coop. I'm sure they'll enjoy having you here in town."

"Those cousins of mine couldn't have scattered any further if they'd tried. With Ben in New York, Jane in Miami, and Cory in Dallas, it keeps Aunt Amelia busy planning trips to visit them."

Josh laughed, feeling oddly at ease around Jenna. He fought the urge to reach out and tuck a stray lock of hair behind her ear as they continued hiding on the balcony, secluded from the party crowd. Instead of giving in to his longing to touch her, he offered her a charming smile.

"So, Miss Jenna Keaton, you mentioned starting a new job on Monday. If it isn't too presumptuous, may I ask where?" Josh liked this niece of the Grangers, much more than his common sense told him he should. He had no intention of getting involved with anyone, especially a girl as sweet and appealing as the one playing hooky from the party with him.

"I'll be working in the human resources department at the new state building. I enjoy the work and it was a good time for me to get out of Seattle. So here I am, at a boring party with a bunch of stuffy people all bent on impressing each other with their money, credentials, or lies." Jenna's eyes took on a teasing twinkle, and she tipped her head

4

to the side, studying Josh. "Which category would you fall into?"

"I beg your pardon?" Josh wasn't sure how to respond to this straight-talking girl with an engaging, bright smile.

"Are you here to impress people with your money, credentials, or fabricated stories?" Jenna repeated, tossing a sassy grin in his direction.

"None of the above." Josh gave Jenna a questioning glance. Uncertain what information she hoped to unearth about him, he had no idea what motive spurred her to ask such a thing. "Your uncle will tell you I'm a terrible liar. My only credentials are that I'm good at what I do, and I try to be an honest, upright kind of guy. As for the money I slave away to earn, it would be pocket change for many of the people inside."

Jenna laughed and motioned for him to take a seat on one of the patio chairs. They watched inky darkness encompass the evening, talking much longer than they realized.

They both turned with a start when Amelia finally breezed outside and sighed dramatically, hands thrown into the air.

"Well, good gracious. Phil and I have looked everywhere for you two, and here you are. I'm so glad you met each other. Jenna, you did meet Josh, didn't you? Isn't he just the nicest boy?" Amelia gushed as she waited for Josh and Jenna to return inside the kitchen.

"Yes, Aunt Amelia, we met. It seems I'll be working just a few blocks from him, so we planned on meeting for lunch Thursday."

"Splendid." Amelia clapped her hands together gleefully as she waltzed through the kitchen back to the crowd in the living room.

While Jenna watched her aunt's theatrics, Josh glanced at her. Although she wasn't a raving beauty, something about her captured his interest, something he found very appealing and attractive. She looked fresh, unaffected, and altogether alluring.

Hastily sticking his hand into his coat pocket, Josh pulled out one of his business cards and handed it to her. "If you need anything, please feel free to give me a call. It can be hard getting established in a new place."

Jenna took the card and placed it in the small evening bag she retrieved from a kitchen chair along with her sweater. "Thank you. I appreciate your offer and I look forward to having lunch with you next week," she said as they walked out of the kitchen. "As soon as I tell Amelia and Phil goodbye, I'm going to call it a night. It really was very nice to meet you."

"If you don't mind, I'll come with you to find your aunt and uncle and say good night." Josh looked down at her with a smile that brought the dimple in his cheek out of hiding and had persuaded any number of women to surrender to his charms.

Phil and Amelia stood at the front door, chatting with a couple ready to leave.

"Thank you both for this evening, but I'm going back to my apartment," Jenna said as she gave first Amelia and then Phil a hug.

"I need to be going as well." Josh shook Phil's

hand and kissed Amelia's cheek. "Thank you for inviting me. As always, it's a pleasure to see you both."

"Anytime, Josh." Amelia walked with them out the door into the hall. "Jenna, dear, why don't I have someone drive you home? I don't want you out alone after dark, especially since the city is so new to you."

"I'd be happy to take Jenna home." Josh heard himself volunteer as they arrived at the elevator. He hadn't planned to see her home, but now that he'd offered, it seemed like a great plan. He liked the idea of spending more time with the engaging woman. "I think her apartment isn't that far from mine, so it wouldn't be any trouble."

"If you're sure?" Amelia questioned. When Josh nodded, she turned to Jenna, "Would that be agreeable to you, dear?"

"Yes, Aunt Amelia, it would be just fine." Jenna kissed her aunt's cheek and strode into the elevator. Josh kept step close behind her.

As they rode down to the lobby, he talked about some of his favorite places in the neighborhood near their apartments. When they sauntered out of the building, Josh held Jenna's sweater for her while she slipped it on. Gently, he placed his hand on her back and guided her to a shiny black sports car parked across the street. The innocent contact made his fingers burn and tingle.

"Nice wheels." Jenna appeared impressed as she surveyed his car. He held the door open for her and gave her a hand as she settled onto the leather seat. "What is it you said you did for a living?"

"I sell cars." Josh grinned as he slid behind the wheel. "I find this particular machine makes a great mobile business card. People ask me all the time where I got my car. It's easy to segue into where I work and what I do."

"Very smart," Jenna agreed, surveying their surroundings as Josh started the car and the engine roared to life. "That's how you know my aunt and uncle, isn't it? They buy new cars as often as most people buy shoes. You must do well selling cars."

"I get by," Josh said, with his sincere humbleness.

He worked hard to be the best in his career. He built relationships with his clients, getting to know them not just as people who provided a healthy income, but also on a personal level. Years ago, he learned that caring about his clients resulted in their loyalty and gave him a sense of purpose. That simple work ethic made him the top salesperson for five of the eight years he'd been at a luxury car dealership in Portland.

Fresh out of college with a degree in business management, Josh charmed his way into a job as a novice car peddler. The combination of his honesty, business savvy, good looks, and friendly personality quickly pushed him to the forefront as a man people trusted, a novelty in the world of car salespeople.

He had a reputation for only selling people what they wanted or needed and had never talked anyone into something he didn't think would be a good fit for them. The six-figure income he earned was icing on the cake.

"Give me directions to your apartment and I'll

take you there." Josh pulled into traffic. "Unless there's anywhere else you want to stop."

Jenna looked at Josh in her matter-of-fact manner. "Actually, I'm starving. Would you want to join me for dinner? The food Aunt Amelia serves at her parties is absolutely ridiculous."

Laughter burst out of Josh and he gave her a conspiring glance. "Just for that, I'm buying. Where would you like to go?"

"Anywhere, as long as its edible." Jenna grinned at him as he sped through the evening traffic.

Ten minutes later, he pulled into the parking lot of his favorite steakhouse.

As they stepped inside, the hostess greeted Josh by name. "Good evening, Mr. Carver. Nice to see you again. Table for two?"

"Yes, please," Josh said as he and Jenna followed the hostess to a booth.

"Will this be satisfactory?" the hostess asked.

"This is perfect, thank you." Josh waited for Jenna to sit down before sliding into the booth.

"You must either leave quite an impression or come here often." Jenna picked up a menu and glanced around the restaurant.

"Maybe both," Josh teased, as he took a sip of water.

Enthralled with each other, they lingered long after they'd finished their meal. Finally realizing the lateness of the hour, Josh took Jenna home, walking with her to her apartment door, making sure she arrived safely.

"Thank you for having dinner with me," Josh

said, as she unlocked the door. "It was a very pleasant surprise to meet you tonight."

After opening her door and flipping on the light, Jenna turned to Josh. "Thank you for feeding a starving newcomer to the city and for extending your friendship. I really appreciate it."

"You're most welcome. It's the least I can do." Josh began to lose himself in the warm chocolate pools staring back at him. Scrambling to think of some reason to keep her talking, he couldn't come up with a single thing. Briefly, he considered what she'd do if he kissed her, but forced his feet to move back a step.

She moved inside and started to close the door. Before she did, she looked up at him with a happy smile. "I'm already looking forward to lunch Thursday. Thanks again and good night."

After closing the door, Jenna released a long breath and leaned against the wood. Her knees felt as solid as overheated gelatin and she needed a minute to gather her composure.

When she'd looked up at the party and saw Josh, the description "tall, dark, and incredibly handsome" entered her thoughts. She chided herself for thinking in terms of clichés, even if it was true.

Josh Carver was a gorgeous man. Despite several attractive males in attendance at the party, it was hard to overlook his broad chest, impeccably covered by an expensive pewter-gray suit jacket, crisp white shirt, and deep blue silk tie. His face was worthy of a magazine cover, highlighted by luminous gray eyes and raven black hair. Generous lips parted in a smile that revealed a deep dimple in his left cheek and rendered her lightheaded.

The hours they'd spent together hadn't told her a lot about him, but she'd already discovered him to be mannerly and kind. He was younger than she thought at first. At dinner, she'd learned he was thirty, the same age as her, but he seemed older and wiser than his years.

And he was breath-stealing handsome, not that looks mattered, but she couldn't help but admire his. Josh was the kind of guy who could get under her skin and into her carefully guarded heart. Urban, successful, gorgeous, and fun with a charismatic personality were characteristics she assumed she'd never find all in one man. Josh's unique combination created a temptation she might find hard to resist.

Regardless of her concerns, it didn't take long for Josh and Jenna to begin seeing each other regularly. In spite her plans to stay focused on her career and his vow to avoid involvement in a committed relationship, they couldn't stay away from each other.

Spring progressed to summer as he took her to plays and concerts. They visited museums and art galleries, savored meals at bistros, strolled through parks, and wandered through some of the most exclusive boutique shopping districts in town. They dined and danced, enjoying all the urbane adventures the city had to offer.

He took her to a few family gatherings an hour away in Tenacity, Oregon, where he learned Jenna didn't possess any enthusiasm for country life. Josh grew up in the small rural community where his family maintained their agricultural roots. He enjoyed the trips home. It gave him an opportunity to savor deep breaths of clean air, hear the birds chirp, and look out over miles of fields without a single skyscraper in sight.

One weekend, he drove with her to Seattle to meet her family and see where she had grown up in the midst of all the cultural charms offered in the city. Jenna embraced the excitement and hustle, the steady motion of moving crowds, the sounds of traffic, and the smells wafting in from the waterfront. There was no doubt in his mind she was a city girl.

On a warm Saturday in early fall, Josh asked Jenna to go for a drive and told her to dress casually. They headed out of Portland, enjoying the sunny day and one another's company.

Jenna assumed they were going to visit Josh's family and he made no effort to correct her. He had other plans. Big plans. They were nearly to the road to turn toward his sister's house when he pulled off the highway onto a paved road. They drove for a few miles before turning down a gravel road.

Josh drove up to a dilapidated farmhouse and stopped the car.

He hurried around to the passenger side, opened her door, and gave Jenna his hand. She stepped out of the car, appearing cute and casual in a pair of jeans and sneakers. Clearly curious, she looked around.

"What are we doing out here, Josh?"

Fully aware of her aversion to dust, dirt, and anything rural or remotely countryfied, he offered her an encouraging smile and squeezed her hand. Jenna gave him a long, studying glance, as though she just noticed he was dressed in faded jeans, scuffed boots, and a western shirt instead of the suits she was accustomed to seeing him wear.

"Josh? What's going on? Why are we here?" she asked, frowning at the derelict house and ramshackle barn in the background.

"I've got something I want to ask you and something I need to tell you." Nervously, he removed the ball cap on his head and ran a hand through his thick black hair.

As he stared into her mesmerizing brown eyes, Josh tried to remember the speech he'd worked so hard to prepare but couldn't bring to mind a single word. Determined, he put his hat back on and took her hands in his. Without his speech, he decided to speak from his heart.

"Jenna, you may or may not know how much I've come to dislike living in the city. I hate the crowds, the traffic, the noise, the superfluous trappings and activities. I can't breathe there anymore. I knew all along that I didn't want to be a car salesman forever. It was just a means to an end. A way to save money until I figured out what I want to do with my life. Now I know." Josh gazed at Jenna with a pleading expression that begged her to understand.

"I had no idea how much you hated your life in the city," Jenna said, genuinely surprised. "I suppose you've mentioned some things in the past and I may not have paid as much attention as I should have. Do you really dislike Portland so much?"

"I do."

"But, Josh, things have been so perfect these past months. Like my perfect dream of the perfect romance."

"I'm glad to hear that, Jenna," he smiled at her with tenderness, struggling to hold onto his courage. "You see, I… um…"

"If this is your way of breaking up with me, you sure picked a rotten, pathetic place to do it," she said, flapping a hand at the house behind them.

He couldn't believe she'd just suggested he'd dragged her all the way out here to end their relationship. "I'm not breaking up with you. Just the opposite."

She eyed him warily. "Go on."

"You're a straight-shooter, you tell it like it is, so I'm going to do the same." Josh willed his heart to stop pounding as he shared his dreams with the woman he had come to love. "I can't keep living in the city. The one place in this world where I am happiest is outside, in the country. This may come as a shock, but I want to farm. I want to live here, where it's peaceful, where the air is clean, where I can hear myself think. I want to buy this land, this very piece of land we are standing on, build a house and a barn, and farm."

Jenna's eyes grew wide and her mouth formed a perfect "O" as she stared at him like he'd started speaking in languages she didn't comprehend.

When she regained the ability to speak, she narrowed her eyes and shook her head. "Does this have anything to do with the two weeks when you came back here during the summer?" Jenna referred to the time Josh spent helping his brother-in-law's family during wheat harvest.

Every year, he took time off work to help. He finally realized he enjoyed those two weeks of hard work more than anything else he did the rest of the year. Josh liked the physical labor, the smells, the sounds, everything about it. This year after harvest, when he returned to his job and life in Portland, he couldn't stop thinking about how much he really wanted to farm.

"Yes, Jenna, it does. It helped me figure out what I really want to do with my life. I want to work the land, out in the fresh air, and live life as a farmer." Josh prayed Jenna would at least try to understand why he needed to make this life-altering change. "But there is more than that."

"More?" Jenna questioned, looking at him as though he'd gone off the deep end and lost his mind. He could almost see her thinking only someone completely mad would plan to abandon a fruitful career to be a farmer, of all things.

Mindful of the questions and doubt on her face, Josh had to plunge ahead or face losing the best thing that had ever happened to him.

"I not only want to buy this land, build a house, and try my hand at farming, but I also want you here beside me." Josh dropped down on one knee and pulled a small velvet box from his pocket. When he opened the lid, a beautiful diamond glittered in the sunlight. "Jenna, I love you. I love everything about you. I'm deeply, madly, and completely in love with you. Will you please marry me?"

Still down on one knee, Josh waited for Jenna to say something, anything. Instead, she stared at him and the ring while tears gathered in her eyes.

Caught completely off-guard by his declaration and proposal, Jenna couldn't think let alone speak.

He wanted to marry her.

That was the only part of the entire crazy conversation penetrating the fog in her brain.

Slowly nodding her head, she took Josh's free hand in hers and gave it a tug. He stood and slipped the ring on her finger then gave her a kiss that made her forget everything. In his arms, she found the one place in the world where she truly belonged.

Regardless of her misgivings, Jenna was about to make peace with all things rural and become a farm wife.

The country boy had won her city girl heart.

Chapter One

Six and a Half Years Later

Josh Carver kept an eye on the hay he swathed as it fed into the front of the machine. He loved the smell of fresh cut hay, loved to watch a field fall into neat windrows as he went through an honest day's work as a farmer.

The best thing he'd ever done was purchase the farm and quit his job in Portland as a luxury car salesman.

Correction. The second best.

The single best thing he'd ever done was convince Jenna Keaton to become his bride. It had taken no small amount of effort on his part.

Even though she agreed to marry him, she decided she would never, ever adjust to life as a farmer's wife. She called off their engagement three times before Josh convinced her she could continue to work in the city. He promised to take her to plays and concerts. He even refrained from burning his suits so he'd have something to wear when they attended one of her aunt and uncle's parties.

After resigning from his position at the car

dealership, he traded in his sports car for a new extended cab pickup and a used flatbed truck. Josh poured his savings into the land he purchased right after he proposed to Jenna.

He added a shop so he could start making repairs and progress on the land. As soon as spring arrived, work began on the house. It was finished just a few months after their wedding before the first hard frost that fall. The next additions were a barn and storage shed followed by a hay shed.

When the fifteen acres at the end of their road came up for sale, Josh purchased it, giving them nearly five hundred acres of hay and wheat ground as well as pasture for the herd of registered Hereford cattle he worked diligently to build.

The business of farming proved more of an investment than Josh anticipated. Although he owned the land and structures, it took a sizeable loan to purchase the farm equipment he needed, and that was buying everything used. He started a custom haying business on the side. The income from that helped whittle away the debt.

Before they wed, Jenna declared not one penny of her hard-earned money would go into the farm. She insisted they maintain separate banking accounts and nearly separate lives. She kept her apartment, refusing to leave until the new house was completely finished.

If Josh wanted to see her, he did so on her terms. For months, he commuted to Portland, eager to be with his bride. The day they moved into the spacious new home, almost a year after he proposed, Jenna's resistance to the farm began to waver.

As Josh started spring farm work and tried to find ways to involve her, she became more interested in the farm. The newborn Hereford calf he gave her for Easter that spring obliterated her resolve to stay out of the farming business. She merged their accounts and, in so doing, finally committed to fully entwining their hearts and lives.

Josh grinned as he thought about his wife. She'd gone from her manicured nails, high heels, and a fear of all things rural to being able to drive the tractor, set irrigation water, and wear ugly rubber boots and a ball cap without having a meltdown.

Jenna learned to put up with the dust and dirt of country life and became a real help to him as he pursued his dreams.

Not that she'd given up her own dreams. She poured herself into her career and it paid off. Recently promoted to a training and development specialist for the state, Jenna would travel extensively in her new career, visiting various branch offices throughout Oregon while training individuals and offering support services.

Her first trip in the position was to Washington D.C. for three weeks of training before she assumed full duties of the new position. It nearly doubled her salary, but Josh wasn't sure he could get used to her being gone so often.

She was due back tomorrow afternoon and he'd missed her tremendously. Although she occasionally traveled with her former position, gone for a day or two at a time, he would never get used to having her away for days on end. Three weeks was approximately twenty days more than he wanted to think about her being gone. The house and farm seemed so lonesome without her there.

He glanced across the road, proud of the house he built for his bride. Painted light tan with dark red shutters and white trim, the Dutch-gabled farmhouse looked homey and inviting with a deep porch and wide front steps. An attached garage kept Jenna out of the weather and her car relatively clean.

When they moved into the house, Josh half-jokingly told Jenna he planned to fill every one of the upstairs bedrooms with babies.

She glared at him as though he'd physically struck her. "No kids, Josh. I can't do kids and a career. I just can't," she said and walked away.

He supposed children, or her lack of interest in them, might have been a good topic to discuss before they got married. Nevertheless, he figured when the time was right, Jenna would come around. He'd been patient, waiting for just the right time to broach the subject again, but in the past five years, the time hadn't seemed right.

Since they were both in their mid-thirties, he hoped to make some headway soon. However, Jenna's new job would definitely put a damper on his baby-making plans.

Lost in his thoughts, Josh jolted back to reality when the swather made a loud clunking noise, indicating a problem. He shut down the machine and climbed out of the air-conditioned cab, closing the door to keep the cool inside. It took him no time to dig out a plug then look to make sure everything else was in good working order.

He found a piece of barbed wire wrapped around the sickle bar and gently tugged it loose. Annoyed, he wondered how many years it would take before he finally picked up all the junk the previous owners randomly tossed out around the place.

One field on the back of the original homestead had been full of golf balls. He didn't want to know how they came to be there, but his nieces, Audrey and Emma, had a great time running around picking them up in baskets like Easter eggs. He still occasionally unearthed one when he irrigated the field.

Tin cans, metal scraps, and old appliances scattered across another field. He hauled truckload after truckload off as scrap metal before he could work and plant the ground. It was no wonder he got such a great price on the place.

His family jumped right in and helped him clean up the unbelievable mess the former owners left behind. His sister, Callan, and her husband, Clay, provided hours and hours of free labor along with equipment borrowed from Clay's parents who owned one of the biggest ranches in the area. Clay's cousin, Jake, often came and lent a hand, as did Josh's dad, Big Jim.

Josh didn't give too much thought to the fact his older brother, Bob, had yet to set foot on the place. Bob was nineteen years his senior and Josh had never liked or respected the man. The less he saw of Bob, the better. He and his wife, Donna, weren't the kind of people anyone enjoyed being around.

When Josh first introduced Jenna to his family, she and Callan hit it off immediately. Now, they were close friends and often planned fun activities together. Clay and Josh had been friends for years and, as Josh learned about farming, he appreciated the experience and wisdom his brother-in-law offered.

Carefully climbing out from under the machine, Josh took off his ball cap and gloves, setting them on the swather step. He tugged off his T-shirt and wiped at the sweat streaming down his face and chest. It was certainly warm for early May. With a mild winter and an early spring, the hay had been ready to cut earlier this year than usual.

Hot and thirsty, Josh wished he'd remembered to bring along something to drink. Rather than take a break, he decided to get back to work and finish this field along with one at the end of their road today. He wanted to have plenty of time to spend with Jenna when she arrived home.

He swiped his soggy shirt across his face and looked across the road again. A profusion of colorful flowers bloomed in baskets hanging from the porch and in beds along the front of the house. He promised Jenna he would faithfully water her flowers while she was gone and so far had only forgotten to water them twice. Although he had farming in his blood, Jenna had gardening in hers. He willingly gave her full credit for doing all the work in the yard that made their house an inviting home.

Josh thought he might be hallucinating from the heat as a familiar figure walked across the lawn in his direction.

It couldn't be Jenna. She wasn't due home until tomorrow. Maybe he'd lost a day somewhere. He frantically tried to remember if he'd left any major messes in the house and concluded only his lunch dishes in the sink and yesterday's dirty clothes on the bedroom floor could get him into trouble.

Convinced he wasn't seeing things and it really was his wife, he jumped over the fence and jogged across the road.

"Babe." His voice sounded husky as he swept Jenna into a tight hug and swung her around in a wide circle. He breathed in her warm vanilla scent, soaking in the sight of her. "I'm so happy to see you. You've been gone for half of forever."

Jenna laughed as he held her close, enjoying the feel of being in his arms again. There was no place on earth she liked better than in Josh's strong and capable arms. Three weeks was too long to be away from him.

"Oh, I bet you didn't miss me at all." She offered him a teasing smile when he finally set her back on her feet, feeling a little off-balance by his affectionate welcome. She inhaled his unique masculine scent, mixed with sweat and the smell of fresh cut hay. The combination was oddly appealing.

"You have no idea how very much I missed you," Josh said in a gravelly voice. He placed his hands on either side of her face and lowered his head, claiming her lips in a kiss that assured her how very much she was missed. "I love you so much. Always have, always will."

"Josh, what's gotten into you?" She took a step back and tried to catch her breath as her heart began to beat in an accelerated tempo.

Her training wrapped up a day early and she couldn't wait to see Josh. She flew into Portland that morning, ran by the office to complete some required paperwork, stopped at the grocery store, then hurried home. As she drove down their road, she watched Josh slide under the swather. After unloading the groceries, she traded her business suit for a T-shirt and shorts, made a pitcher of lemonade, and started over to see if he could take a break.

As she walked across the front yard, she was surprised he jumped across the fence shirtless and hatless. She wouldn't ever grow tired of watching him move and work. Swarthy was the word that best described him. If he had a flowing white shirt, sash at his waist, and an eye patch, he could easily be mistaken for a swashbuckling pirate.

Tall and muscular with olive-toned skin, broad shoulders, and narrow hips, she had mistakenly thought he was a dignified urbanite when they were dating. Little did she know that beneath those expensive tailored suits hid a finely sculpted body of someone accustomed to hard physical labor.

Josh could be polished and refined when he dressed in his "city duds," as he liked to call them.

Despite what she thought she wanted when they were dating, she much preferred seeing him relaxed and at peace in the country. Jenna long ago decided that her husband was most wickedly handsome when he was dressed as he was today in snug jeans, shirtless, with scuffed boots.

The swanky goatee he grew while she was gone pushed his raw appeal up to a completely new level and drew her attention from his bare chest to his chin.

She took another step back to study it and tilted her head from side to side, trying to decide if she merely liked it or absolutely loved it.

Josh caught her studying gaze and stuck out his chin, rubbing his whiskers with his hand. He turned his profile to her and smirked.

"What do you think? Does it add to my dashing good looks?" He shot her a roguish grin.

"You are too cocky for your own good, Josh Carver," Jenna said in a feigned huff. "Just for that, you can get back to work while I enjoy a glass of cold lemonade."

Jenna turned and managed to take two steps toward the house before Josh grabbed her around her waist and swept her into his arms.

"Not without me you don't." His lips plundered hers as he carried her into the house. He loved holding Jenna close in his arms every bit as much as she enjoyed being held close to his heart.

After walking inside the front door, Josh set Jenna on her feet then stooped to pull off his boots in the foyer, leaving his soggy T-shirt there as well. He followed Jenna through the cool of the house to the kitchen, surprised to see a plate of sugar cookies on the counter along with two glasses.

"Looks like you were expecting company,"

Josh teased, raising an eyebrow at the treat. As he stepped over to the sink to wash his filthy hands, he noticed the trail of hay leaves and dust floating behind him. Shooting his wife a panicked glance, he started to backtrack and apologize but Jenna waved her hand at him.

"It's fine, Josh. Wash up and sit down. A little hay and dust won't throw me completely off kilter." Jenna smiled as she poured the lemonade.

Surprised at her acceptance of the dirt, Josh washed his hands then sat on one of the swiveling bar stools. Jenna usually pitched a fit if he dragged any mess inside the house, but she didn't seem concerned at all today. Maybe she missed him more than she cared to admit.

"I want to hear all about your trip." Josh leaned back and munched on a cookie. He listened to her talk about the training, the people she met, and places she visited. He sensed there was something she refrained from telling him, but she'd get around to it when she was ready. Josh glanced at the kitchen clock and decided he better get back to swathing. The afternoon was half-gone and he still had a lot of work to do.

"Thanks for the break, babe." Josh set his dirty glass in the sink and wrapped Jenna in another hug. "I'm so glad you're home. If you want, I'll take you out for dinner tonight."

"I'd rather stay right here, with you." Jenna pulled his head down for a sizzling kiss that made them both struggle to catch their breath when they finally broke apart. "I can't tell you how nice it is to be home. The peacefulness of your wretched farm has finally gotten to me. I'd forgotten how loud cities can be at night."

"That just goes to show what good clean living can do for you," Josh joked as he walked to the front door. While he tugged on his boots, she ran into their bedroom and snagged a clean T-shirt for him.

"Your other shirt doesn't look like it will make it through the rest of the day and we can't have you showing off all your goods to anyone who might drive by," Jenna teased, holding out the shirt, emblazoned with a logo from a popular implement dealer.

Josh yanked on the shirt and smiled down at her. "Who would drive by since we're the only people who live on this dead-end road? You're not worried about unexpected visitors. The problem is you've been gone so long, Mrs. Carver, that you've forgotten just how irresistible your husband can be. Admit it. You're utterly overwhelmed by my dashing good looks and considerable charm."

"Oh, you conceited thing." Jenna swatted the seat of his attractive posterior and gave him a shove toward the door. "Don't you have some hay that needs your attention?"

Before Josh sauntered out the door, he turned back and gave Jenna one more long kiss, their lips tasting of lemonade and sugar. "I love you, babe. Welcome home."

She watched him jog across the road and waved when he climbed back in the swather's cab.

Josh finished cutting the field just before dinner and called Jenna on his cell phone.

"Hey, babe, can you come pick me up? I want to move the swather to the field across from the Harold place so it will be ready to go in the morning," Josh asked when Jenna answered the phone.

"Sure. I'll be right there," Jenna said. Josh heard the clatter of a lid on a pot in the background. "Just let me turn off the oven."

Josh drove the swather to a field at the far end of their property. The acreage he'd purchased at the end of the road belonged to a man named Henry Harold, so now he and Jenna referred to the property as the Harold place.

In addition to the small acreage, it included a four-room house and a barn with a corral. When Josh hired extra help, the house would come in handy. As it was, he hoped to hire some help for the summer and planned to discuss the possibility with Jenna.

After shutting down the swather, he climbed out and walked across the culvert at the entrance into the field. He waited a few minutes for Jenna to arrive. When she failed to appear, he started walking toward home. Although it wasn't quite a mile, he was tired and didn't relish the thought of trekking home in the heat. He'd gone about a quarter-mile when Jenna charged down the road on their four-wheeler.

The first time he tried to get her to drive it, she refused to go faster than ten miles an hour because it stirred up too much dust. Now, she drove it with dust billowing around her, as if she was in some kind of race and planned to win. She turned the four-wheeler around, stopped in front of him, and slid back so he could drive.

"I thought maybe you forgot about me." He looked over his shoulder at her as he shifted into gear and drove home. "Either that or you decided to make sure I was exhausted by the time I got in the door and too tired to consider any extra-curricular activities this evening."

"Neither one." Jenna hugged him around the waist and scooted closer, resting her cheek against his back. "Callan called as I was walking out the door and I couldn't hang up on her."

"Why not?" Josh questioned jokingly. "It's not like the two of you don't talk every day as it is."

Josh stopped by the back door and gave Jenna his hand as she climbed off the four-wheeler. He stepped off and stomped his boots to dislodge some of the dust then they walked into the mudroom. He removed his dirty clothes before entering the house.

"Do I have time to take a shower?" He paused in the kitchen as Jenna washed her hands at the sink.

"If you make it quick. Dinner is more than ready. I'll have it on the table in a minute," she said, hurrying to dry her hands and push a pan back onto a warm burner.

"Quick, got it." Josh hustled into their bedroom, jumped into a shower, and washed away the dirt and grime of the day. He might not mind being hot, sweaty, and dirty most of the time but he liked to be clean when he ate dinner and spent time with his best girl.

In five minutes, he was back in the kitchen,

dressed in clean jeans and a T-shirt, smelling of soap and his aftershave. Jenna wondered how he could have possibly shaved that fast and quickly looked to make sure he still sported the goatee. To her relief, it still beckoned to her. She might have to mention to Josh how much she liked it.

After setting their plates on the counter, they sank onto the bar stools and Josh gave thanks for their meal.

"So, what did that sister of mine want?" Josh asked as he picked up a piece of warm buttered bread and took a bite.

"She had some good news." Jenna turned to him excitedly. "Some very good news."

"Is it final?" Josh set down his fork and bread, looking at Jenna. "It's all finished?"

"Yes! The judge finalized the paperwork this afternoon. Isn't it amazing?" Jenna sighed in happiness over the good news Callan shared.

For the past sixteen months, Callan and Clay had been guardians of their two young nieces. They spent the better part of the last year trying to adopt the girls. The proceedings would have gone smoothly and ended quickly except for the involvement of Callan and Josh's brother Bob and his wife. For unknown reasons, they fought the adoption every step of the way.

Bob and Donna's only child, Melanie, ran off with a drummer she met in a club in Portland. She left behind signed divorce papers as well as documents granting all parental rights for her two daughters, Audrey and Emma, to her husband. Ted tried to keep the girls for a few weeks but finally asked Callan and Clay if they would watch them for a while until he got back on his feet. Another month went by before he signed over parental rights to them and moved away.

Callan and Clay were thrilled. Not that Melanie and Ted abandoned the girls, but that they would finally be able to give Audrey and Emma a stable home. Since they were unable to have children of their own, they had often taken the girls on fun outings or invited them to spend the weekend.

Resolved to making the change permanent and legally binding, Callan and Clay filled out the necessary paperwork to adopt the girls.

With parental rights already signed over by both parents, it should have been a simple process, but Bob and Donna refused to let it happen. They didn't want to care for the girls, but they were adamant that Clay and Callan not adopt them. For months, they'd been tied up in court.

A few weeks ago, Callan and Josh's dad, Big Jim, had a little talk with Bob and Donna. Josh wished he could have been present to hear what his dad said. Whatever it was, Pop must have driven his point home because Bob and Donna suddenly decided it would be just fine for Callan and Clay to adopt the girls.

The judge made everything legal and official that very afternoon.

Josh was excited for Clay and Callan, but also for Audrey and Emma. Melanie and Ted had been unfit parents in every way imaginable. Despite what he, Jenna, Clay and Callan tried to do to help the girls, he knew they would probably always have some emotional scars from the time spent with their natural parents.

"Babe, that is awesome news," Josh said, picking up his fork and taking a bite of the casserole Jenna made for dinner. "We should celebrate this weekend."

"Callan is one step ahead of you, as always." Jenna tossed him a saucy grin. "They're planning a big barbecue at their place tomorrow evening and I said we wouldn't miss it. Do you think we should get a little present for the girls?"

"That's a great idea." Josh thought of ideas for an appropriate gift for two little girls who'd been awarded a new set of parents. Since he wasn't that familiar with what little girls liked, he deferred to Jenna. "Did you have something in mind?"

"I do, but I'm not sure we can find it in town. I may have to run into Portland to get it." Jenna stirred the food around on her plate. Josh generally had too much work to do to run into the city for no reason and disliked shopping almost as much as attending one of her aunt's lavish parties. "I don't suppose you could take the day off tomorrow and come with me. We could have lunch and enjoy the day."

"Babe, I wish I could, but the hay won't cut itself." Josh watched Jenna's big brown eyes fill with disappointment and changed his mind. "You know what, one day won't hurt. I'd love to spend tomorrow with you."

Jenna's eyes lit up and she gave his hand a squeeze. Leaning close to his ear, she kissed his cheek. "I'm so glad, Buck. I promise to make it worth your while."

Josh turned his full attention to his wife. She nicknamed him Buck, short for buccaneer, right after they wed. Once she'd gotten over the fact that he truly was not a city boy and had a bit of a wild rugged streak, she informed him he could have come right out of some pirate movie.

One day, he'd have to find an eye patch and sword and see what she thought of that. In the meantime, he enjoyed hearing her use the name. She didn't say it very often, but when she did, it always worked in his favor.

As he offered her a slow, sexy smile, he let himself fall into the warm chocolate depths of her eyes.

Jenna could feel the warmth start to pool in her belly and spread out to her fingers and toes when Josh turned the full power of his smile on her. She didn't know if she could handle him with that goatee. Maybe she didn't want to take him with her tomorrow. She wasn't sure she could stand to see other women gawk at him all day.

Intentionally ignoring her feelings, she took a deep breath and turned back to her rapidly cooling meal.

"Eat your dinner, Josh. It isn't going to get any warmer or better," she said, taking another bite of the casserole.

Josh continued to stare at his wife, watching a blush color her cheeks and wondering what was going on in that pretty head of hers.

It hadn't taken him long in his role as a

husband to realize that this woman's thoughts would remain a mystery no matter how hard he tried to understand her. He was okay with that. It kept things lively and exciting.

He returned his attention to dinner and asked Jenna more questions about her new job and upcoming travel plans.

"I'm not scheduled to go out on the road for a couple of weeks. I guess they figure by then I should know what I'm doing," Jenna said with a laugh. "Or at least that is the hope."

"You'll do great." Whatever Jenna did, she would do well and give it her best. "You're extremely intelligent and very talented, so don't sell yourself short."

Jenna gazed at her husband with love and admiration. "Thank you."

Her travel schedule was going to be hard on them both, but she appreciated Josh letting her follow her dreams. She knew he had some lingering guilt over dragging her out to live on the farm when she was a confirmed city girl. That guilt worked to her advantage because she did pretty much whatever she wanted with Josh's encouragement and support.

The truth of the matter was that she liked the farm and the country way of life. She loved how relaxed, open and real Josh was on the farm. In the city, Josh had been like an actor doing a splendid job of playing his part. Here on the farm, though, he was in his element. It was where he belonged and she belonged with Josh, wherever that may be.

Since she worked in the city, she didn't really

miss any of the conveniences she thought she would. Josh still took her to plays, concerts, and museum exhibits on occasion. Once in a blue moon, they both summoned the strength and fortitude to attend one of Phil and Amelia's parties, after which they would stop at their favorite steakhouse and enjoy a nice dinner.

Jenna snapped out of her musings and noticed Josh began cleaning up the dinner dishes. She looked down at her half-eaten plate of food and realized she wasn't hungry. As jet lag caught up to her, she was incredibly tired. She leaned her chin on her hand and watched Josh load the dishwasher, cover the leftovers and store them in the fridge, then wipe off the stove.

He walked over to the counter and gave her a questioning look. "Don't you feel well, babe?" After touching the back of his hand to her forehead, he decided she didn't have a fever.

"I'm fine, just tired. The time difference is starting to catch up with me." Jenna covered her mouth with her hand, attempting to stifle a yawn.

"Three hours difference can throw you for a loop." Josh picked up her plate and scraped her uneaten dinner into a scrap bucket before setting the dish and her utensils in the dishwasher. He wiped down the counter, tossed the rag in the sink, and looked around the orderly kitchen.

"Do I get a gold star for my exemplary efforts?" he asked, moving next to her barstool.

She smiled warmly, gazing up at him with sleepy eyes. "Maybe two if you're a good boy."

"Oh, I'm always good." His deep baritone

voice rumbled in his chest as he picked her up and carried her to their bedroom. "Very, very good, Mrs. Carver."

Chapter Two

Josh couldn't stop staring at his wife. He missed her so much while she was gone and had no idea how he'd handle her new travel schedule once it started.

For now, he watched her sleep. Although it was long past time for him to be out of bed, he talked himself into staying beside her for a while longer.

Reluctantly, he slid out of bed, grabbed the jeans and T-shirt he'd left on the floor last night, pulled socks out of his chest of drawers, and softly shut the bedroom door. After dressing in the kitchen, he drank a glass of milk and ate a banana. In the mudroom, he tugged on his boots, picked up his gloves, and settled his ball cap on his uncombed hair.

He hurried outside and pushed the four-wheeler toward the barn so the noise of it starting wouldn't wake Jenna. Finished with the morning chores and irrigating in record time, he decided he could swath a while before he returned to the house.

Josh made good time cutting two rounds around the outside of the field, creating a back swath, so he started swathing rows. As he neared the end of the windrow, he glanced at the position of the sun and decided he had better get back to the house or Jenna would have his head.

After shutting down the swather and rushing back to the house on the four-wheeler, he pulled up at the back door. He left his boots, gloves, and cap in the mudroom before washing up in the kitchen, expecting to find Jenna impatiently waiting. Instead, the house was eerily quiet.

A glimpse of the clock confirmed it was after nine. Since Jenna was usually an early riser, he was surprised to return to their bedroom and find her still sleeping. Exhausted from her trip, he didn't have the heart to wake her. Josh removed his clothes and climbed back under the covers, snuggling close to Jenna. His eyes grew heavy and he soon joined her in slumber.

An annoying chirping sound woke Josh from his dreams. As he sat up in bed, he realized it was Jenna's phone. He grabbed it off the nightstand and hurried into the bathroom. The caller ID showed the name Dennis Gillman. Josh had no idea who Dennis Gillman was but decided to answer.

"Jenna's phone."

"May I speak with Jenna?" A male voice asked, sounding annoyed and irritated.

"She isn't available. May I help you?" Josh didn't like the tone of the man's voice.

"Tell her The Gillman called," then the call disconnected.

Josh stared at the phone, wondering who "The Gillman" was to Jenna.

What a jerk.

Josh turned off the phone and walked into the bedroom, surprised to see the clock read ten-thirty. He set the phone on the nightstand and slid back into bed. He couldn't remember ever lazing away a day in bed.

Lying on his side, he watched Jenna slowly awaken. She stretched and rolled on her side before opening her big brown eyes, staring at him for a moment before a smile spread across her face.

"Hi," she whispered, reaching out a hand and placing it on his cheek.

"Hey, babe." Josh smiled, gently rubbing his hand up and down her bare arm. "Are you feeling better today?"

"I feel great." Jenna rolled over to glance at the clock. When she saw the time, she bolted upright in bed. "Good grief, Josh, you let me sleep away half the day. We'll have to hurry if we're going to run into the city, find a gift, and get back in time for dinner."

She would have jumped out of bed but Josh pulled her back down.

"Let's not get in too big of a hurry." Josh's voice was husky and enthralling as he trailed kisses along Jenna's neck. "I bet Laken will have something perfect and then we won't need to rush."

"But Josh, what if she doesn't, then we'll really have to hustle and I…" Jenna lost her train of thought when Josh kissed her long and slow and sweet. Maybe the gift hunting would wait for a little while longer.

After they ate lunch, Jenna called On a Lark, a gift shop in the Tenacity Mall owned by Callan's best friend, Laken Johnson. The three women sometimes got together and did fun things like manicures or shopping.

"On a Lark, this is Laken. May I help you?"

"Laken, this is Jenna. How are you?" Jenna asked.

"Great, Jenna. What can I do for you?" Laken knew Jenna wouldn't call the store unless she needed something.

"I'm looking for a special gift for Audrey and Emma. I'm hoping you might have something in your store. I want it personalized with their new names on it, but I didn't know what you have available," Jenna explained.

"I've got just the thing. I've only had it a few weeks, but come in and check it out. I think you'll really like it," Laken said, sounding excited.

"Great, Josh and I will be there soon. See you in a bit."

Jenna disconnected the call and turned to find Josh smiling at her.

"Told you Laken would have something."

Jenna picked up her purse and car keys, walking toward the garage. "Don't get your gloat on yet," Jenna teased as they headed out the door.

A short while later, they walked into On a Lark. Jenna admired the work Laken put into her displays, making the store look friendly and welcoming. She immediately spied the woman behind the cash register. Even if she hadn't spotted her there, Laken's infectious laughter gave her away.

Laken smiled at them and finished with her customer. As soon as she was free, she rushed over, giving Jenna a hug and Josh a pat on the back.

"Well, Jenna, how did you manage to get this ol' farmer out of the field today?" Laken teased, knowing Josh preferred to be at the farm than the mall.

"He promised to take me to Portland shopping and reneged on his deal, so he gets to tag along with me anyway." Jenna gave Josh a heated look that let him know exactly how pleased she was to spend the day with him. "I'm dying to see what you've got that you think would work as a gift for the girls."

Laken showed them a new computerized program with a special printer that allowed her to print custom vinyl lettering in a variety of colors and styles. Jenna liked the idea of making the girls signs with their names on them and selected a background with blue sky, green grass, and butterflies for Emma, who loved bugs and frogs and all things outdoors. For Audrey, she chose a pink background with curlicues and sparkly flourishes. Laken printed the customized designs then carefully transferred the artwork onto pre-made signs.

Josh was impressed and Jenna was thrilled.

As they browsed around the store, Jenna found one more gift she had to buy for Callan. The leather bound scrapbook that said, "Our Family" offered page after page to record family memories, holidays, birthdays, and insert photos. Several of the pages had inspirational quotes that centered on family life. It was perfect for the newly formed Matthews family.

"Can you wrap this up too, Laken?" Jenna asked, setting the book on the counter next to the signs.

"Absolutely." Laken gave her a big smile. "I was toying with the idea of giving Callan one of these so I'm glad you picked it out."

"She'll love it, babe," Josh said, his silvery gray eyes glowing with warmth. "Callan will be ecstatic."

Laken and Jenna both laughed. "I don't know about that, but I think she will be pleased." Jenna squeezed Josh's hand, glad he took an interest in the gifts.

"Do you two have any other stores to visit? I can wrap these up and have them waiting for you," Laken offered.

"Sure, we can look around for a few minutes," Josh said, tugging Jenna toward the door. "Thanks, Laken, we really appreciate it."

"Anytime." Laken waved as she hurried into her back room to find boxes for the signs and the book.

Josh and Jenna meandered around the Tenacity Mall. Although not large by any standard, it offered a nice selection of stores for local shoppers, providing an alternative to driving into Portland.

Josh wandered into the sporting goods store while Jenna browsed through a trendy clothing store. When they met in the food court, he bought them both a Dr Pepper then they sauntered back toward Laken's store.

After collecting the beautifully wrapped packages from Laken, Jenna suggested they run by the grocery store and pick up a few things to make for the barbecue that night. Josh readily agreed.

He grabbed a cart and started throwing things in before Jenna could formulate a grocery list. She quickly surmised he wanted her to make a chocolate bundt cake along with seven-layer taco dip.

Josh carried in the groceries while she got out everything to make the cake. While she prepared the batter, he washed tomatoes and readied the avocado for the dip. His years of living in the city had taught him how to cook a few things, cake not being one of them.

He loved all things chocolate, as did Callan, and never passed up an opportunity for Jenna to make her special chocolate cake - a moist chocolate bundt cake topped with a rich chocolate glaze. His mouth watered just thinking about it.

Jenna only had to slap his hands half a dozen times to keep him out of the cake batter. Once she finished spooning the batter into the pan, she gladly gave him the bowl to lick clean.

"You're worse than six little boys all together," she laughed at Josh as he sat at the counter, contentedly licking every speck of chocolate out of the bowl.

Josh didn't answer. He looked up long enough to flash his you-can't-refuse-me-a-thing grin before turning his attention to one last tiny drop of chocolate clinging to the edge of the bowl

"Josh, you're impossible," Jenna chided, taking the empty bowl away from him and setting it in the dishwasher. While the cake baked, she led Josh to the great room where they sank into the comfortable cushions of the couch and talked about their plans for the next few weeks.

"By the way…" Josh stretched out on the long couch and rested his head on her lap. "Who is Dennis Gillman?"

"Nobody important. Why?" Jenna stiffened and her voice took on an edge Josh hadn't heard before. Quickly sitting up, he looked her full in the face, trying to figure out what bothered her. Something made her uncomfortable, that much was certain.

"I answered your phone when it rang this morning. He said to tell you 'The Gillman' called." Josh attempted to analyze Jenna's reaction to his words. "I forgot to tell you earlier."

Jenna took a deep breath and released a sigh. "He's just someone from work. I'm sure it wasn't anything important or someone would have called me back."

"Are you sure there isn't something you need to tell me?"

"No. He's a new-hire experiencing some difficulty figuring out how things work at the office."

Josh decided to let the discussion go for now. However, he fully intended to find out everything he could about Dennis Gillman.

They discussed farm details until the cake finished baking. After giving it time to cool, Jenna frosted it then they packed up the food to take to Clay and Callan's.

As they pulled into the Matthews' driveway, Jenna smiled at Callan's yard full of beautiful flowers. Cully, the family dog, barked from the backyard where Audrey and Emma no doubt played with him.

Jenna carried the gifts while Josh took care of the cake and dip. With both of their hands full, Josh rang the doorbell with his elbow and waited for someone to answer. It didn't take long for Callan to open the door, beaming a huge smile.

"Hello, hello! Come on in," she said in welcome, taking the cake out of Josh's hand and kissing his cheek. "I'm glad you two came over early. I haven't seen either one of you for a while and we need to catch up on life."

Only a year apart in age, Callan and Josh were close. Both tall, they possessed beautiful smiles that popped dimples out in their left cheeks. Where Josh was dark in both coloring and hair with silvery eyes, Callan had fair skin with a tendency to freckle, auburn hair, and bright emerald green eyes. Despite the differences in their coloring, it was easy to see a resemblance in their features.

Callan tended to be more serious while Josh was something of a jokester, although he had a hard time keeping up with Callan's husband, Clay, in that department. He seemed to maintain the upper hand when it came to pranks.

Jenna set the presents down in the front room before walking into the kitchen where Josh placed the taco dip on the counter. Callan came right over and gave her a hug.

"Jenna, you look wonderful. The new job must agree with you," Callan said with a warm smile.

"So far, so good." Jenna returned Callan's hug, then took a step back. "We brought a little something for the girls. Would it be okay to give it to them now, before all the rest of the company arrives?"

"Oh, you didn't need to do that, but I'm sure the girls will be thrilled. Now would be a great time to have them open presents." Callan walked through the family room and opened the patio door. She said something Josh and Jenna couldn't hear and soon returned to the kitchen with Audrey and Emma.

"Uncle Josh! Auntie Jenna!" The girls squealed as they ran into the kitchen and gave them both hugs and kisses. Jenna never ceased to be amazed at how much alike the two girls appeared. Although three years apart in age, the girls looked exactly alike with big china blue eyes, perfect rosebud lips, and heart-shaped faces topped with a mop of curly blond hair that fell in perfect ringlets. Since they'd been living with Clay and Callan, they were always dressed adorably. Today was no exception.

Jenna picked up six-year-old Emma and gave her an extra warm hug. "How are you today, Miss Sweet Pea?" she asked, tickling the little girl's side.

"I'm wonderful, Auntie Jenna," Emma said between giggles. "Did Auntie Callan tell you? We get to belong to her and Uncle Clay forever and ever. I'm so glad."

Jenna smiled at Emma and pulled her little head close to her own. "I know, Sweet Pea, and I'm so happy for you. It's exciting, isn't it?"

"Yep," Emma agreed, hanging onto Jenna's neck.

While she picked up Emma, nine-year-old Audrey wasted no time in launching herself into Josh's arms then swung around to cling on his back like a monkey.

"If you two girls can behave for a minute or two, we might have a present for you to open," Josh teased.

"For real?" Audrey asked, squeezing him around the neck. "Can we open it?"

"You bet, if you don't choke me to death first." Audrey giggled as Josh carried her into the living room and deposited her on the couch.

Jenna sat down next to her and held Emma on her lap while Josh passed a gift to each girl. They eagerly tore away the wrapping paper and opened the boxes.

"Oh, look, Auntie Callan," Audrey gasped in pleasure at her sign. "It says 'Audrey Matthews' and Emma's says 'Emma Matthews.' They have our new names on them, Emma."

"Yippee!" Emma clapped and tossed her head, setting her curls to bouncing. "Our new names are the bestest names of all."

The adults laughed while the girls ran to their shared bedroom to find somewhere to display their signs. Josh handed Callan the third package.

"We thought you might like this, Callan," Jenna said as Callan sat down beside her and removed the wrappings covering the beautiful scrapbook.

"This is lovely, you two." Callan's voice was quiet as she swiped at a tear. "Thank you so much. We'll enjoy filling every single page."

Josh leaned down and gave his sister a hug. "We're so proud of you and Clay. Not everyone would have wanted the girls much less fought for so long to keep them. You two have done a wonderful thing."

"Josh, you're going to make my mascara run," Callan said through her tears, squeezing her brother's hand. "You both have been so supportive and encouraging. Clay and I appreciate it so much. Those girls are a blessing to us and I'm grateful every day to have them."

Jenna began sniffling so Josh decided it was time to lighten the mood. "And you both are darn lucky to have someone extra special like me." He struck a super-hero pose and gave them a cocky grin before looking around the room. "Speaking of extra special, where's Clay?"

"He ran to the store to pick up more ice and another tank of propane. Of course, as soon as he decided to fire up the grill, it spluttered and died," Callan said, regaining her sense of humor. "He should be back any minute, though."

The three of them returned to the kitchen where Jenna and Callan worked together getting food ready for dinner. Josh wandered into the girls' bedroom. They both sat on Audrey's bed, admiring their signs.

"What are you two up to?" he asked stepping into the room that sported white furniture accented with pink curtains, bedspreads and throw pillows. It was definitely a princess room meant for little girls. He picked up a chair from their little corner table, turned it around and attempted to straddle it with his long legs nearly up to his ears. The girls broke into peals of delighted childish laughter.

"Uncle Josh, you're going to break our chair." Emma ran over to him and tugged on his hand.

"You can't sit there. You're oodles too big."

"Oh, I'm sorry." Josh attempted to look serious. He feigned confusion and glanced around the room. "Where can I sit?"

"On the bed, silly." Emma flopped down on her sister's bed and patted a spot between the two of them. "You can sit right here between me and Audrey."

"Sit on you and Audrey?" Josh teased, starting to sit down on top of them both.

"No!" they yelled in unison, shoving at him to stand up. "Not on top of us."

Josh stood and scratched his head, pretending to consider his options. "Are you sure I can't sit on you?"

"Very sure," Audrey said, nodding her head for emphasis. "You know better, Uncle Josh."

"I do?" He leaned over and grabbed both girls then started tickling them. They wiggled and giggled, gasping for breath. When he finally let go, they jumped on top of him and pulled him down on the bed. All three of them dissolved into laughter.

"What's going on in here?" Clay's deep voice filled the room. Although he sounded stern, his big smile gave away his mirth.

"Uncle Clay, you're home!" Emma leaped from the bed into his arms. "We missed you!"

"I was gone less than an hour, Sweet Pea. You couldn't have missed me that soon."

"Oh, but we did." Emma kissed Clay on the cheek then turned to Josh. "Did you see what Uncle Josh and Aunt Jenna brought us?"

"What did you get?" Clay asked, setting Emma

49

down. He offered all the appropriate words of praise when the girls showed him their signs.

"These are great, Josh. Thank you." Clay nodded to his brother-in-law. They struck up a friendship when Clay and Callan started dating and had been close ever since.

"It was Jenna's idea." Josh reached out a hand to shake Clay's. "We're really happy for you all. It's about time this was behind you so you can move forward as a family."

"I agree," Clay said with a solemn nod before giving Josh a devilish grin. "You might want to think about starting your own family one of these days in the not so distant future."

"That is a topic currently not open for discussion." Josh glared at Clay and motioned his head toward the girls. Clay nodded back in understanding.

"Right," Clay said, pointing his finger in the direction of the hall. "Girls, I bet we're going to have a house full of company any minute. Let's go see what we can do to help your two aunties."

"Okay," Audrey said, running toward the kitchen with Emma right behind her.

"So the topic of a family is seriously not open for discussion?" Clay asked, sincerely interested as he and Josh stood in the pink domain of his adopted daughters.

"Not by me, by Jenna. The last time I broached the subject of babies, it didn't go so well." Josh raked a hand through his dark hair at the memory.

Clay slapped him good-naturedly on the back as they walked out of the bedroom. "Maybe you just need to turn on the full force of your powers of persuasion." Clay waggled his eyebrows suggestively and grinned.

"Maybe," Josh agreed with a laugh. "Maybe I do."

When Jenna got past her fear of all things rural, she learned to appreciate time spent with Josh's family. She watched as Josh's dad, Clay's parents, Clay's Aunt Maggie, Uncle Tom, and cousin Jake walked inside the house, bringing smiles and laughter. Laken, her husband, Tyler, and their two kids along with numerous friends and neighbors converged at the Matthews' home all bearing plates of food and some bringing gifts for the girls. It seemed like half the Tenacity community dropped by at some point during the evening.

Bobbi and Steve, Clay's parents, were giddy with joy at officially becoming grandparents. Clay was their only child and since Callan was unable to have children, they'd given up hope of ever having grandchildren. They insisted the girls call them, "Grammy and Gramps."

Jenna loved being around this family, filled with people who were so genuine, honest, and kind. She sat back and smiled as Clay carried his two girls around. Audrey hung on his back while Emma wiggled in his arms.

Truthfully, it was a miracle to see him walk.

Two years ago, they had all been out at Bobbi

and Steve's ranch working cattle when a pen full of cows stampeded and Clay suffered severe injuries. He'd been so badly hurt, they weren't sure he would make it. After two weeks in a coma, he spent months in therapy. A hoof-shaped scar on his head and a plate in his leg were the only visible reminders of the accident.

Jenna breathed another prayer of thanks for Clay's continued health and that Josh wasn't injured since he was in the pen with Clay when it happened.

The accident seemed to change both Callan and Clay. They lived each day with a deep and underlying sense of gratitude. Maybe that was why they both seemed to love their new roles as parents.

Having known Clay for quite a few years, Jenna would never have pictured him as such a doting father.

Clay was a huge man, barrel-chested, and taller even than Josh, with thick muscled arms and legs. Despite his intimidating size, he possessed a deep dimpled grin, warm blue eyes, and one of the biggest hearts she'd ever encountered. The fact that his sun rose and set with his wife just endeared him even more to those who knew and loved them.

From what Jenna understood, he was an excellent teacher in his position as dean of the agricultural department at the community college. She knew from personal experience he was a big tease, but also compassionate. It was no wonder he had turned out to be an excellent father.

Callan was motherhood personified. She seemed to love everything about being a mother. Once she quit her job as the creative director at the local convention center last year and focused only on her event planning business, she had much more time to devote to the girls and fully embrace the role of parenting. She was a natural at nurturing and encouraging with just the right amount of discipline.

Reflective, Jenna sighed, knowing she would make a miserable parent. The thought of being stuck at home with little people demanding her attention made her chest tighten and stomach ache. She knew, to the very depths of her being, that she was just not motherhood material.

As much as Josh wanted a family, children were the one thing she refused to give him. She had career goals and raising babies didn't fit into her carefully structured plans.

Forcibly shifting her thoughts away from babies and parenthood, Jenna rejoined the conversation around her.

On the drive home from the party, she and Josh shared conversations from the party, news they heard, and discussed how much they enjoyed the evening.

"Did you save me a piece of chocolate cake?" Josh asked, concerned it may have been all gone.

"You already had a piece, you oinker," Jenna teased. When Josh looked truly stricken at the thought of not getting another piece, she relieved his misery. "Yes, I saved a piece for you. Good grief, Buck. Its only cake."

Grabbing Jenna's hand and kissing it in gratitude, Josh smiled at her. "It isn't just cake. It's your chocolate cake and I absolutely need another piece."

"What am I going to do with you?" Jenna laughed at the boyish grin on his face.

Josh's voice grew husky and he placed a moist kiss to her palm. "I have a few ideas."

Her cheeks tingled with heat while her stomach fluttered so she decided to change the subject.

"It was nice to see Jake," she said of Clay's younger cousin. Jake, also an only child, worked to finish classes at Portland State University and would soon graduate with a degree in biology. He came home most weekends to work with the herd of registered quarter horses he raised and help on his parent's small farm. When he had time, he also helped on Steve and Bobbi's sprawling ranch.

"He said he has two more weeks until graduation then he'll be home for the summer or at least until he finds a job." Josh let Jenna change the subject to Jake because it was a topic he wanted to discuss. "We're really going to need a hired hand this summer and I was thinking about offering the job to Jake. What do you think? If he wanted, he could live in the Harold house or he could drive out from Maggie and Tom's place."

"I think that's a great idea," Jenna smiled at Josh. She wasn't going to be much help to her husband on the farm all summer with her hectic travel schedule. She'd worried how he would handle all the work by himself. A hired hand for the summer months made perfect sense. They both liked Jake. From experience, they knew he was honest and a hard worker.

"Why don't you call him tomorrow and see if he'd be interested. If he wants to live in the house, we could fix it up a little. I'm sure it's been overrun with rodents and creepy crawlies."

As Jenna said the last words, she shuddered. Mice, snakes, and spiders were things she would never become accustomed to or even accept as part of rural life. Josh worked hard to make sure their house and outbuildings remained rodent and reptile free, but he couldn't control their presence in the yard.

Whenever Jenna came across a snake, Josh was convinced anyone residing on that end of the county knew about it from her frantic screaming.

The first time she'd screamed like the world was about to come to an abrupt and surprising end, Josh had been working in the shop on a piece of equipment. He dropped the heavy piece of metal and narrowly missed maiming his foot as he ran full-tilt toward the house to see what horrendous tragedy had befallen his wife.

Winded and afraid of what he would find when he arrived in the yard, he discovered Jenna standing on the porch steps, clutching a shovel and jabbing it in the direction of a flowerbed. He thought maybe there was a nest of rattlesnakes coiled up there for all her pointing and gasping, but upon investigation, he found one tiny little garter snake.

After that, he didn't get quite as excited when he heard her scream. He always ran to the rescue, just not as fast and furiously as he did that first time.

"Great. I'll give Jake a call tomorrow. I'd ask him after church, but I somehow doubt we'll see him there." Josh gave Jenna a knowing look. Jake's flagrant disregard for his Christian upbringing was a source of great contention within his family. He was a good kid, polite, responsible, and thoughtful, but he refused to attend church with his parents and was often seen hanging out with a crowd of questionable reputations.

Josh remembered what it was like to be twenty-one, popular with the girls, and have the world by a string. He couldn't say he blamed Jake one bit. Then again, he wouldn't trade his current life for anything.

Jenna was perfect for him and he absolutely loved the life they built together.

Chapter Three

A quick call to Jake the next day confirmed he not only would enjoy working for them for the summer, but would also take them up on the offer of a place to live.

Jake hesitated to live with his parents, but he didn't have too many choices. He planned to continue paying rent for the apartment he shared with three other guys in Portland, and that left him with limited funds for summer housing.

Callan and the girls arrived early the next Saturday to help spruce up the Harold house. Jenna loaded her vacuum and a variety of cleaning supplies as well as rags and garbage bags into the trunk of her car. She drove down the road to the house, fully engaged in the chatter of Audrey and Emma from the back seat.

As they parked in front of the house, Jenna realized she and Josh should have done a better job of maintaining the place. The yard was overgrown and weeds grew everywhere. They removed the cleaning supplies out of the trunk and trudged to the front door, brushing at the cobwebs that seemed to be everywhere.

When Jenna opened the door, a blast of smelly, hot air greeted them. Jenna gave Callan a dismayed look. "This may be worse than I expected."

Jenna stepped inside, followed by Callan. A bullsnake slithered across the front room floor in pursuit of a mouse and flicked his tongue at them in greeting.

Both women screamed and hurriedly retraced their steps out the door. Outside, they continued screaming as shudders ran over them both.

Since they didn't know what had happened, Emma and Audrey began screaming, too. Callan picked up Emma and ran to the car while Jenna tugged Audrey along with her.

Safe inside the car, Callan and Jenna eyed each other then started to giggle.

"That was an interesting start to our cleaning," Callan said with a smile. "I think we're going to need some reinforcements before we can do anything in there."

Jenna pulled out her cell phone and called Josh. He'd gone over to help at the Matthews ranch that morning.

"Hey, babe. You aren't all done cleaning, are you?" he teased, knowing she, Callan, and the girls barely had time to get started.

"Actually, we've got a problem and require your immediate assistance," Jenna said, not giving away any details.

"What kind of problem?" Josh sounded distracted.

"A big enough problem the four of us are

trapped in the car for reasons of personal safety."
Jenna glanced toward the door of the house, half-
expecting the vermin to escape and swarm her car.
She thought she saw something furry run outside
and tamped down the urge to scream again. "Would
you please get over here as quickly as possible and
bring some weaponry with you?"

"Are you joking with me, babe? We're kind of
in the middle of things and I can't run over there to
brush down a spider web for you," Josh cautioned.
His wife's idea of a big problem and his were
usually entirely different.

"I assure you, we have already brushed down
the cobwebs from the door and the problem isn't
something Callan and I can handle." Irritated that
Josh didn't offer to run right over, she needed his
support. If one of the men didn't rapidly deal with
the problem, her concern would move straight into a
state of panic. "Josh, please. You have to come help
us. Please?"

She heard Josh say something muffled in the
background then he returned. Relief washed over
her at the sound of his pickup starting. "I'm on my
way. Don't move."

Certain she didn't want to know how fast Josh
drove, within ten minutes he pulled up behind her
car. Both pickup doors opened and Clay got out
along with Josh. They sauntered up on either side of
the car and stuck their heads inside the open
windows.

"What's got you four hiding out in the car?"
Josh asked, winking at Audrey and Emma.

"Uncle Josh, it was awful. It made us all

scream!" Emma said before Audrey clapped her hand over her sister's mouth.

"Auntie Callan said to let them see for themselves, remember?" Audrey hissed at her little sister, known for having a big mouth.

"I forgot. Sorry. Yep, go see for yourself. It's scary!" Emma said, bouncing on her seat.

"I'm sure it is terribly frightening." Clay smirked as he stepped away from the car and followed Josh inside the house.

The men were gone just a few minutes before they hustled out the door. Looks of horror filled their tanned faces, replacing the sarcastic smiles they'd sported as they entered the house.

"Why didn't you mention the infestation?" Josh asked, catching his breath. "There are nests upon nests in there."

"Nests?" both Jenna and Callan yelled, causing the girls to start screaming again.

"We only saw one mouse being chased by a very large snake," Callan said as Clay leaned against the car, appearing to need a moment to wrap his head around the state of disaster in the house.

Clay looked across the top of the car at Josh. Since his brother-in-law owned the place, it was his duty to inform the women what they found in the house. When Josh continued staring at him, he nodded toward the women and gave the man a look that said he had to be the one to break the news.

"Well, girls, it um… it appears that maybe we should not have left the house unattended for quite so long. There seems to be a few dozen mice in residence along with several snakes, three wasp nests, and I'm pretty sure we saw a bat in the bathroom."

Jenna and Callan both turned white and looked at each other.

"Get a torch and let's burn it to the ground," Jenna said, meaning every word. There was no way she would set foot in the house. She sure didn't know how anyone could live in it.

"Now, babe, calm down. We can take care of the problem. It's just going to take a little time. This is an older house, so we'll have to clear it out, seal any cracks and holes, set traps and make sure they stay empty, and then you girls can clean. Plan on it being next weekend before you can get any work done here."

"Are you crazy?" Jenna got out of the car long enough to shake her finger under Josh's nose. "You are completely insane if you think I will ever, in a million years, set foot in there again. I think that snake smiled at me!" She shuddered just remembering it and had to tamp down the urge to jump into Josh's arms where she knew she'd be safe.

"We can get it cleaned out and it will be fine. No problem," Clay said, trying to reassure Jenna and Callan as well as himself. He wasn't fond of snakes. When they came across the bat, he and Josh were both caught off guard. They nearly pushed each other down in their haste to get out of the house.

Jenna pointed to her cleaning supplies and vacuum, and asked the men to load them in her trunk, which they did. She started her car and gave

Josh a look of warning. "When you can promise me there isn't one creepy anything left in that house, we'll talk about coming back to clean it. Deal?"

"Deal," Josh said, hoping Clay would be game to help him. He sure didn't want to tackle the job on his own. "Why don't you girls do something fun today while Clay and I work on this project."

"That sounds like a great idea," Callan said, waving a hand out the window at them. "We'll see you boys later."

Jenna turned the car around and headed home.

After the girls left, Josh and Clay drove into town and bought a dozen mousetraps of varying sizes and styles, a few gallons of bug spray along with bug bombs, and asked at the feed store for ideas on catching snakes and bats.

While giving them odd looks, the old timers that tended to gather there on Saturdays were full of wisdom and offered no less than thirteen ways to catch snakes and remove bats. Josh settled on a dozen snake traps instead. He and Clay gathered up bags full of supplies and ventured back to the house, armed with their arsenal of weapons for the removal of rodents, bugs, and snakes.

Cautiously stepping inside the house, the front room seemed still and quiet so they started setting out mousetraps. Two traps were the mouse hotel style that would hold several mice at once. They emptied those two traps numerous times throughout the day and each time they did, they both fought down the urge to be sick. An old metal burning barrel collected the contents they dumped out of the traps, and they set fire to it as they worked on the odious project.

The snakes took a lot more work to catch. By noon, they had evicted nine of them. Neither one of the men felt like they could eat anything, so they came up with a game plan to get rid of the wasp nests. Using a long rod and a gunnysack, they decided the fastest way to get the nests out of the house would be to knock the nests into the sack, twist it closed and haul it outside where they would douse the whole thing in a bucket of bug spray. Their plan was a success with the first nest. Clay had just knocked the second nest into the sack while Josh twisted it closed when the bat flapped out of the bathroom and flogged Josh's ball cap-covered head. He dropped the sack in an attempt to shield himself from the bat and the wasps swarmed out.

He and Clay ran pell-mell out into the yard and took refuge in the pickup. Once the wasps settled down, they returned inside. Clay used the rod to carry the sack outside and dunk the nest in a bucket of the bug spray. They quickly repeated the process with the third nest. When they finished, they could at least work without dodging wasps along with the snakes and mice.

As they turned to check the mousetraps again, Josh and Clay watched in mesmerized revulsion as a snake slithered into the mouse hotel, stuck partway in the hole.

"You better take that outside now." Clay pushed Josh in the direction of the trap.

"Me?" Josh stared at Clay as if he'd lost his mind. "You're so much better at dumping that thing than I am. Why don't you take it?"

"I don't think so, man. This is your place, your mess, and your snake-filled mouse trap." Clay gave Josh another nudge.

Josh ended up retrieving their wasp nest rod and scooting the trap outside. He couldn't bring himself to look when he dumped the trap, knowing he wouldn't want to see what came out of it.

He started back inside, but Clay nearly bowled him over, flapping his arms around his head as the bat followed in hot pursuit. Josh ducked as the bat winged through the open door and flew off.

"At least we don't have to figure out a way to evict it now." Josh glanced at Clay as he continued to brush a hand over his hat-covered head.

Although there were still mice and snakes running amuck in the house, they had endured about all they could for one day. After setting off three times the recommended amount of bug bombs for the square footage, they closed the door and sat on the pickup tailgate trying to muster the energy to go home and clean up.

Callan dropped Clay at the ranch that morning and he was certain she wouldn't let him in her car as filthy and smelly as he was. He couldn't get the stench of mice out of his nose and from the way Josh kept breathing through his mouth, he most likely experienced the same problem.

"We've got to pull ourselves together and go home, you know." Clay stated the obvious as they tried to forget every single thing they had seen and experienced since arriving at the house after Jenna called for their assistance.

"I know." Josh nodded his head in agreement.

"I need a few minutes before I face the girls. Do you suppose this is what they feel like when they see one mouse or snake?"

"I don't know," Clay mused. Callan wasn't afraid of too many things, but she absolutely couldn't handle seeing a mouse. She jumped for the highest object and screamed bloody murder. "If so, I won't ever make fun of them again."

"Me either," Josh said, looking up as Jenna's car pulled into the drive.

The girls returned to Jenna's house where they decided to treat themselves to a spa day. They soaked their feet in dishpans filled with fizzy peppermint foot soak, painted their fingernails and toenails, and ate quiche for lunch.

Jenna and Callan gave each other neck massages then applied a thick coat of oozing facial cream that would eventually dry and peel off. With a slice of cool cucumber on their eyes, they relaxed in the living room, sipped lemonade through straws and listened to the sounds of the Audrey and Emma as they watched *Mary Poppins*.

"We should feel a little guilty, shouldn't we, for enjoying such a relaxing day while the guys are down there mucking out that mess?" Jenna didn't feel guilty enough to see how their husbands fared with the project.

"I suppose we should, yet I'm having a hard time mustering any guilt." Callan's voice held a teasing lilt. "Probably because of all the times they've made fun of us for having a fit over a mouse or a snake. If we haven't heard a peep from them in, say, another hour, we can go check on them."

"Sounds like a plan," Jenna said, taking another sip of her lemonade.

By the time she and Callan peeled off their masks, made more lemonade, and whipped up a batch of cookies, two hours passed so they loaded the girls in the car and drove back to the Harold place. As they pulled into the driveway, Clay and Josh sat on the tailgate of Josh's pickup. Covered in dust, sweat, and cobwebs, they looked exhausted and overheated.

Jenna handed cups to Audrey and hefted the jar of lemonade while Callan picked up the plate of cookies then they walked over to the exhausted men.

"You two look terrible," Jenna said, setting the lemonade on the tailgate between them as she trailed her gaze over them both. Josh and Clay looked like they'd been dragged through a knothole and barely survived the trip. "What happened?"

"You don't want to know," Josh managed to grumble. "You really don't want to know."

Jenna poured lemonade for them while Callan held out the plate of cookies. Both men looked down at their filthy hands and passed on the cookies. They gulped down the lemonade and held their cups out for more.

"You could go inside and wash," Callan innocently suggested.

"No!" Josh and Clay yelled simultaneously.

"We, um… we set off bug bombs and need to wait for the air to clear before we go back in," Clay explained. A haunted look flashed across his face.

Jenna could have sworn she saw both of them shudder. She wondered what had really gone on at the house today, but decided she was better off not knowing.

"You could at least rinse off at the faucet over there." Jenna pointed to a freeze-proof faucet located at the side of the house.

"Right." Josh slid off the tailgate and walked over to the faucet. He grabbed the handle then suddenly let go, slapping at his leg and jumping back. As he stomped the ground, Jenna guessed he'd found a spider.

Turning on the faucet, Josh let the water run over his hands for a while before he rubbed them together. As he scrubbed away the grime, Clay joined him and soon they had mostly clean hands before they started dashing cold water on their faces. Both of them had cobwebs all over their ball caps, on their jeans, and across the backs of their shirts. As Josh bent over to rinse his face off again, Clay thumped his hand down hard across his back. He pulled his hand back and rinsed off the remainder of a squished spider under the water while Josh ripped off his shirt.

"I can't take anymore," Josh said under his breath to Clay, holding his T-shirt in a tight wad. "I think we should have let Jenna burn the house down when she suggested it."

"I'm not going to argue with you," Clay

whispered, casting a glance at the girls as they sat on the tailgate munching cookies. "By the time we come back tomorrow, most of what's in there will either be dead or gone. It won't take long to seal the holes, clean out the mess, and be done."

"I know, but if one more thing crawls across my foot or flaps around my head, I might start screaming like a girl," Josh mumbled, shaking his head.

"After today, I don't think anyone could blame you." Clay laughed and gave him a shove toward the girls.

Callan agreed there was no way she'd let Clay ride home in her car looking and smelling like he did. Josh let him take his pickup home to clean up and then come back for dinner. While Clay was gone, Jenna and Callan worked on dinner preparations, Audrey and Emma set out plates and cutlery, and Josh took a long shower.

Clay returned looking refreshed as Callan and Jenna set dinner on the table. Although exhausted, Josh and Clay joined in the lively conversation, highlighted by Audrey and Emma's retelling of the movie they watched and the fun things they'd done with their two aunts.

Later, as he carried a sleeping Emma out to the car, Clay assured Josh he would come back after church the following day to help him finish the job of cleaning out the house.

Audrey hugged both Josh and Jenna. "I had so much fun today, Auntie Jenna. Maybe we can do this every Saturday."

"I sure hope we don't," Josh muttered darkly

while Jenna shot him a glare.

"Audrey, honey, as fun as that would be, I don't think we can do it every Saturday. I look forward to seeing you all next Saturday, though. We'll try cleaning the house then. Thank you for spending the day with me." Jenna walked Audrey to the car and made sure she was buckled in before shutting the car door.

"Thanks so much for a lovely day, Jenna," Callan said, giving her a hug. "We'll get the house whipped into shape next weekend."

After shaking Clay's hand, Josh thanked him again for his help. For some reason, their day spent in the trenches made him appreciate his brother-in-law even more. Not everyone would have stuck it out like Clay had, right to the bitter bat-filled end.

When Clay arrived the next afternoon, he and Josh both steeled themselves for whatever they might find when they opened the door at the little house. They weren't quite prepared for the mass of corpses on the floor that included everything from spiders and flies to mice, snakes, and what looked like a lizard. After retrieving two scoop shovels from the shop, they donned facemasks, and soon had the floor cleaned. They pulled out the carpeting and tossed it in a heap out back, then began the task of finding holes and sealing them.

Clay added weather-stripping around the front door to keep anything from coming in under or around the door edges. Jenna sent along bottles of bleach spray, so Josh sprayed down all the cupboards, the counters, the kitchen sink and floor as well as nearly the entire bathroom. They reset all the mousetraps, set fire to the mess out back, and called it a good day's work.

Josh checked the traps each day and didn't find any more mice in them. He also noticed there weren't any more mouse droppings in the house, taking that as a good sign that they'd evicted all the rodents.

One afternoon, he took a scythe and worked down the weeds closest to the house then drove the tractor with the mower over the yard.

When Callan and the girls arrived early Saturday, Josh confidently stated there were no surprises in the house and it just needed a good cleaning. After finishing his irrigating, he checked in on the women. Since they were busy scrubbing the bathroom and kitchen, he decided it was safe to head over to the ranch for the rest of the day to work.

Jenna and Callan were quite pleased with their efforts as they dumped the last bucket of water they used to scrub the house from top to bottom. Although the floor really needed to be sanded and refinished, the hardwood was in good condition and would serve Jake well. The house was only about five-hundred square feet with a living room, kitchen, bedroom, and bathroom.

The tiny bathroom was located off the bedroom. If Jenna stood sideways in it, she could touch her fingers on both walls at the same time. At least the tub had a showerhead. She doubted Jake would appreciate taking baths all summer.

Since it wouldn't take long to paint the inside walls of the small house, she and Callan quickly rolled on a thick coat of white paint. Even though it was boring as far as home interiors went, it looked fresh and clean. They finished their efforts by giving the floors one more scrubbing, effectively mopping up any paint splatters.

Jenna worried about furnishing the house. There wasn't a stick of furniture in it and if there had been she would have insisted Josh burn it.

As Jenna and Callan looked around the empty house, Callan remembered an ad she saw in the previous evening's newspaper.

"Jenna, let's get cleaned up and run into town. I have an idea..." Callan hustled out the door and called to the girls as they pulled weeds around the yard.

They loaded all the cleaning supplies and returned to Jenna's where they washed up and climbed into Callan's car. She drove them back to town and out on the other side where a huge yard sale took place. Despite starting earlier in the day, there was still a large selection of merchandise.

Jenna spotted a bedroom set in great condition at the price that made her smile. Quickly pulling off the price tag, she couldn't believe the owners wanted so little for the bed including the mattress set, a dresser, and a chest of drawers. It was too good to be true.

She approached an older couple operating the payment table, and set down the tag. When she told them she'd take the bedroom set and wasn't finished shopping yet, they told her to keep looking while they taped a "sold" sign on the dresser mirror.

Callan found a recliner and end table along

with a small dining table with two chairs.

The girls ran over, excited about finding a refrigerator. Not a new model by any means, it did appear to work. Jenna picked up a few dishes, bowls, a set of glasses, and a couple of coffee mugs, adding them to her growing pile. The last thing she purchased was a large area rug in excellent condition. Her total bill came in just over three hundred dollars.

She asked the couple if they could come back later to pick everything up and they assured her it would be fine. After visiting with them, she and Callan found out they had no children and were no longer able to take care of their home, so they were moving to a retirement center. Their rooms at the center were furnished, so they needed to get rid of their house full of belongings. Jenna was extremely grateful for her good fortune in finding so many things they needed for the house that would soon be home to Jake. After plunking down cash, Jenna told them she'd come back when they were ready to move to take their stove and a small love seat.

On their way home, Jenna called Josh and gave him the address of the yard sale. She asked if he and Clay could pick up everything when they finished work that evening. Callan suggested they both take their pickups.

"Just exactly what did you buy?" Josh asked, envisioning the shopping spree Callan and Jenna were capable of taking.

"Just a few pieces of furniture for Jake's house," Jenna said, referring to the Harold place as Jake's, since he would move in the following weekend. "You won't believe the deals we got. Oh, there'll also be a few more pieces to pick up on Thursday."

"Okay," Josh said, disconnecting the call. When he and Clay arrived at the address, they introduced themselves to the elderly couple who pointed out the pieces they needed to take. It filled both their pickups.

After pulling up at Jake's house, Josh and Clay walked inside to see what the girls had accomplished that day.

"Wow, are we in the right place?" Clay asked, looking around at the freshly painted walls and sniffing the clean-smelling air. "Those two sure got a lot done today."

"Boy, I'd say." Josh walked from room to room. Everything looked move-in ready, so he and Clay hauled in the furniture and set it up. After setting the refrigerator in the kitchen, he admired how the house started to look like a home.

Josh noted a few things they would need to purchase before Jake moved in, but overall, the house looked good.

Outside, they could see someone pulled the remaining weeds around the house and even swept the sidewalk, giving it a tidy appearance.

"I think our girls outdid themselves," Josh said as he and Clay walked back to their pickups. "Maybe we should take them out for dinner."

"Great idea," Clay said, thinking Jenna and Callan had more than earned it.

Jake moved in the following Saturday.

By then, Jenna had hung blinds in the windows,

added a few throw rugs, brought in two sets of sheets, blankets, and a comforter along with bath and kitchen towels and purchased a small microwave and television set. Rummaging through some of the things she and Josh had in storage, she found art to hang on the walls, added throw pillows to the loveseat and made Josh install a small window air-conditioner in the bedroom.

The place was as ready as they could make it.

Jake was thrilled to have a place to himself and couldn't thank Josh and Jenna enough for providing room and board. They invited him to eat meals with them as well as have the use of their washer and dryer.

The first few days Jake was at the house, he loved it.

He liked Josh and Jenna, enjoyed the good meals she had provided and settled into the new routine. Monday through Friday Jake worked full days, and until noon on Saturdays. It left him with plenty of time to take care of his horses, hang out with friends, and continue his hunt for a job. The small barn and corral by the house allowed him to bring a couple of horses with him to train during his free time in the evenings.

As he sat in the recliner one evening, watching the news, he thought he saw something move out of the corner of his eye. When he turned his head, he could have sworn he saw a tail slither around the corner into the bedroom, but decided he was seeing things.

The next morning, he knew his imagination wasn't conjuring things that weren't there when a snake slithered under the bathroom door while he brushed his teeth. Spewing toothpaste all over the mirror, he watched the snake disappear into the bedroom before he gathered his wits enough to chase it. He searched the small bedroom from top to bottom and didn't find the snake anywhere. Moving furniture around in the living room didn't turn it up either. He had no idea where the snake could have disappeared to, and decided he wasn't going to stick around to find out.

That evening he again sat in the recliner, hoping the snake had gone, when he saw it wiggle beneath the closet door. Jake willed himself not to freak out and opened the closet, broom in hand. Ready to send the snake to its demise, he couldn't find it. Used to people around, he questioned his sanity. Maybe the solitude of the place was getting to him, causing him to have snake hallucinations.

The following morning when he found a bullsnake curled up the bathroom rug, he grabbed the garbage can to trap it, only to turn around and find it gone. He hustled to Josh and Jenna's house and hastily knocked on the back door before hurrying inside. Jenna was gone on a business trip, but Josh was in the kitchen making breakfast. Jake could smell the bacon frying as Josh expertly cracked an egg into a hot skillet.

"Josh, do you know how to trap a snake?" Jake asked.

The egg in Josh's hand hit the floor. "A what?" Josh turned around, his face pale beneath his tan.

"A snake. There's a snake in my house and I don't think I can spend all summer living with it.

Do you know a way to trap it?" Jake tore off a paper towel and wiped up the splattered egg. "I can't quite bring myself to grab it with my bare hands."

"I'll get something today," Josh said, then started muttering about rodents and reptiles. Jake didn't know what had Josh all worked up and decided to leave well enough alone.

True to his word, Jake arrived home that evening to find a snake trap in each room. Apparently, a smell inside the box attracted snakes and glue in the bottom held them captive once they got inside. Jake sincerely hoped it would work.

Exhausted from a long day of hard work, he took a shower then climbed into bed. Nearly asleep, he felt something by his foot. He remained perfectly still and realized he not only felt something by his foot, but the something moved. With a startled yell, he jumped out of bed, turned on the light, and yelled again when the snake slithered across his bed and disappeared behind the headboard. Jake grabbed his jeans and keys then raced to Josh's house and pounded on the door.

Josh answered, his hair still wet from his evening shower and a towel wrapped around his waist.

"What's wrong, Jake? You look awful." Josh opened the door wider so Jake could come inside.

"The snake was in my bed." Jake shuddered. Just thinking about it made his skin crawl all over again.

Josh stared at him with his mouth open. When he finally spoke, he shook his head and put a hand on Jake's shoulder.

"I'm really sorry. I thought we caught all the snakes. Evidently, one is quite an escape artist. I'll go over tomorrow and make sure it is taken care of. I'm so sorry, man." Josh walked Jake into the living room. "Why don't you sleep in one of the upstairs bedrooms tonight? Take your pick."

"What do you mean you thought you caught all of them?" Jake asked, suddenly curious how many had been in his house.

"There were, um… a few in there when the girls went to clean. Clay and I sealed all the holes so it shouldn't be a problem," Josh said, turning on the stair light, illuminating the steps up to the second floor. "Sleep tight."

The next morning, when the two of them went to the house, a thumping noise greeted them as they walked in the door. Caught in one of the traps, the snake let them know how much it didn't like the arrangement. Josh took great pleasure in removing it from the premises.

Just in case any more snakes decided to take up residence, Josh left the other traps in place. While they didn't have any more problems, Jake developed an acute fear of snakes.

Chapter Four

Josh settled into his recliner, picked up the evening's paper and prepared to enjoy the quiet of day's end when the phone rang. Jenna was outside watering her flowers, so he picked it up on the third ring.

"Hello." Josh barely contained his anger as he recognized the name on the caller ID.

"I want to talk to Jenna," a male voice that was becoming all too familiar demanded.

"I don't think so. What do you want?" Josh stewed with barely repressed anger.

"Tell her Dennis called. I need to speak with her." With that, the line went dead.

Josh felt like throwing the phone into the fireplace. Dennis Gillman had called Jenna every evening for the past week and a half. Sometimes on her cell, other times on their home phone. She never answered and never said anything about the calls. The whole situation made him irate, frustrated, and suspicious.

Anytime he asked her about Dennis or his calls, she seemed nervous and defensive. Josh wondered what, exactly, was going on.

Jenna would be traveling again the following week and he didn't want to think about Dennis calling her every evening while she was gone. He looked outside and watched his wife water her flowers. He had no idea what to make of Dennis Gillman's sudden obsession with her.

By refusing to talk about the problem, she certainly didn't alleviate his concerns.

Outside, Jenna savored the last rays of sunshine as she watered the flowers around the house. As she held the hose above a big planter at the corner of the porch, her cell phone rang. She pulled it out of her pocket and sighed before turning it off. Gillman, again.

Dennis Gillman was a new hire at the office. He, along with Jenna and two others, traveled together to Washington D.C. for training. When they weren't in classes, he seemed to think she was his personal escort.

Well into his forties, Dennis Gillman appeared to possess the maturity of a hormone-ridden teenager. With a pretty-boy face and a suave manner, he operated under the assumption that no woman could resist him. When Jenna completely ignored him, he took it as a personal challenge and had been in relentless pursuit of her affections ever since. It only spurred him on when she pointed out she was married and uninterested.

Jenna hoped returning from the training and settling into a work routine would calm him down, but if anything, his behavior worsened. She knew Josh was irritated with the phone calls. Good thing he never saw her emails, or he'd come unhinged by some of the suggestive messages Dennis had sent.

Not wanting to get her coworker in trouble, or possibly fired, Jenna thought she could handle the situation. Unfortunately, Gillman proved to be more difficult than Jenna imagined. She planned to try one last time to set him straight. If that didn't work, she would go to her supervisor with a copy of the emails and a record of the phone calls.

She turned off the hose and decided tomorrow would be soon enough to worry about Mr. Gillman.

Down on her knees pulling weeds out of the flowerbed in her front yard, Callan glanced up as Josh parked in her driveway. Surprised to see him when she knew he was busy haying, she thought it odd that he would show up at her house mid-morning on a Friday. He normally called if he planned to come over and he never came when there was fieldwork waiting for him at home.

Quickly standing, she brushed dirt from her jeans, pulled off her gloves and walked over to meet him at the front door.

"What brings you by today?" Callan asked, giving him a hug. "Is this a social call or is something going on?"

Josh removed his ball cap and toyed with the brim, looking tired and worried. "Can we go inside and talk?"

Immediately, Callan knew something was wrong and bothering her brother. Rarely serious, the fact that he wanted to go inside to talk set off her inner alarms.

Callan led the way inside the house to the kitchen. She motioned Josh to sit at the table while she washed her hands and poured glasses of cold sweet tea.

"What's up? Something is wrong." Callan placed a glass in front of Josh and sat down across from him. "Let's hear it."

"I think Jenna may be having an affair," Josh finally said, tracing circles on the tabletop with his finger, unable to look Callan in the eye.

Shocked, Callan fixed him with a disbelieving glare. "What? Are you insane? What in the world would make you think that?"

"This guy, Dennis Gillman, keeps calling for her. It started the day after she came back from D.C. He calls every evening. If I answer, he hangs up or is extremely rude. Last night he called and hung up. Right before bed he called back and Jenna answered. She didn't know it, but I picked up the phone. Their conversation was very interesting, to say the least."

"What did Jenna say?" Callan asked.

"I didn't actually hear her on the phone, but I heard Gillman tell her he missed her and couldn't wait to lay his eyes on her 'luscious bod.'" Josh made quotes in the air with his fingers and released a disgusted sigh. "I hung up after that. I'm about ready to let Gillman know exactly what I think of him."

Callan tried to look at the situation from a different angle. She placed a gentle hand on Josh's where it rested on the table. "Don't do anything you'll later regret. Did you talk to Jenna? Did you ask her about it? Maybe it isn't what it seems."

Josh shook his head. "I've tried talking to her about it multiple times, but she gets defensive and clams up. What am I supposed to think?"

"I agree it sounds incriminating, but Jenna would never cheat on you. She loves you," Callan tried to reassure him.

"Would you talk to her, Cal? Please?" Josh pleaded. He looked dejected and wounded, uncertain what to do, and entirely unlike himself. "Would you see if you can find out what's going on? Even if she isn't having an affair, there's definitely something not right about the whole situation."

"I agree. There is something peculiar about it all. I'm happy to talk to her. Maybe you could come over for dinner this weekend," Callan suggested, trying to think of a way to broach such a delicate subject with her sister-in-law.

"Could you please talk to her today? Please?" Josh begged. "I can't take not knowing, Cal. I need to know what's going on now. You could go out to lunch and talk to her."

Callan wasn't sure what to say. This was so unlike Josh. He rarely asked her for favors and she'd never seen him look so upset and discouraged.

"Let me see if she'll meet for lunch. If so, I'll go talk to her. If not, we'll have to think of a different plan," Callan said, dialing Jenna's number.

Josh could tell from the one-sided conversation

that Jenna agreed to lunch and Callan would meet her at the office at noon.

"All right. I'm going to have to hustle to get cleaned up and to her office before noon," Callan said, standing from the table and punching in another phone number. When she hung up from speaking with the school secretary, she turned to Josh.

"You're going to have to take care of the girls today. Clay has classes all day, so you need to pick up Emma at school at a quarter to noon on the dot. You can't be late or she gets upset. I called to let the school know it's fine for Emma to leave with you. You need to be here at a quarter past three to meet Audrey when the bus drops her off in case I'm not back yet. I planned to run into Portland early next week to pick up some things for an event next weekend, but I'll pick them up today since I'll be in the city."

"Okay. I got it. Emma before noon, Audrey after school. No problem. I can take care of it." Josh stepped over to the sink and set his empty glass in it.

"Emma will need lunch and Audrey likes to have an afterschool snack. You can either stay here with the girls or take them back to your house. I'll call you as soon as I'm almost home," Callan said, walking Josh out to his pickup.

She pulled Emma's booster seat out of her car and fastened it into the backseat of Josh's pickup. "Now, get going so I can get ready."

"Thanks, Cal." Josh gave her a warm hug, "You're the best."

"Don't forget it," she teased as she ran back inside the house, convinced Josh was wrong about his suspicions.

In the mood to celebrate, Jenna looked forward to lunch with Callan, deciding her sister-in-law had perfect timing in her request to meet for lunch.

First thing that morning, Jenna walked up to Dennis Gillman and demanded he leave her alone or she would take the issue to her supervisor. His response was to ask her what color underwear she wore and attempt to kiss her.

Fed up with his inappropriate shenanigans, she marched back to her office, printed off his offensive emails, retrieved a list of her incoming cell phone calls, and took the evidence to her supervisor. After a brief discussion, Gillman was relieved of his duties, given a few minutes to clean out his desk, and escorted out of the building with a dire warning should he ever darken the doorstep again.

With a heavy weight lifted from her shoulders, Jenna couldn't wait for Callan to arrive. A few minutes before noon, the receptionist called to let her know she had a visitor. Jenna snatched her up her purse, hurried out to the reception area, and gave Callan a warm hug.

"This is such a pleasant surprise, Callan. Your timing is perfect." Jenna looped her arm through her sister-in-law's as they walked out the door and onto the busy sidewalk. "What are you in the mood for?"

"A big green salad and a nice quiet place to talk," Callan said, giving Jenna a pointed look.

Not sure what Callan wanted to discuss, Jenna suggested they go to a nearby restaurant that offered private outdoor seating areas. They soon found themselves sitting outside in the pleasant afternoon, enjoying the sunshine and good food.

"You might as well get to the point, Cal," Jenna said, taking a sip of her iced tea. "You didn't just happen to be in the city today and want to have lunch. We've been friends long enough, I can tell something's on your mind. Spit it out."

Callan occasionally forgot Jenna's gift for being plain spoken and driving right to the point.

"Josh came to see me this morning, quite concerned about you." Callan set her fork down on her plate and focused her attention on Jenna. She still couldn't imagine the woman ever cheating on Josh. She loved him too much. "Jenna, Josh... well, he thinks... Josh thinks you might be having an affair."

Jenna choked on the bite she swallowed. The tea she gulped to help wash it down made her cough even more. Callan thumped her on the back, uncertain what else to do. When Jenna could finally speak, sparks flew from her brown eyes.

"Josh thinks what? That idiot! How could he think that?" Jenna slumped against her chair, thoroughly incensed that Josh would ever question her commitment to him. "I would never, ever do such a thing."

Relieved by Jenna's declaration, Callan let her tense shoulders relax. "He said some guy named

Dennis Gillman keeps calling. Josh heard him say something rather inappropriate to you on the phone last night."

Jenna's mouth flattened into a tight seam. She knew she should have taken care of the problem sooner rather than ignoring it and hoping it would go away. With a frustrated sigh, she explained to Callan what happened, including discussing the problem with her supervisor and the termination of Gillman's position that morning.

"Well, merciful stars, Jenna! Why didn't you say something? Why didn't you tell Josh?" Callan was incredulous that Jenna wouldn't tell someone, anyone, about the unacceptable circumstances.

"I didn't want to seem weak for not being able to handle the problem. I'm a business professional and I should be able to take care of situations without involving anyone else. I train employees how to deal with problems exactly like this. It was embarrassing that I couldn't handle Gillman," Jenna quietly explained. "Besides, you know Josh. He would have flipped a gear and done something he shouldn't have."

"I can see why you didn't tell Josh. I probably would have done the same thing with Clay," Callan agreed, knowing her husband would have been infuriated if someone harassed her like Gillman had done to Jenna. "But you should have let someone at work know when it first started. You had no reason to be embarrassed, Jenna. He was the one who did something wrong, not you. It isn't a sign of weakness. It's a sign of being human."

Callan reached across the table and squeezed

Jenna's hand. "I told Josh there was more to this than he knew. I'm glad that, once again, I can prove my little brother wrong."

Jenna smiled at Callan as an idea formed in her head.

"I agree the evidence gave him reason to think something was going on, but he should know me well enough to not jump to conclusions. Crazy man," Jenna said, starting to grin in a way that meant she plotted something. "I think we need to teach him a lesson."

A wide, mischievous smile blossomed on Callan's face. "I'm all ears, what have you got in mind?"

Josh arrived at Emma's school five minutes before she got out for the day. As he stood outside with other parents, he watched for her little blonde head to bob along with students rushing down the sidewalk.

He spotted her as soon as she stepped outside. She happily chatted with two other little girls, dragging a bright purple backpack behind her.

"Emma!" Josh called as she skipped his direction. "Emma Matthews."

Emma's head came up and she looked around. When she spotted Josh, she bid a hasty "bye" to her friends and ran toward him, curls flying while the backpack slapped against her legs.

Josh hunkered down and held out his arms to

her. "Hey, Sweet Pea. You mind spending the afternoon with me?"

Emma threw her arms around his neck and gave him a tight hug. "Really, Uncle Josh? I get to spend the day with you? Just me?"

Josh stood with her still in his arms and carried her to his pickup. "Yep. It's just the two of us until your sister gets home from school."

"Yippee!" Emma gave Josh another tight hug. She climbed into her booster seat in the back of the pickup and fastened her seat belt.

Josh slid in the driver's side, started the truck, and drove to a fast-food restaurant. "Can I interest you in some lunch, Sweet Pea?"

"Yep. I'm starving." Emma beamed as she gazed fondly at her uncle, excited to spend time with him.

Josh smiled at her as they pulled into the parking lot then went inside. Emma wanted the kid's meal with a hamburger. Rather than eating her lunch, she played with the toy that came in the meal.

"Emma, eat first, then you can play. Okay?" Josh scooted her forgotten hamburger closer to her and took the toy away.

"Okay, Uncle Josh." Emma looked displeased, but she obeyed. She hurriedly ate her hamburger, took two bites of her fries then turned her attention back to her toy. Josh let her play for a few minutes while he finished his meal and her fries.

"Are you ready to roll?" Josh cleaned up their table and dumped the trash into the garbage.

"Let's roll," Emma said, grabbing his hand and

swinging on it.

If he wasn't careful, Josh could get used to the feel of a tiny hand in his big one. He smiled as he looked down at Emma's curly head.

Callan nicknamed her Sweet Pea when she was just a few weeks old and the name stuck. If anyone in their circle of family and friends mentioned Sweet Pea, everyone knew the name referred to little Emma.

He picked her up and set her in the booster seat, waiting until she buckled her seatbelt to close the door. He had no idea how he was going to entertain her all afternoon, but supposed he could figure something out. Jenna kept a box of toys somewhere in the house because he'd seen the girls playing with it before. They also had some Disney movies that Emma might like to watch. How hard could it be to keep a six-year-old entertained?

Two and a half hours later, Josh had exhausted his repertoire of child-appropriate stories, watched cartoons and, despite his heated protests, played with Barbie dolls. He made Emma promise not to tell anyone he sat on the floor and pretended to be Barbie's friend Misty. She had finally fallen asleep on the couch so he left her there and sat down to take a break in his recliner.

Although he knew he'd have to leave to pick up Audrey soon, he closed his eyes, for just a moment. Josh woke himself up when his chin hit his chest. Quickly opening both eyes, he looked at his watch and panicked.

He had less than ten minutes to get to Callan's house before Audrey would arrive. If he hustled, he could make it.

Springing out of his chair, he scooped up a sleeping Emma, ran out to his truck, and belted her limp body into the booster seat. After speeding down the gravel road, he barely stopped at the stop sign, raced to the highway, and zoomed toward Callan and Clay's.

As he pulled into the driveway, he watched the school bus turn down the road. Perfect timing. When Audrey stepped off the bus, Josh stood at the end of the driveway waiting for her.

"Uncle Josh! What are you doing here?" Audrey gave him a big hug.

"Auntie Callan had to go to Portland unexpectedly, so she asked me to take care of you and Emma for a while." Josh helped Audrey into the back seat of his pickup where Emma still slept. "I'm gonna take you back to my house. Okay?"

"Sure," Audrey said, chatting about school and her friends and how excited she was for summer vacation to start in a few weeks.

After parking by the back door, Josh helped Audrey climb out then carried Emma inside the house. The phone started ringing as they walked into the kitchen. Josh dropped his keys and Audrey's backpack on the counter, then struggled to grab the phone and shift Emma to one arm.

"Hello," Josh said, nearly dropping the phone as Emma woke up and started wiggling.

"Josh, its Callan. I'm running a few errands and will be a little later than I planned. Are you doing okay with the girls?"

"Yes, we're doing fine. I picked up Audrey and

we just walked in the door when you called. Take all the time you need." Josh set Emma on the counter as she opened her eyes and came fully awake. "Did you get a chance to talk to Jenna?"

"I did and what she shared was very interesting. I think we better discuss it in person." Callan didn't give any indication if he was right in his thinking or if something else was going on. "Thanks again for watching the girls."

"No problem. Thanks for your help, Cal." Josh felt even more worried now that Callan got information out of Jenna and wasn't saying anything. "I'll talk to you later."

Josh hung up the phone, looked at the two little girls in his care, and decided they probably could use a snack. He set Emma on a bar stool and helped Audrey onto one, then got out milk and cookies.

"Uncle Josh?" Audrey looked at him with her sweet face and big blue eyes that reminded Josh of a china doll he'd seen at his grandma's house when he was about Audrey's age. "Can I ask you a question?"

"Sure, honey. What's on your mind?" Turning to look at his niece, he wondered what ran through her head.

"Do you think Auntie Callan and Uncle Clay would mind if we called them Mama and Daddy?" Audrey asked quietly.

Josh took a moment to answer. Before he could speak, he needed to swallow down the emotion clogging his throat. Callan and Clay would be thrilled beyond words that the girls wanted to refer to them as their parents.

"I think they would like that very much," Josh said, offering her an encouraging smile. "Have you mentioned it to Auntie Callan?"

"No." Audrey toyed with a cookie. "I didn't know what she would say and I was afraid she might say no. I didn't want her to say no."

Josh pulled Audrey onto his lap and hugged her tight. Carefully, he chose his words. "Audrey, you can talk to Auntie Callan, your new mama, about anything. If she tells you no about something, it would only be because no is what would be best for you. But I promise you, if you ask her if you can call her mama, she won't tell you no."

"Really?" Audrey sounded hopeful, looking up at her uncle with trusting eyes.

"Really." Josh grinned down at her. He looked over at Emma as she played with her cookie and put a hand around her little shoulders. "What do you think Emma? Would you like to call them Mama and Daddy?"

"Yep. It was my idea." Emma nodded her head knowingly. "I told Audrey we had to call them something different than our first mom and dad so that's why I said it should be Mama and Daddy. Auntie Callan, I mean Mama, calls Gampa 'Daddy' and I think it sounds nice. Don't you?"

"Yes, I do. It sounds better than nice." Josh ruffled Emma's hair. "How about you girls come with me out to the barn? I think I saw a new litter of kittens out there the other day. I bet if we tried real hard, we could find them."

"Yippee!" Emma jumped off her barstool and ran to the door. "Let's roll!"

By the time Callan arrived to pick up the girls, Josh was thoroughly exhausted. He'd rather work outside digging ditch all day in hundred-degree temperatures than try to keep two little girls entertained. When Callan walked in the door, they sat on the couch watching *Snow White* while Josh collapsed in his chair, enjoying a few minutes of rest.

"Hello," Callan called as she breezed inside the back door. "Anybody home?"

The girls heard her voice and ran toward her. Callan bent down to give them both a hug.

"Mama, we missed you!" Emma hugged Callan tightly

Josh knew he'd never forget the look on Callan's face when Emma called her Mama. It was a look of joy, wonder, and love unlike anything he'd ever seen.

Callan sank to her knees, pulled both girls to her, and kissed the tops of their heads. "Emma, did you just call me Mama?" Callan asked.

"Yep. Uncle Josh said it would be okay. It is okay, isn't it?" Emma gazed at Callan with her lower lip starting to protrude in a pout.

"Oh, Sweet Pea, it's more than okay. It's absolutely wonderful." Callan kissed the girls again then looked up at Josh with tears in her eyes. She mouthed "thank you" to him over the girls' heads, struggling to keep her tears from overflowing.

Josh grinned. "You're welcome."

Chapter Five

Hot, tired and dirty, Josh returned to the house in a dark mood after a long, hard day working in the fields.

Due to the girls getting Callan wound up over calling her mama the previous afternoon, she whisked them home to share the news with Clay and completely forgot to tell him what she found out from Jenna.

Although he called her multiple times throughout the day, he kept getting her voice mail. Finally deciding to catch her after church the following day, he tried to let go of his overwhelming need to know what Jenna said about having an affair. Callan would have said something if it was all a misunderstanding. The fact she wanted to talk in person had him plenty worried.

Josh opened the door to the mudroom and walked inside, speculating what delicious thing Jenna had made for dinner. After shucking off everything but his underwear, he strolled into the kitchen and found it empty. No taste-tempting aromas of dinner cooking filled the air.

"Jenna," he called, walking through the house.

"Jenna?" He entered their bedroom and noticed the closed bathroom door. He gathered a change of clothes from his dresser drawers and was ready to knock on the door when it opened. Jenna strode into the bedroom dressed for an evening out on the town. She wore more makeup than usual with her hair piled on top of her head.

His gaze fastened on the burgundy cocktail dress that hugged every curve. A pair of strappy high heels drew his eyes to her legs while her perfume wafted around him in a sensual vanilla cloud.

"Whoa, babe! You look fantastic. What are we doing?" He leaned over and kissed her cheek, afraid to get too close and get her dirty.

Jenna laughed, picking up a little evening bag and dropping lip-gloss and a credit card case inside. "*We* aren't doing anything. Don't you remember? I told you weeks ago the girls are having a night out tonight. We're going to dinner and then the movies."

"What girls?" Josh asked, fighting to control his anger. He was certain there were no girls involved in the evening plans. If he were a betting man, he'd wager Jenna was off to meet Dennis Gillman.

"Callan and Laken, of course. Who do you think?" Jenna ignored his frown as she fastened a necklace around her neck, daring a glimpse at him in the dresser mirror. She almost burst into giggles at the sight of him standing in his underwear, hands fisted at his waist and a dark scowl on his handsome face. Barely containing her humor, she focused her attention on adjusting a strand of hair near her ear. "You're on your own for dinner and the evening. We might be late, so don't wait up for me."

"But, Jenna…" The ringing of Jenna's phone cut off anything he planned to say. Although she walked into the front room, he followed close enough to hear the one-sided conversation.

"I know. I can't wait to see you either. I'm wearing your favorite dress. No, he doesn't know. Yes, Giovanni's at seven. Me, too. Bye."

Josh was about to blow a fuse. Jenna *was* having an affair. Moreover, she wasn't even trying very hard to keep it a secret.

If she thought he'd stand by while she violated their marriage vows and walked out on him, she had another think coming. He masked his fury and stepped into the living room.

"Have a nice time." He kissed her cheek then plastered on a fake smile.

"Thanks, Josh, I will." She dropped her phone into her bag and walked out the door with a wave of her fingers.

Josh glanced at the clock on the wall and decided if he hurried he could grab a shower, drive to Giovanni's, and be at the restaurant in time to catch Jenna with lover boy. Just to confirm his suspicions, he called Callan and asked if she had plans for the evening. When she said no, he yelled, "Ha! I knew it!" and hung up the phone.

He ran into the bathroom, shaved and showered in record time. Determined to gain the upper hand, he pulled one of his suits with a crisp shirt out of the closet and rushed to get dressed. After swiping a rag over his good cowboy boots, he tugged them on, and finished knotting his tie as he ran out the door. If he was going to prove who the better man was, he sure wasn't going to do it dressed like a hick from the sticks.

Mindless of breaking the speed limit by several miles per hour, he wheeled into Giovanni's parking lot five minutes before seven. Inside, he went to the hostess station to see if she had seated Jenna, but had to stand in line and wait.

He glanced into the bar and noticed Jenna at a cozy table for two with a big burly cowboy sitting with his back to the door. Dennis Gillman wore a black Stetson, pulled low over his face, along with a black sports jacket. If he didn't know better, Josh could have sworn the guy was a twin to Clay from the back.

Josh marched into the bar, stomped up to the table, and turned a furious glare on his wife.

"Well, isn't this a cozy picture miss night-out-with-the-girls," Josh spat out, keeping his voice low even though his tone screamed his displeasure. Fiery indignation blazed in his gray eyes while his entire countenance oozed anger and disappointment. "How dare you lie to me? How dare you cheat on me? How dare you!"

Jenna gave him an innocent look. "Josh, I…"

Josh cut her off. "Don't you Josh me, missy. You answer my questions. How could you?"

"Now hold on a minute, there, city boy." Jenna's date stood from the table and pushed back his hat. "You might want to stop with the accusations."

Josh's head snapped up at the familiar voice and turned to gape at the face of his brother-in-law. He had no idea what Clay was doing at the table with Jenna, and he was too mad to listen to any explanations.

"So I've been betrayed by not only my wife, but also my best friend," Josh said in disbelief. "This just keeps getting better and better."

Instead of defending themselves, instead of admitting their guilt, they both laughed at him.

Laughed!

"I'm glad you find this so humorous," he said, staring at them with loathing. "Maybe you won't laugh so hard when Callan finds out, Clay. Hmm? Will it still be funny then?"

"Absolutely." Clay's cocky grin made Josh want to punch him in the nose. Clay stretched out his hand toward the bar. Callan slid off a barstool and wrapped her fingers around his as she stepped next to the table.

"Little brother, you have officially been had," Callan said with a big smile. "We got you good."

Confused and angry, Josh looked from Clay and Callan to Jenna then back again. "What is going on here?"

Jenna rose from the table and took Josh's arm, pulling him toward the hostess station. Clay and Callan walked behind them.

"We're ready for our table now," Jenna said to the hostess, who then led them to a table for four back in a corner. Once the girls sat down, the men took their seats. Josh's temper continued to boil.

"Would someone like to explain what is going

on?" he asked through clenched teeth.

"You asked me to find out if Jenna was having an affair and I did. I'll let her give you the details herself, but I told you all along Jenna would never cheat on you. Of course I was right," Callan said smugly. "We decided to teach you a lesson. Of course, Clay was more than happy to help."

"I do what I can." Clay smiled broadly then leaned back in his chair, quite pleased with his part in the prank.

Josh didn't know what to say. Humiliated by his wife, sister, and brother-in-law, he'd made quite a scene in one of their favorite restaurants. Now, they expected him to eat dinner, all nice and civilized, when he could hardly see straight.

He glanced at Jenna, realizing he should have talked to her instead of jumping to conclusions. Regardless of his abhorrence of conflict, he should have pressured her to discuss the problem at home. It certainly would have been better than the drama in the bar a few minutes ago.

Gently lifting Jenna's hand in his, his temper cooled and remorse settled in. He raised her hand to his lips and kissed her palm.

"I'm sorry, babe. You've never given me a reason to doubt you and I should have known you wouldn't cheat on me, but this still doesn't make sense. Who is Dennis Gillman? I know it wasn't Clay calling our house non-stop and hanging up on me when I answered the phone."

After a server took their orders, Jenna told the story of being harassed by Gillman. She explained how she finally turned the problem over to her supervisor the previous morning, before Callan met her for lunch.

"I'm sorry, too, Josh. I should have told you what was going on, but I wanted to handle it by myself. I didn't want you to worry and I didn't want you to fight my battle for me." Jenna stared down at her hands, nervously twisting the napkin on her lap.

"That's what husbands do, Jenna. We live to fight battles for the honor of our women. Isn't that right, Clay?" Josh asked, looking to his friend for support.

Clay grunted like a cavedweller and nodded his head. "Ugg and Zoog here to protect women."

Callan and Jenna laughed and the remaining tension around the table quickly dissipated.

"Who was on the phone earlier?" Josh asked as they ate the dinner. "Someone called right before you left."

"That was me," Callan said with a sly smile. "Jenna hid in your bathroom and called me when she heard you come in. The plan was to wait a few minutes then call her back pretending to be Gillman. We knew you'd be furious and follow her, and here we are."

"Thanks for behaving according to plan." Jenna patted Josh's hand.

He might have let his anger rise again if he hadn't looked into her eyes and started to fall into the their intoxicating depths.

The four of them relaxed and relished a rare evening out together. They were all dressed up, eating at the best restaurant in town, enjoying one another's company. Bobbi and Steve kept Audrey and Emma overnight. Without any little ones to hurry home to, the foursome decided to go to the movies and then stop for dessert before calling it a night.

As they parted company for the evening, Callan suggested they plan a night out once a month. Jenna readily agreed and they all promised the next time would not involve a joke at Josh's expense.

Josh followed Jenna's car home. The drive gave him time to think of a nice apology speech. He pulled into the driveway while Jenna parked in the garage, rehearsing what he wanted to say.

Even though Jenna thought she'd evened the score by playing the joke on him, Josh knew he owed his wife an apology. Despite incriminating evidence, he should have known, without a doubt, Jenna would never cheat on him. He'd violated her trust, questioned her commitment, and humiliated them both. If she kicked him out of their bedroom for a while, he couldn't blame her. Not in the least.

He walked into the kitchen and watched Jenna set her evening bag on the counter. When she turned to look at him, she kept her expression blank and shook her head. She folded her arms across her chest, leaned against the counter, and waited.

Josh cleared his throat and took a step toward her. Apologizing seemed a lot easier driving home than it was turning out to be in reality.

"Jenna..." He stared at his boots. Jenna stuck an index finger under his chin and pushed upward, bringing his gaze up to meet hers. Releasing a sigh, Josh took her hand in his and started over. "I'm so sorry, babe. I should have trusted you and never doubted you. Rather than jumping to conclusions, I should have discussed my concerns with you. I should have known you would never cheat on me. I'm the most jealous, stupid husband in the world and can only beg for your forgiveness. Please?"

"I don't know." Jenna tipped her head and studied him with her eyes full of unshed tears. "How could you, Josh? How could you ever think that I'd have an affair? How could you think I'd take our vows so casually? Disregard our love? I would never, ever do that and it hurts to know that's what you thought. You have absolutely no faith or trust in me."

Josh pulled her into his arms and rested his head on top of hers. "Jenna, that isn't true. I think I knew deep down that you wouldn't cheat on me, but in case you haven't noticed, I can get a little jealous and slightly unreasonable. What was I supposed to think when that guy kept calling?"

"That your wife had a problem and she didn't know how to handle it," Jenna said quietly. "Josh, I should have told you from the start what was going on. I was just so ashamed that I couldn't stop it and then I was afraid what you'd do if you found out."

"What did you think I would do?" Josh asked, suddenly curious to know how his wife thought he'd handle a problem like someone stalking her.

"I thought you'd get unreasonably angry and go beat him up, or show up at the office and make a scene. I'm truly sorry." Jenna hugged him tightly.

Josh smiled inwardly. Jenna wasn't far off in her assumptions of what he would have done, or at least felt like doing if she'd told him the truth.

"I'm as much to blame as you for not discussing the problem," Jenna said, trying not to cry. "I know you hate to engage in anything remotely resembling conflict and getting defensive was a way of shutting you out. I should have been willing to discuss it with you."

"Tell you what, babe. Next time you have a problem, you talk to me about it right away and I promise I won't go all cavedweller on you or jump to conclusions. Deal?" Josh rubbed his hands soothingly up and down Jenna's back, enjoying the feel of her silk dress beneath his hands. Her perfume teased his nose and he suddenly hoped they could forget about this incident and end the evening on a good note.

"Deal," Jenna said, pulling back to look up at him, her eyes molten and inviting. She lowered her voice and gave him a flirty smile. "I think now would be a very good time for you to kiss me."

Josh bent his dark head toward hers, kissing her slowly, teasingly, thoroughly with a passion that left them both breathless.

"I love you, Jenna." His lips brushed her ear, breath warm on her neck. "Always have, always will."

Chapter Six

After traveling for the last month with her new job, Jenna experienced some trepidation about her recent promotion.

In the past thirty days, she'd only been home for five. She worked late last night, rose extra early that morning, and hoped to arrive at the office by eight if she drove straight through without stopping for breakfast.

She hadn't bothered to drive home the previous weekend because it would have been an eight-hour drive one-way. After one day at home with Josh, she would have been back on the road Sunday. Instead, she hung out in a hotel, missing Josh, and wishing she were home. They talked or texted several times a day, but she still missed him, more than she ever imagined possible.

Josh had all he could do to keep on top of the summer farm work. When he wasn't working on their place, he did custom haying or helped Steve and Clay at their ranch. He liked to help there when he could because when he needed assistance, they were always quick to provide whatever he needed, be it equipment or free labor.

Jenna sighed as she watched the sun brighten the horizon on a beautiful June morning. The bright orb on the horizon streaked rays of pink and gold across the blue sky, giving the promise of another spectacular summer day.

Today was their wedding anniversary and she hoped Josh would pull his head out of farming long enough to remember.

The few days she had been home, he was so exhausted from farm work, he barely paid her any attention. He ate his meals in a hurry, asking her a few questions about her work before returning outside until dark. When he came in, he took a quick shower then collapsed on their bed, asleep as soon as his head hit the pillow. By the time she woke up, he was long gone out to the fields.

She realized now why Josh tried to talk her into getting married any time other than summer. It really was his busiest time of year and the thought of taking time off for even a short vacation or getaway was completely out of the question.

At the time, she thought he was being ridiculous, suggesting a winter or even early spring wedding. She wanted an outdoor ceremony in the summer and wasn't about to listen to what he tried to tell her.

They spent their first few anniversaries with him out in the field and her at home pouting. He tried to make it up to her by taking her out to dinner and giving her special gifts. After the third anniversary, she finally understood what he'd been saying all along and resigned herself to making the best of it. He always took her on a nice trip in

January when things were quiet and he had extra time to devote just to her.

Determined to make this anniversary special, despite their limited time together, she played over plans as she drove toward Portland. She had to leave again on Monday for another two weeks out of town, but hoped to make the weekend one Josh would remember.

Jenna enjoyed her work, even if it kept her separated from Josh more than she anticipated it would. Summer would be her heaviest travel time. By fall, Josh's workload would lighten and she would be home more. They just had to make it through September.

Jenna pulled into the office parking lot a few minutes before eight, picked up her purse and briefcase, then hurried inside. The quicker she finished up at the office, the sooner she could go home.

An hour later, she filed her last piece of paperwork. She ran a few errands before heading out of town toward Tenacity.

Surprisingly, the closer she got to home, the grayer the sky became. If it continued at this rate, they might receive a summer rainstorm. She hoped Josh had the hay all in. Although an afternoon rainstorm would help her plans immensely, rain on the hay would not make Josh happy.

After parking in the garage, Jenna wondered where she could find Josh. His pickup was home and the flat bed truck was parked down by the barn, so she assumed he was out somewhere on the four-wheeler.

Since he would come to the house for lunch, she hustled to put away groceries and get ready for his arrival. Josh wouldn't expect her to be home until late that evening, so she had the element of surprise working in her favor.

At a quarter past noon, Jenna heard the back door open and footsteps in the house. Quietly sneaking out of the bedroom, she tiptoed down the hall and into the kitchen. A pair of long, muscular, Wrangler-clad legs poked out from behind the open refrigerator door. Jenna smiled to herself, anticipating Josh's reaction when he turned around.

On her way home, she stopped at the mall to pick up a gift for Josh, one that she now wore. The transparent black lingerie was not something she would normally choose, but she decided to walk a little on the wild side for Josh. She applied an additional coating of mascara, donned a pair of strappy black heels, and gave herself a spray of his favorite perfume.

Provocatively leaning against the counter, she lifted her lips in an inviting smile and used her most sultry tone of voice. "If you're hungry, I've got something much more satisfying than anything you're going to find in there."

A plastic bottle of soda pop hit the floor and splattered everywhere. The head that popped out from behind the fridge door caused Jenna to blush five shades of red and snatch the dishtowel off the counter to hold in front of her.

After an initial ear-shattering scream, Jenna gasped. "Jake! What are you doing here?"

How could she have forgotten Jake was at the

farm?

Shamed beyond anything imaginable, Jenna hoped he hadn't seen anything. Jake was like the younger brother she never had. Despite her fervent pleas, the floor didn't open up and swallow her whole.

Jake turned red from the top of his head past the neck of his shirt. He spun around with his back to her while Mountain Dew soaked his legs and dripped on his boots. He'd seen enough to know he didn't want to see any more, especially when the scantily clad woman behind him was like an older sister.

"Dang it all, Jenna! What are you doing?" Jake spluttered, horrified. "I… we… Josh sent me in to make some lunch."

While watering Jenna's flowers, Josh heard a scream from inside the house. He tossed down the hose and ran inside as fast as humanly possible. When he plowed into the kitchen, he took in Jake's red face turned toward the wall. Jenna clutched a dishtowel to her chest and slowly backed out of the kitchen. Her outfit, at least what he could see around the dishtowel, made his eyes widen in astonishment.

Glad he wore a shirt that snapped up the front, Josh yanked it loose, slipped it around Jenna, and swept her into his arms. There was no way she could beat a hasty retreat down the hall in the shoes she wore. After carrying her to their bedroom, he kicked the door shut and dropped her on the bed. He stood and gaped at her for several long, silent moments.

"What are you doing?" he finally asked in a rough voice. As he ogled his wife, he felt confused, annoyed and wildly excited all at the same time. "You aren't supposed to be home until this evening."

"I wanted to surprise you." Jenna clutched Josh's shirt to her chest as her carefully styled hair fell across her face. She pushed it back and let out a ragged breath. "I completely forgot Jake was here. I certainly didn't plan on finding him in the kitchen."

Josh continued to stare at her. Just looking at his lovely wife, whom he hadn't seen in more than two weeks, caused his heart to pound while his blood thrummed through his veins. The fact that Jenna wore something so tempting made it hard for him to think beyond his sudden desire to grab his shirt and the dishtowel away from her so he could have an unobstructed view of her new outfit.

"Without a doubt, we're all surprised. What did you think would happen? It's the middle of the day and I've got more work to do than I can handle." Josh sounded gruffer than he intended.

Jenna really caught him off-guard and he was more than a little perturbed thinking about just how much of his wife Jake may have seen. As he took a step closer to the bed, a burst of thunder shook the house. He glanced out the window and frowned as rain began pouring down in sheets.

Tears pooled in her eyes when Jenna looked up at Josh.

"That is exactly what I hoped would happen. You can't make hay in the rain." She inclined her head toward the window. "Although I never dreamed Jake would be the one in the kitchen. Honestly, I didn't even think about him being here. I'm so sorry. I'm going to positively die from embarrassment."

"It's okay, babe. I don't think you'll die. I'm pretty sure you weren't what Jake expected to find when I sent him in to make sandwiches." Josh chuckled, suddenly finding the situation amusing, now that the initial shock had passed. "As a matter of fact, I'm guessing his eyeballs are feeling somewhat scorched right now."

He bent down to give her a kiss meant to be brief and welcoming, but it quickly turned into something heated and filled with longing. He leaned one knee on the bed while she wrapped her arms around his neck, drawing him closer.

"Babe, don't move. I'll be back in a minute," Josh whispered with his lips against her ear before opening the door and walking down the hall to the kitchen.

Jake suffered from acute embarrassment and looked unsettled as he wiped up the last of the spilled pop.

"I'm sorry, man. I didn't see anything." Jake tossed the paper towels into the garbage while his neck and ears continued to glow a shade of bright red.

"No need to apologize, Jake. Jenna forgot you were here. Honest mistake, that's all." Josh pulled his wallet out of his back pocket and fished out a twenty-dollar bill. After handing it to Jake, Josh thumped him on the back and pointed him toward the door.

"We aren't going to be able to finish anything in this rain. Why don't you run into town and get yourself some lunch? Take your time. On your way back, if you wouldn't mind stopping by the tire store to see if the tractor tire I ordered came in, you can charge it to my account. I'll meet you in the shop at three. Will that work for you?"

"Sure." Jake regained his sense of humor as he approached the back door. A wicked grin rode his lips as he opened the back door. He couldn't keep from teasing Josh. "Dude, enjoy your... um... lunch. Jenna mentioned something about it being quite satisfying."

Josh shoved Jake outside and turned off the hose he'd left running then hurriedly removed his boots, washed his hands, and hustled back to the bedroom.

Jenna was nowhere in sight. His shirt was on the bed and her shoes were on the floor halfway to the bathroom. She'd closed the blinds over the windows, throwing the room into shadows.

He hoped she hadn't changed. Josh relished the thought of fully exploring the little black number she wore, now that he'd warmed up to the idea of a few hours spent inside on a rainy afternoon.

"Jenna," he called, hoping she'd quit hiding behind the partially closed bathroom door. "Jake's gone, so come on out."

When she pulled the door open and stepped out, she wore her soft cotton bathrobe, much to his disappointment. She appeared mortified as she stared at him with tears in her eyes.

When he opened his arms to her, she buried her

face against him. Her tears dripped down his bare chest.

"Babe, don't cry. It's okay," he said soothingly, rubbing her back. "Don't worry about it. It was just a mistake."

She mumbled something inaudible against his chest so he used his thumb to push her chin up far enough he could hear her. "What did you say?" He wiped at her tears with the dishtowel she'd left on the bed and blotted the trails of mascara on his chest.

"I said I'll never be able to face Jake again. I'm so ashamed." Jenna sniffled. "I will never, ever do something like that again as long as I live."

Josh grinned and leaned down so their noses practically touched. "Now, let's not get carried away. I have to tell you, I wouldn't mind coming in and seeing you dressed like that from time to time. Just make sure Jake isn't around. I think I would have enjoyed the show much more than he did."

Jenna let out a choppy laugh and smacked Josh on the arm. "You're terrible, you know."

"I don't know anything of the sort." Josh wrapped his arms back around her and pulled her close. "Happy Anniversary, Jenna."

"Happy Anniversary." She raised her lips to his in a kiss filled with love and longing.

When Josh reached down and untied her robe, she let him. He pushed back the sleeves to reveal the filmy little gown that caused all the commotion. His gaze slowly traveled over every inch of her and he knew she could see the appreciation written across his face.

"This just might be the best anniversary present ever."

Later, after eating lunch, Josh walked Jenna around to the back patio where a gliding wood bench waited, tied with a big blue bow. She ran her hands over the smooth wood, taking in the detailed craftsmanship. Someone had burned the words, "*Give me your forever, not a day less will do*," into the wood on the backrest of the bench in a beautiful script.

"Josh, this is wonderful." Jenna removed the bow and tugged Josh down to sit beside her. "Where did you get it?"

"I made it, with some help," he answered, pleased she liked her gift. "Despite what you think, I did remember our anniversary and thought about it weeks ago. According to the information I researched, we're supposed to give wood or iron for this anniversary, so I decided to go with wood. Clay, Pop, and Jake helped me make the bench and then Bobbi and Callan helped with the wood burning. I guess you could call it a group effort."

"It is beautiful, thoughtful, and perfect." Jenna leaned against Josh's side as he wrapped an arm around her. "I can't thank you enough. Every time we sit on it, I'll remember today, remember how much I love you right at this very moment."

"And don't forget scorching Jake's eyeballs," Josh teased, giving her a cocky grin. "You can't forget that."

Jenna blushed and ducked her head. "I'm sure even if I could forget it, you'll keep reminding me."

Josh kissed her again and cuddled her close for

a few minutes before he looked at his watch and stood. They walked back inside the house and Josh turned to look out the kitchen window as Jake pulled his pickup in by the shop, a large tire bouncing in the back.

"I told Jake to meet me at the shop, so I better get moving." Josh yanked on his gloves and settled his ball cap on his head. "Do you want to go out for dinner tonight?"

"I think I'd rather stay home," Jenna said, kissing his cheek. "I'll see you later and please give Jake my apologies. I don't think I'm quite ready to face him myself."

Jenna managed to avoid seeing Jake the rest of the weekend and was glad she didn't have to face him. Every time she thought of what had happened, her face flushed red and a wave of humiliation swept over her. Even admitting the blunder could have happened to anyone, it didn't help her feel any less shamed. She argued with herself that most women would not prance around in their unmentionables in the middle of the day, trying to beguile an over-worked husband.

When it came time to leave Monday morning, Jenna dreaded the next month. She had two more weeks on the road, three days off, and then another two weeks before she would be home to stay for a few weeks. In spite of what she kept trying to tell herself, she was really starting to dislike her new job.

Chapter Seven

Josh hated Jenna's new job. He could count on his two hands the number of days she'd been home since she started it.

He missed her with an ache that began in his heart and spread out to every part of his being. He missed her laughter, her smile, and her witty conversation. He missed coming in from the fields at night to see her cooking dinner and knowing something delicious would be ready to eat by the time he got out of the shower. He missed the subtle fragrance of her perfume lingering around him, even after she'd left the room. He missed seeing her shoes kicked off under a kitchen barstool and her purse sitting on the chair by the back door. He missed looking into her eyes and getting lost in the dark depths.

Most of all, he missed her presence, her spirit. The house seemed so empty, cold, and unwelcoming without her in it.

For him, Jenna was home.

At night, he could barely sleep without her beside him. He was used to her warmth and the funny little sounds she made while she slept.

The additional income she made was nice, but he'd rather they both be completely broke than have to spend all this time apart. Although she enjoyed the challenge of her position, he didn't know how much longer he could stand having her gone.

She arrived home Friday afternoon for what was supposed to be three days off. Instead, she got a call Friday evening asking if she could fly to Boston Sunday for a meeting. When she returned from it, she would be back on the road for another week and a half before coming home. Josh worked long hours Friday and came in so late he did nothing more than eat dinner and collapse on the bed. The custom haying job he had to finish Saturday kept him working late, so they hardly saw each other at all.

Exhausted and disappointed, they went to bed with barely a kiss good night and fell into a deep sleep. Josh got up as she hurried to dress and leave for her early flight, giving her a kiss filled with desperation and longing as she walked out the door.

"Jenna, I love you. Always have, always will. Don't forget that." He held her close and breathed in her scent one more time before she left.

Struggling to hold back her tears, she kissed him with a sense of urgency that bordered on despair. "I love you, too, Josh. I miss you so much. I promise in a couple of weeks, we'll spend some time together."

Jenna fought overwhelming exhaustion during her trip to Boston. She woke up in the mornings tired and sometimes with a headache. For the first time in her life, she thought she might throw up on her flight back from Boston. It took every ounce of fortitude she possessed to keep herself from being violently ill. Immediately after landing, she headed out for her next assignment. As she struggled with a queasy stomach, she wondered if she might have a touch of the flu, but quickly decided the stomach flu wouldn't linger this long.

Tomorrow, she would be home and had two weeks reprieve before she was scheduled to head out on the road again. She couldn't wait to relax in her own home, sleep in her own bed, and see Josh.

Late the next afternoon, she drove into the garage. When the door to the mudroom opened before she turned off the motor, she was surprised to see Josh hurry out to open her car door. Without a word, he pulled her into his arms.

Kissing her deeply, he gathered her close and held her there, trying to fill the emptiness that had loomed in him since she left.

"Babe, I missed you so much." He buried his face in her hair, breathing in her scent. "Please tell me you're home for more than a day or two."

She hugged him tightly and soaked in his warmth while the smells of sunshine, hay, and his aftershave teased her nose. "I don't have to go anywhere for two weeks."

Josh picked up her suitcase and carried it inside while maintaining his hold on her hand. He seemed reluctant to break contact with her.

"Is everything okay?" she finally asked. He acted so strange, oddly clinging.

"Yes. No... I missed you more than I thought humanly possible." He dropped her suitcase and again pulled her into his embrace. "I wish you didn't have to leave again. Ever."

"I know, Josh. Part of me wishes that, too. The other part of me loves what I'm doing and I'm learning more than I ever dreamed." Jenna hoped he understood how much it meant to her to be able to succeed in her work.

"Well, darn it, Jenna. Do you have to be so good at everything you do?" His teasing smile worked its way up to his glowing gray eyes.

She smiled at his compliment and sat down on a kitchen barstool while he poured two glasses of iced tea.

"What are you doing in the house on a beautiful day like today?" she asked, taking a sip of the sweet tea. "I assumed you'd either be out in the fields or off on a custom job."

Josh took a long drink of his tea before answering.

"I sent Jake over to do the Tuttle's baling. He should be done in another hour or so. I was working on some repairs in the shop and remembered I had some picking up to do in here before you got home." Josh shot her a sheepish smile. He'd been hustling for the last hour, throwing dirty clothes into the washing machine, wiping down the kitchen, putting fresh sheets on the bed, and straightening their bathroom. The house looked good, if he did say so himself. He'd just finished loading the dishwasher and turned it on when he saw Jenna's car pull into the drive.

"Everything looks wonderful." Josh generally did a good job of keeping the house up despite his busy farm schedule. She hoped he knew how much she appreciated all his hard work and his willingness to let her try this new career.

"I wasn't sure if you remembered, but we're supposed to go to dinner and then a play with Clay and Callan tonight. If you're too tired, warmthey'll understand." Josh leaned across the counter as he spoke, his eyes intent on her tired face. He almost hoped she would cancel because he wouldn't mind staying home with her this evening.

"Oh, I did forget, but I'd still love to go. I've got time to get ready, don't I?" Jenna glanced at the kitchen clock.

"Plenty of time." Josh kissed her on the cheek. "I'll call Cal and let her know we're still on. Why don't I have them meet us here and we can ride together."

"Sounds great." Jenna finished her tea then tugged her suitcase into the bedroom. The bed looked so inviting, she wanted to sink onto it and sleep for a week. Instead, she drew a bath, deciding she had time for a short soak. She hoped it would ease the achiness that had plagued her the last several days so she could enjoy the evening ahead.

Jenna awoke to Josh knocking on the bathroom door.

"Babe, you better get a move on. Clay and Cal will be here in half an hour." Josh stuck his head around the bathroom door. "Have you been in the tub all this time?"

Jenna couldn't believe she fell asleep in the tub. That was definitely a first. She glanced at her shriveled fingers and wondered how long it would take them to look normal again. Frantically grabbing a towel, she got out of the tub then plugged in her blow dryer and flat iron.

"I'll be ready in a flash," she said, blowing her hair dry. "Want to time me?"

"No need. I'll still be ready before you are." Josh laughed, taking clothes out of the closet and laying them on the bed before he jumped in the shower.

Josh beat her getting ready by a full five minutes. She walked into the living room just as Clay and Callan strolled in the back door.

After deciding to go in Callan's car, they enjoyed catching up on the drive into Portland. Clay pulled into the restaurant parking lot where they sat at a cozy booth for four and savored a delicious meal. At the play down the street, they ran into Jenna's aunt and uncle.

"Jenna, sweetie, we haven't seen you forever," Amelia said, embracing her in a hug and a fog of perfume.

"I know, Aunt Amelia. I've been kind of busy with my new job." Jenna wrapped her arm around her aunt's as they walked inside the theater. It turned out Phil and Amelia's seats were just a few rows over from them, so they visited until it was time for the performance to begin. After the play, a great comedy, Amelia and Phil invited them over for dessert.

"I didn't have time to bake today, Jenna, so I picked up something from that wonderful bakery you always liked so well," Amelia explained. "One of their chocolate creations."

"I don't think it would hurt for just a short visit,

would it Jenna?" Josh was more than willing to eat chocolate cake as long as Amelia didn't make it. He turned to his sister, convinced he could count on her support. "What do you think, Callan?"

"That sounds lovely." Callan smiled in agreement.

Josh knew she wouldn't let him down when it came to chocolate.

Over chocolate cheesecake with raspberry sauce, Clay carried most of the conversation with Amelia and Phil while Callan and Josh savored every bite of the treat. Jenna looked like she could barely stay awake as she leaned over her untouched dessert.

On the drive home, Jenna fell asleep against Josh's shoulder. He slipped his arm around her and pulled her close.

Callan glanced back and shook her head. "Is she feeling okay, Josh?" Concern filled her voice. "She looked so pale and tired this evening, I wondered if she was sick."

"I'm not sure." Josh stared down at his wife. It certainly wasn't like her to be fatigued and lack energy. Generally, she was a ball of fire, running circles around him. "She fell asleep in the tub when she got home and then had to rush to get ready before you two arrived. I wonder if she's just exhausted from all the travel and stress of her job."

"Probably," Callan commented as they turned into Josh and Jenna's driveway. "She should have said something and we could have done this another time."

"I know, but she really did want to go." Josh

unfastened both his and Jenna's seatbelts, waking her up.

"Oh, are we home already?" Jenna sat up, looking disoriented. "Sorry. I didn't mean to conk out on you guys."

"Don't worry about it." Callan smiled from her spot in the front seat. "We had a great time and it's your turn to pick our outing next month. Just tell us when and where to show up."

"I will. Thanks again for this evening. It was so nice." Jenna tried unsuccessfully to stifle a yawn.

"I better get her inside or she might just curl up on the step," Josh teased, giving Jenna his hand as she climbed out of the car. "See you both later and thanks again."

Jenna's head barely touched her pillow before she sank into a deep sleep. Josh watched her in the moonlit shadows and worried about what was wrong with his wife.

Chapter Eight

Although she slept most of the weekend, Jenna was exhausted. She lacked the energy to do more than shuffle into the kitchen to get a drink or eat something before shuffling back to the bed and sleeping for hours on end. Nearly in a panic by the time Monday morning arrived, Josh hovered by her side.

"Babe, let me take you to the doctor this morning," he said, sitting on the edge of the bed. While Jenna slept through the weekend, he kept watch, trying to figure out what could make her so tired. Shadows hung beneath his bleary eyes as he fidgeted with the edge of the sheet. "Please? Something isn't right and I really think you should let the doctor take a look."

"I have an appointment tomorrow. One more day won't make any difference." Jenna struggled to keep her eyes open long enough to talk to Josh. "I'm sure I'll feel better soon."

"Right," Josh said without any conviction. He leaned over and put an arm on each side of her head. He stared into her eyes, willing the sparks he often saw there to flare to life. Instead, all he saw was weariness. "I've got my phone if you need me today, okay? Promise you'll call me if you don't feel better or if you need something."

"I promise." Jenna lifted her arms to hug him around the neck, offering him a soft kiss. "I love you."

"I love you, too, babe." Josh stood, unconvinced it was a good idea to leave her alone.

"Go on, Josh. I'll be fine," Jenna tried to reassure him. After summoning a smile, she shooed him in the direction of the door. "I'm sure Jake is wondering what happened to you. Get going, Farmer Man."

Josh walked backward to the bedroom door and smiled at her before he turned and left. If she didn't look better when he returned, he would personally escort her to the doctor.

Jenna couldn't keep her eyes open and drifted back to sleep. She awoke at noon when she heard a noise in the kitchen. Unable to muster the energy to shuffle down the hall, she raised her voice. "Josh, is that you?"

She heard more noise, like something being set down on the counter, then footsteps approached the bedroom. A soft knock preceded a dark head peeking into the room. It was Jake.

"Josh went over to the Weaver's to finish swathing." Jake stood in the doorway, looking uncertain. After the last lunchtime fiasco, she couldn't blame him for acting hesitant around her. "Can I get you something, Jenna?"

"No, thank you, Jake. I'm fine. I heard someone in the kitchen and thought it was Josh. Go ahead and eat your lunch. Don't mind me." Jenna was embarrassed for anyone to see her looking like such a tousled mess. She hadn't showered since Saturday. If she looked even half as bad as she felt, she must make quite a sight.

"Are you sure I can't bring you something to drink or eat?" Jake gave her a worried glance. "Josh said you've been under the weather. I could make you some tea or soup."

"Thank you, Jake. I appreciate the offer." Jenna smiled at his eagerness to help. Someday, a lucky girl would find herself blessed to snag Jake Chandler, if he was ever of a mind to let someone catch him. "If it wouldn't be too much trouble, I'd love a glass of iced tea and some toast."

"No problem. I'll be right back." Jake hustled to the kitchen. She heard him banging around and in no time he was back with a glass of tea, a plate with two pieces of toast, buttered and sliced, and a napkin on a tray. Jenna scooted back to sit against the pillows and pulled the sheet up to her chin.

"Where do you want this?" Jake asked, walking over to the bed. Jenna took the tray out of his hands and placed it on her lap. She offered him a weak smile, but one that held gratitude.

"This looks wonderful. If you don't mind eating in here, I'd love to hear some news of what's been going on in the world while I slept away the last few days," Jenna said as Jake stepped away from the bed.

"Sure, Jen. Just give me a minute." Jake returned to the kitchen. He reappeared with two sandwiches, a pile of chips, and a mound of grapes on a plate along with a big glass of tea. Jenna motioned him to a small side table beneath the window.

"Set those books on the floor and drag the table and chair over here." Jake followed her direction. In no time, they laughed and visited, just like old times. Jenna forgot about her exhaustion for a little while.

Jake took the last bite of a sandwich when Jenna heard a voice call from the kitchen.

"Hello, anybody home?"

"We're in the bedroom. Come on in," Jenna replied.

Callan entered the room carrying a vase of summer roses. "I thought you might like something to cheer you up." Callan set the flowers down on the dresser and looked around the room.

"Well, goodness, Jake, how are you? I haven't seen you forever since you enlisted to be Josh's summer slave labor." Callan grinned.

Jake stood up and gave her a warm hug. "Josh keeps me plenty busy, but I enjoy it," Jake said, picking up his plate and glass.

"You know, I think you just get more handsome every time I see you," Callan teased, playfully pinching his cheek and watching his ears and neck turn red. "But don't let it go to your head."

Jenna and Callan both laughed as he hurried into the kitchen. He returned to move the side table and chair back under the window, replacing the books on top.

"Okay, I'm out of here and back to the field. Despite my heart-stopping good looks, Josh will still expect some work out of me today. Jen, it looks like you're in good hands this afternoon." Jake gave Callan another hug. In all the years he'd known her, she'd become like a second mother or well loved sister to him and he enjoyed spending time with her.

Jenna held out her hand to him, giving his a light squeeze when he engulfed her fingers in a rough hand. "Thank you for coming to my rescue, Jake. I very much appreciate it. Have a great afternoon."

"You're welcome. Bye ladies." Jake walked out the door.

Callan sat down on the edge of Jenna's bed and looked at her intently. After studying her for a few minutes, she leaned back and smiled.

"Your husband was convinced you were on your deathbed this morning and asked me to check on you," Callan explained. "The girls went with Clay to Steve and Bobbi's so I thought I'd spend the afternoon, if you don't mind. Josh said you've been down in bed all weekend. Where do you feel sick?"

"That's the problem," Jenna said, exasperated by both her strange illness and Josh. She appreciated him wanting to take care of her, but to ask Callan to babysit her was going too far. "I don't really feel sick anywhere. I'm just tired. Bone tired. I sleep and sleep, wake up and think about doing something, then fall back asleep before I can get up."

"Maybe your travel schedule just has you exhausted. You've been on the road so much the past couple of months and it has been so hot, maybe you got dehydrated as well," Callan said, trying to think of reasons why Jenna might not feel well.

"I tried to tell Josh I have a doctor's appointment tomorrow, so I didn't see any reason to get all worked up, yet." Jenna slid back down in the bed as her eyes grew heavy.

"Is there anything you'd like me to do?" Callan knew Jenna was about to go back to sleep.

"No, I'm fine. You really don't have to stay," Jenna said softly as her eyes drifted shut and she fell asleep.

Callan picked up Jenna's lunch tray and returned it to the kitchen. She gathered up all the dirty clothes she could find and started the laundry then went outside and watered Jenna's garden and flowers.

When she finished, she returned inside to check on Jenna. The woman continued sleeping, so Callan returned to the kitchen. After digging around in the freezer, she pulled out some meat and planned dinner.

By the time Josh returned home, Callan had completed three loads of laundry, picked up the house, and made dinner along with a chocolate cream pie. Jenna had taken a shower and sat in bed wearing a T-shirt and shorts, sipping from a glass of lemonade.

Josh pecked Callan on the cheek, washed his hands at the kitchen sink, and looked around in appreciation.

"I didn't know when I called you that a miracle worker was going to come over," Josh said with a grin. "Honest, Cal, I didn't expect you to work all afternoon, just keep an eye on Jenna."

"I know, Josh, but she was tired and needed to sleep. I couldn't sit around doing nothing," Callan said as she pulled a pork roast out of the oven.

While Callan put dinner on the table, Josh walked into the bedroom and looked down at Jenna. "How are you feeling, babe? Want to sit at the counter or the table with me?"

"I think I do feel better and I would love to see something besides these four walls." Jenna scooted to the edge of the bed. Josh started to pick her up but she insisted on walking. "I feel like my legs need to stretch." She wrapped her arm around Josh's trim waist as she walked into the kitchen.

Callan dished up the food and prepared to leave. "Everything is ready. You two enjoy. I better get on home and feed my own hungry troops." Callan gave Jenna a hug. "If you need me to come over tomorrow, just say the word. I expect a phone call as soon as you find out anything from the doctor."

"Will do, Cal." Josh walked her to the back door. "Thanks again for coming today. I really appreciate it."

"Anytime." Callan gave him a big smile as she walked out the door. "I'm sure I'll think of some way for you to repay me."

Jenna's doctor appointment was for late morning in Portland. Josh rose extra early and completed as much work as he could before returning to the house, showering, and helping Jenna out to her car. As they drove an hour into the city, he hoped the doctor could discover what made Jenna so tired. She did look better today and her color was definitely improving. Maybe it was a flu bug like she suggested, but he somehow doubted it.

When Jenna arrived, she explained to the nurse that she was there for an annual check-up, but didn't feel well and wanted to speak with the doctor about what caused her exhaustion. Josh stayed in the waiting room while the nurse took her blood pressure, weighed and measured her, then collected fluid samples.

By the time the doctor finally walked into her exam room, Jenna fought fatigue. The doctor took one glance at her and knew something wasn't right. She looked in her eyes, nose and throat, had her breathe and swallow. While she proceeded with the exam, the doctor kept up a friendly chatter, asking several questions.

The nurse returned to the room, smiling excitedly as she handed a folder to the doctor. The doctor completed the rest of the exam then told Jenna she'd like to have her come to her office. While Jenna dressed, the nurse escorted Josh from the waiting room then led them both to the doctor's office.

As they sat facing the doctor, Jenna felt Josh take her hand in his and squeeze it lightly. The warmth of his fingers wrapped around hers made her feel protected and loved.

"Jenna, after your exam and looking at your test results, I can tell you that your condition is temporary. It should completely right itself in about seven months." The doctor offered them both a pleased smile.

"She can't make it like this through seven more

months," Josh said, letting go of Jenna's hand and leaning forward on his knees. Was the doctor crazy or completely lacking in empathy? "Can't you do something for her?"

"I assure you, she can. Women have been doing it since the beginning of time. I don't think you have anything to worry about, Daddy." The doctor gave Josh a pointed look.

"Well, what does..." Josh suddenly looked from Dr. Meliah to Jenna then back to the doctor. She grinned and nodded her head. "Daddy? Do you mean she's... that Jenna ... that we're gonna have a baby?"

"That is exactly what I mean. Congratulations to you both. It looks like Jenna is about seven weeks pregnant," the doctor said enthusiastically. She picked up some brochures and a prescription pad, scribbling something across it before handing the information to Josh while she turned to Jenna.

"Jenna, you're going to need to take these vitamins. It's important that you get enough rest and stay hydrated. From what you said earlier, your new job is very stressful, demanding, and you're out on the road a lot. That is going to have to change. You may need to look at cutting back hours or turning in the suitcase for a desk job. You certainly won't be able to do the traveling in the late stages of your pregnancy. As for your exhaustion, it should get better as long as you don't push yourself and rest when you feel tired. It isn't uncommon for expectant mothers to need naps."

While the doctor spoke and Josh absorbed all the information, Jenna seethed. She could hear voices droning on around her, but she couldn't bring herself to join in the conversation.

Pregnant! How could this have happened?

Well, she knew how it had happened, but she didn't want it to have happened. She didn't want to be a mother, didn't want to quit her job, didn't want to be forced into the role of parenting.

Even admitting she did not want this baby, she knew she was having it. For her, and most certainly for Josh, there weren't any other options. From the look of pure joy on his face, he was thrilled with the news.

"Thank you, doctor. This is the best news," Josh said, unable to stop smiling. He picked up Jenna's hand again and rubbed his thumb along the back of it. What had felt comforting to her minutes ago now irritated her.

Josh turned to look at Jenna as she stared out the doctor's office window, lost in her thoughts.

This unwanted baby would completely change her life. Josh's would continue on much like it always had, but she was the one who would give up her career and her dreams while her body morphed into something neither one of them would recognize.

"Jenna, you're awfully quiet." Dr. Meliah studied her intently. "Do you have any questions?"

"No," Jenna finally managed to say, turning her gaze from the window back to Dr. Meliah. She didn't think the doctor would appreciate questions like, "Why wouldn't you just let me have one more month of pills?" or "How can you spend years on birth control and get pregnant two weeks after you quit taking them?"

Josh watched emotions fly across Jenna's face and felt acute disappointment at what he witnessed. He registered her anger, frustration, and fear. Nothing he saw said she was happy or excited, or even the tiniest bit pleased at the miracle they had created together. Although unplanned, their baby was a miracle of life and one he planned to celebrate.

"How about you, Josh? Any questions?" Dr. Meliah asked, turning to him.

"I was just wondering how often women get pregnant while they're taking the pill. I mean, it won't hurt the baby will it?" Josh asked, concerned.

"Jenna, maybe you better answer his question." Dr. Meliah was under the assumption that Jenna and Josh both knew she hadn't filled her prescription for a while.

"I ran out of pills a couple months ago. With my new schedule, I kept forgetting to make an appointment to come in for a new prescription. And here we are." Jenna's tone sounded clipped and peeved.

"But..." Josh looked at Jenna then turned back to the doctor. "So Jenna didn't have any medication in her system when she got pregnant?"

"Not enough to be effective. Normally, it takes a while to get pregnant once you quit taking birth control pills, but sometimes it happens quickly. Everything should be just fine, Josh," Dr. Meliah assured him. The doctor wrote down some notes and handed Jenna a slip of paper to give to the receptionist.

"I'd like to have you come back in five weeks. We'll do an ultrasound then and you'll be able to listen to the baby's heartbeat and see your first photo of the little one. You might want to wait until then to start spreading the news of your baby's upcoming arrival. Most danger of miscarriage is past by then," the doctor explained. "Because of your age, Jenna, I would put you into a higher risk group, especially since this is your first baby. We generally do that with anyone over thirty-five. Since you're thirty-six, you definitely fall into that bracket. Make sure you start on those vitamins right away and get plenty of rest. I'm sure this husband of yours will take great care of you."

"I plan on it, ma'am." Josh wrapped his arm protectively around Jenna as they walked out the door. He wanted to jump up and kick his heels, shout from the rooftops that they were finally, finally going to have a baby. He couldn't have been any more excited if someone had told him he'd just won the lottery.

Jenna, on the other hand, still hadn't said a word. However, her silence screamed at him as they walked to the car. After holding her door open for her, he waited until she fastened her seatbelt to lean down and kiss her. She stiffened against him. He stared into eyes filled with contempt and anger.

Unsettled, he shut her car door and walked to the driver's side, trying to think of a way to avoid the fight he sensed was coming. He absolutely hated conflict of any kind.

After growing up with a cruel, spiteful mother who thrived on keeping everyone at odds, he avoided engaging in arguments. It reminded him too much of the years he and Callan spent with their deranged mother while their dad worked to keep a roof over their heads and food on the table. Even though his mother passed away several years ago from cancer, Josh still hadn't fully overcome the trauma of his childhood.

Unable to bear Jenna's silent wrath, Josh turned on the radio on the drive home. Jenna stared out the passenger window, clenching her hands together until they turned white before folding them angrily across her chest.

"Do you want to go to the pharmacy before we head home or would you rather I run in after dropping you off?" Josh asked as they neared their turn-off.

Jenna was so angry, she felt like screaming and kicking her feet. How could she have been so stupid? She knew better. She absolutely knew the risks involved. How could she have assumed it would take months for the effects of the birth control pills to wear off before she'd need to worry about it? The only person she was angrier with than herself was Josh. How dare he be so happy about this knowing how much she didn't want to be a mother. This was entirely his fault.

"I'd rather I wasn't pregnant at all, but since that can't be changed, I might as well go with you," Jenna said through clenched teeth. Her jaw was set in a way that made Josh cringe.

On what should be one of the happiest days of their married life, Jenna refused to see the blessing of this pregnancy, wallowing in pity over what she viewed as her broken dreams.

Josh drove into town and parked outside a superstore. He thought about going to the small pharmacy in Tenaity where everyone knew you by name, but decided for the sake of Jenna's privacy, it would be better to go somewhere it was easy to blend into the crowd.

He hurried around the car, opened her door, and held his hand out to her. She sent him a cold glare before refusing his hand and stalking toward the entrance. Josh grabbed a cart and followed along behind. When they got to the vitamin section, he pulled out the list the doctor had written on the prescription pad and handed it to Jenna. He watched as she read labels and carefully selected each bottle. She may not like what had happened, may be furious at him without cause, but she would take care of herself for the baby's sake.

Josh pushed the cart and followed her as she headed toward the grocery section. She loaded up on fruits, vegetables, cheese, milk, and lean meats. Josh couldn't pass by a tray of brownies in the bakery and added them to the cart, earning himself another glare. If she planned to make him suffer, he'd endure it with chocolate in hand.

They made it to the checkout line without running into anyone they knew. While Jenna dug around in her purse, Josh tossed in a few magazines on parenting and pregnancy. It seemed to him that at least one of them should take some interest in the little life growing in Jenna and figure out what they needed to do in each coming stage.

When they arrived home, Jenna didn't wait for

him to open the car door. Instead, she hustled inside and veered into the guest bathroom. By the time he had all the sacks of groceries inside, Jenna sat at the counter looking worn out and defeated.

She helped pull a few things out of bags and happened across the magazines. She glanced at the covers, slapped them on the counter, marched to the bedroom, and slammed the door.

That went well, Josh brooded as he continued putting away the groceries. He'd just finished when his cell phone rang. From the caller ID he knew it was Callan.

"Hey, Cal." Josh attempted to sound much more upbeat than he felt. He wasn't sure how to harness joy and happiness with dismay and distress.

"What did the doctor say?" Callan's concern carried in her tone. "Is Jenna okay?"

"Not exactly." Josh was unsure what to tell his sister. He didn't want to lie to her, but he wasn't convinced telling her the real reason for Jenna's fatigue was the best idea, especially in light of Jenna's reaction to the news.

"What's wrong? Is it something serious?" Callan sounded on the verge of tears. "It's not something major, is it?"

"It, um, is definitely major and absolutely serious, but nothing that won't cure itself in a few months time," Josh answered ambiguously.

"Josh, you aren't making a lick of sense. Let me talk to Jenna."

"I don't think she's much in the mood for talking," Josh said with honesty.

Releasing a sigh, he decided to be upfront with

his sister or she wouldn't give him any peace. "Jenna's pregnant. We had no idea. She forgot to mention a few things to me over the course of the last couple of months. She's less than thrilled about the whole situation. As a matter of fact, she is currently not speaking to me and I may be sleeping upstairs for a while."

"Oh, Josh," Callan said, her voice wavering. "I don't know what to say."

Josh knew his sister would have given almost anything to be able to have a baby of her own. Instead, his wife was pregnant and didn't want the baby. Ironic how life often makes such interesting turns and twists.

He heard Callan suck in a gulp of air. If he knew his sister, she was wiping tears off her cheeks and straightening her spine.

"What can I do to help?" Callan asked with sincerity. "Do you want me to talk to her?"

"Not yet." Josh explained that Jenna was only seven weeks pregnant and they wanted to keep it quiet for another month. Callan promised to keep it a secret and encouraged Josh to pray about the best way to help Jenna come to terms with the pregnancy.

"Thanks, Callan. If there's anything you can do that'll help, I'll let you know." Josh disconnected the call and leaned against the counter, staring down the hall at the closed bedroom door. He sent up a quick prayer for direction and wisdom.

Aware that Jenna needed to keep hydrated and take her vitamins, he thought she should also eat something. He assembled a tray with cheese and crackers, a glass of sweet tea, and some sliced melon. He carried it to the bedroom door and managed to hold the tray in one hand and open the door with the other.

Jenna sat on the window seat, staring out at the backyard. She didn't even look up when he walked in.

"I thought you might like something to eat and drink." Josh set the tray on the bed. He walked over to stand beside her and reached a hand out to touch her arm. When he did, she pulled back and turned on him with a fury he'd never expected.

"How could you do this to me? You know how hard I've worked to be successful at my job, to build my career. Now it's over. Completely over! Life is never going to be the same again and it is your fault!" Jenna screamed at him, ignoring the look of pain that flashed through his eyes and the betrayal that filled his face.

She wasn't in the mood to be rational. She wanted to lay the blame somewhere other than herself and vent her anger. Josh just happened to be the one available.

"Jenna, this is not my fault. You never told me you ran out of pills. That might have been a good detail to share with me, don't you think? You never once mentioned that getting pregnant was a possibility," Josh defended himself, taking a step back from Jenna as she jumped up from the window seat.

"Don't you blame me, you... you... Casanova," Jenna yelled, wagging her index finger in his face. "You run around here half-naked, all bronzed and beautiful with those rippling muscles and swarthy good looks. You know exactly how this happened, you… seducer."

"Babe, can we please sit down and talk about this rationally?" Josh placed his hands on her arms, wishing she'd stop whipping her finger around in his face.

She jerked away from him. "Don't you babe me, you… man. It's all fine and dandy for me to be pregnant because I'm the one who has to give up my career and my dreams. I'm the one whose body will never be the same. I'm the one who has to change everything. Life for you will continue uninterrupted," Jenna ranted, pacing back and forth across the bedroom.

"No, Jenna. Life changed this morning when you looked at me with hate and disgust in your eyes." Josh lost the tenuous hold he had on his temper. His eyes turned the color of cold gunmetal while a vein throbbed at his temple. He grabbed Jenna's arms again and held her still.

"Just stop it, right now. Maybe a part of you wanted to get pregnant. Did you think of that? Why else would you skip taking your pills? You can tell yourself whatever you want, but you can't ignore the truth. You made this choice." Josh continued holding onto her arms, his own jaw set in determination as he narrowed his gaze.

"The fact of the matter is that we made this baby together because we love each other. You can't deny it. You can't change it. We are having this baby. We can do it together as a team or you can fight it every step of the way, but the result is going to be that in seven months we are bringing home a baby. He is never going to know that his mother didn't want him. Not ever. Do you hear me, Jenna?" Josh grabbed her chin with his hand, forcing her to look at him. "We will never do that to our child. Never! Is that clear?"

"Perfectly." Jenna matched him glare for glare. "Now let go of me," she hissed, shaking off his hands and running into the bathroom before slamming the door.

"Very mature, Jenna. Why don't you stamp your foot and stick out your tongue, too?" Josh yelled then stomped back out to the kitchen. He wanted to shout, he wanted to kick or punch something. Instead, he pounded his fist on the counter and sank onto a barstool. Burying his hands in his dark hair, he leaned his elbows on the counter and willed himself to calm down.

A few minutes later, Jenna stormed out from the bedroom, dragging her suitcase behind her. Josh blocked her path as she tried to go past him out the back door.

"What do you think you're doing?" Steel edged the roughness of his voice as he fisted his hands at his hips and glared at her. If he had to, he would bodily carry her back to the bedroom and force her to stay.

"I'm leaving." Jenna wouldn't make eye contact with him. "Get out of my way."

"Jenna, don't do this. Don't walk out that door." Josh reached out for her, only to have her slap his hands.

"Don't touch me. Just let me go." She made the

mistake of looking at Josh, seeing the pain tearing through his face, the hurt in his eyes.

Her own eyes filled with tears and her fury passed. Regret flooded through her.

With a softened voice and heart, she turned to Josh. "I… I need some time to think. Please? Give me a little time to adjust to all this."

"Where are you going to go?" Josh folded his hands across his chest to keep from reaching out to her again.

"Aunt Amelia will let me stay with them. She won't ask too many questions. I'm not up to telling her I'm pregnant and I really don't want anyone to know right now anyway." Jenna stepped around Josh and filled a bag with her vitamins. She pulled a bottle of water out of the fridge and walked back to grab her suitcase.

Josh picked it up and carried it out to her car without saying a word. She followed behind him. Part of her wanted him to hold her tight and tell her everything would be fine. The other part of her wanted to pound his chest and scream at him for ruining her life. It was best for her to spend some time away from him until she wrapped her head around the notion that she was truly having his baby. It wasn't his fault, so until she could quit unfairly blaming him, she needed some time to herself.

She opened her car door and dropped the bag of vitamins, water bottle, and her purse on the passenger seat. Before she could climb inside, Josh engulfed her from behind in a hug. In his arms, she felt his desperation, anxiety, and heartache.

On a day they should both be celebrating, Jenna instead felt like a part of her had died. With a deep sigh, she turned and wrapped her arms around Josh, holding him tight. He drew her even closer and took several ragged breaths. He held her that way for a few minutes before pulling back and kissing her forehead.

"Do you want me to drive you?" he asked in a voice raw with emotion.

"I'll be fine. I'll call you when I get to Aunt Amelia's." Jenna bit the inside of her cheek to keep from crying. "I'm sorry, Josh, I just need some time."

"Take all the time you need, but remember I'm right here when you're ready to come home," Josh said, as she slid into the driver's seat and started the car. "I love you, Jenna. Always have, always will."

Tears poured down Jenna's face as she put a hand on Josh's cheek. "I love you, too."

Chapter Nine

As she drove back to the city, Jenna's energy level flagged before she reached the halfway mark.

She fought to keep focused on the road and breathed a sigh of relief when she reached her aunt and uncle's neighborhood.

Dragging her suitcase across the street and up to Phil and Amelia's apartment took every bit of strength she had left. She rang the bell, standing on weak knees outside their door, hoping she'd make it to their guest room before she collapsed.

The door finally opened. "Jenna, dear, what are you doing?" Amelia asked with a welcoming smile, before leveling a questioning glance at Jenna's suitcase.

"I know it's extremely bad manners, Aunt Amelia, but may I please stay with you for a while? Josh and I… we… um… I just need a little time to think and I can't do that at home." Jenna pulled the suitcase inside while Amelia closed the door.

"Jenna, you know you're welcome to stay any time you need to." Amelia took the suitcase handle from Jenna and pulled it down the hall to a guest room.

The large bed, comfortable rocker, private bathroom, and windows that let sunlight stream inside made it one of the most welcoming guest rooms Jenna thought she'd ever seen. Gratitude flowed through her at Amelia's willingness to let her stay.

"If you need someone to talk to, I'm always willing to listen. You can stay as long as you need to," Amelia said, giving her a comforting hug. "Does Josh know you're here?"

"Yes. I promised I'd call and let him know I made it." Jenna sank onto the bed in exhaustion. She flopped back against the mattress and instantly fell asleep.

Amelia shook her head as she swung Jenna's legs onto the bed, pulled off her shoes, and draped a light throw over her.

After closing the curtains and the door, she walked back to the kitchen, wondering what had driven Jenna away from Josh.

Although Jenna seemed rather quiet during dessert, they'd been so happy Friday when they spent time together before and after the play.

Hesitant, Amelia placed a call to Josh. She didn't have to wait long for him to pick up.

"Hi, Amelia." Josh didn't give anything away by his tone. "I'm guessing Jenna is there or you wouldn't be calling."

"She is Josh. Poor thing sat down on the bed and said she needed to call you. Before I could blink, she'd fallen asleep." Amelia was curious what caused her niece to run to away from him. "I didn't want you to worry, so I thought I'd let you know she arrived safe and sound. Is she okay? She doesn't look well."

Josh hesitated before answering - long enough for Amelia to know he was thinking about how to respond to her question.

"We went to the doctor this morning. Apparently, Jenna's new job is more demanding than either of us expected. The doctor diagnosed her with exhaustion and cautioned her to slow down. She's not too happy about the prospect of giving up her new job."

"And I take it you wouldn't mind her giving up the new job for one that didn't involve her traveling," Amelia asked innocently.

"Darn right." Josh's tone was rough, laced with conviction. "That job is ruining her health along with a variety of other things. I want her to take care of herself but right now, she's plenty ticked at me. From our last conversation, it became glaringly apparent Jenna isn't particularly open to discussing options with any degree of reason at the moment."

Amelia laughed, surprising Josh. "Well, you know Jenna is related to her Uncle Phil and the Granger family. You'd be hard-pressed to find a bunch of more bull-headed people. She doesn't want anyone making decisions for her and she likes everything to be on her terms. Give her time, Josh. Once she gets her head wrapped around the problem, things will be fine. I'll try to keep you posted. If you need to talk, call me anytime."

"You're the best, Amelia." Warmth filled his voice as he experienced a wave of thankfulness for Jenna's aunt and uncle. "Thanks for everything."

"You are more than welcome."

The tractor bounced across a badger hole, yanking Josh from his gloomy thoughts as he drove the baler into a neighbor's field, ready to begin another custom haying job. His cell phone rang and he hurriedly pulled it from his shirt pocket.

"Hey, Cal." He turned off the tractor so he could hear his sister. "What's up?"

"I wanted to find out how things are going with you and Jenna. I couldn't help but worry after what you shared. Are you sure there isn't anything I can do?"

"Not now." Impatient and frustrated, Josh jiggled his foot. This wasn't a conversation he wanted to have with anyone, let alone Callan. "She left me. Went to Amelia's and said she'd come back when she had time to think. I had no choice but to let her go. I can't make her want to stay any more than I can make her want this baby."

"Oh, Josh. I'm so sorry." Callan's voice quavered, working to keep her tears in check. "It will work out fine. Just give her some time to let it all sink in. I'm sure the news came as quite a shock to you both, but Jenna has been quite adamant about not having kids. I can't believe she got pregnant."

"Here's the best part," Josh said, as his anger flared once again. "She forgot to refill her prescription for birth control pills, yet claims her being pregnant is completely and entirely my fault. She didn't even bother to tell me she'd been off the pills for a while. If she was really that set against having a baby, wouldn't she have been more mindful of making sure she couldn't get pregnant?"

"That's very interesting." Callan attempted to hide the smile in her voice but it was impossible to disguise from Josh. He knew her too well.

"What's so amusing?" Josh asked in a clipped tone, annoyed with Callan. There wasn't a single thing about this situation that he found humorous.

"Despite Jenna's protests otherwise, maybe a part of her really wanted to have a baby. Maybe part of her didn't get a refill on purpose and didn't tell you on purpose."

"That's what I thought." Josh took off his ball cap and ran a hand over his head before replacing it. "When I suggested that, she slammed the bathroom door on me. I'm thrilled she's pregnant. You know how much I love Emma and Audrey, how much I've wanted to start our own family. I just wish I could share that happiness with Jenna."

"You will. She'll come around and when she does, you can celebrate together, the way it should be," Callan said with an assurance Josh needed to hear. "I better let you get back to work. Are you sure there isn't anything you need? You can come over here for dinner tonight, if you want."

"Thanks, but Jake is here as well. I don't want to overwhelm you with too much charm and stunning good looks in one evening," Josh teased, feeling more like himself.

"Oh, that won't be a problem unless you two

are bringing along someone I haven't met. Just be here around six-thirty. I promise I'll make something chocolate." Callan threw out the promise of chocolate as a bribe, knowing Josh wouldn't refuse.

"We'll be there. Thanks, Cal. Love you."

"Love you, too, little brother."

Arriving at Callan and Clay's right on time, Josh gave a quick knock on the door before he and Jake stepped inside the house. Although no one greeted them, food sat on the counter in the kitchen, waiting to be served.

When the two men walked through the family room, they heard Audrey and Emma giggling from the backyard along with the dog barking and adult laughter.

After opening the patio door, they found Callan reclining on a patio chair with a glass of iced tea while Clay manned the barbecue. Audrey and Emma struggled to pull a small length of rope away from Cully, their Border collie, across the yard. The more they tugged, the more the dog yanked and shook the rope.

"I think you two need to admit defeat," Josh said, moving beside Callan's chair.

"Hi guys." Callan motioned for them to take a seat at the patio table. Before they could sit down, the girls dropped their end of the rope and ran over to see two of their favorite people. Emma launched herself at Josh. He swept her up and tossed her in the air, much to her pleasure.

Jake grabbed Audrey under the arms and swung her around in a big circle.

"Again, Jake, again," Audrey pleaded between giggles. He swung her around a few more times before Emma demanded a turn.

"Whew, you two wore me out," Jake said, dropping onto a chair and fanning himself with his hat.

"Come on, Jake, again," Emma tugged on his hand.

"Girls, that's enough." Callan raised an eyebrow at the two girls. "Why don't you go get Jake and Uncle Josh a glass of tea?"

"Sure, Mama." Audrey ran into the house followed by Emma.

"Are you two just going to sit there while I slave away, melting in the heat, to cook your dinner?" Clay waving his cooking tongs at Josh and Jake for emphasis.

"I fully intend to sit here, dude, and have you wait on me hand and foot," Jake said, with a devilish gleam in his blue eyes. "Hurry it up, would ya'. I'm starving."

Clay pointed at Jake then offered Callan a wide grin. "Callan, no steak for big-mouth. He can have a peanut butter sandwich."

"Yeah, whatever." Jake knew Clay was teasing. The two of them rarely traded anything except jesting comments or insults, and liked it that way.

The six of them enjoyed a delicious steak dinner with baked potatoes, green salad, sliced fruit, and crusty bread. For dessert, Callan brought out homemade chocolate ice cream with all the trimmings including a tray of chocolate chip cookies, strawberries, chocolate sauce, and whipped cream.

"Cal, this is amazing." Josh took another bite of ice cream. On his second bowl of the creamy confection, he'd already eaten at least three cookies. "Thank you for inviting us. This is better than anything we'd make at home. Left to our own devices, Jake may have eaten that peanut butter sandwich after all."

Jake shot Josh a look that said he would have found something better than peanut butter for dinner as he scooped another bowl of ice cream.

"Clay, remember the year at the fair you kept buying me ice cream cones and I ate so many I got sick. Mom was really ticked at you," Jake laughed at the memory. "Wasn't that the summer you met Callan?"

Clay looked up from his bowl of strawberries covered with whipped cream and shared a private smile with his wife. He'd never liked ice cream, but the summer they fell in love, he'd been determined to meet her. When he discovered she peddled ice cream cones for her aunt's sorority club at the county fair, he visited the booth multiple times before he worked up the courage to ask her out. He had to do something with all the ice cream cones he purchased and Jake was a willing recipient.

"Yep, that was the summer I met the most beautiful girl in the world." Clay squeezed Callan's hand. She leaned over and kissed his cheek, eyes glowing with love.

Josh glanced at his sister. He didn't know how it happened, but she and Clay seemed to fall more in love every day. He wished his relationship with Jenna would return to being even remotely that warm, loving, and open. Instead, he felt like she'd erected a wall between them that only she could tear down.

He was happy for Callan and Clay, truly, he was, but seeing them so in love made the ache in his heart hurt even more.

Josh and Jake stayed until Clay declared it time for the girls to go to bed. Audrey and Emma gave both men a tight hug and sticky kiss before Clay herded them toward their room.

Callan walked Josh and Jake to the door. "I'm so glad you two came over."

"Thanks, Callan." Jake hugged her and kissed her cheek. "Anything is better than trying to choke down the slop Josh passes off as food."

"I heard that, you know." Josh nudged Jake out the door, shaking his head. "I assume you don't want to walk home and will keep further commentary about my cooking to yourself."

Jake grinned and waved at Callan as he walked down the sidewalk toward Josh's pickup.

"Thanks again, Cal." Josh settled his arm around her shoulders as she walked down the sidewalk with him. "I appreciate the good food and the company."

"You know you can come anytime. Just hang in there, Josh. Things will get better soon." Callan handed him a plain brown gift bag with blue tissue paper decoratively placed inside.

"What's this?" Josh took the gift in his hands. The bag was heavy and he looked from it to her quizzically. "It's not my birthday or anything."

"I know, but I think you'll like it just the same." Callan offered him an indulgent smile. "Wait until Jake goes home to open it, though, okay?"

"Sure." Josh set it on backseat of his pickup, slid behind the wheel, and started the ignition. "Thanks for being such a great sister."

"You can quit dumping on the flattery, man, she already fed us dinner," Jake grinned and waggled his eyebrows at Callan, making her laugh.

Josh frowned and gave Jake a playful shove as he put the pickup in reverse.

"Bye guys. And see, I was able to survive all your charm and dashing good looks just fine!" Callan teased as they backed out of the driveway.

As soon as they arrived back at the farm, Jake returned to his place.

Josh walked inside the house, turned on the kitchen light, and set the bag from Callan on the counter. When he removed the tissue paper, he was surprised to find several books on pregnancy and parenthood. He looked through the selections and turned over one of the books to read the back cover. Written expressly for expectant fathers, it looked like a great place to start learning what he'd need to know before the baby arrived. He had no idea what Jenna felt or experienced and wanted to understand.

He carried the books into the bedroom and stacked the various titles on the side table. He placed the one for fathers on his nightstand and got ready for bed.

Josh turned on the bedside lamp, climbed

between the cool sheets, and read for more than an hour. He had no idea so much happened to a woman's body, even in the first few weeks of pregnancy.

No wonder Jenna didn't act like herself. *She isn't herself*, he mused. Her body rapidly changed to accommodate the little life growing inside.

Josh sat lost in his thoughts for a while before he turned out the light and rolled over to the empty side of the bed.

Jenna's scent clung to her pillow, so he pulled it close and breathed deeply. Slowly drifting off to sleep, he wondered if the ache of missing his wife would ever go away.

Chapter Ten

Jenna awoke late that evening, disoriented. Reluctantly, she recalled her doctor appointment and all the spiteful, cruel words she'd tossed at Josh.

Disheartened, she wandered out to the living room where her aunt and uncle watched television.

"Hello, Jenna." Phil got to his feet and wrapped her in a welcoming hug. "We saved you a plate from dinner. Are you hungry?"

"Actually, I am." She smiled at her uncle then walked into the kitchen followed by Amelia. "I can get it Aunt Amelia, no need for you to miss your show."

"Phil's watching one of those crime shows with blood and gore. I pretend to watch while I'm reading or stitching," she said with a wave of her hand toward the kitchen door. "Believe me, I don't mind missing the whole thing."

Jenna laughed as her aunt set a plate in front of her with pasta, a hunk of buttered bread, and fruit. It all looked delicious. Tired or not, Jenna realized she hadn't eaten well for days and needed to force herself to eat better.

She still hadn't taken the vitamins they'd picked up earlier in the day and decided she would make them part of her morning routine. So far, she wasn't suffering from morning sickness. She found herself nauseous occasionally, but nothing like what some of her friends or her two older sisters had suffered while pregnant.

"Thank you, again, Aunt Amelia. You can't begin to know how much I appreciate you letting me stay, and taking care of me. I've been a little tired lately," Jenna said between bites of her dinner.

"You know you're always welcome." Amelia sat down across from Jenna at the kitchen table, a cup of tea in her hands. "Josh said you were exhausted and that you might have to give up your new job."

"Did Josh call?" Jenna asked, pushing her pasta around on her plate. Guilt stabbed her when she realized she'd forgotten to call him before she fell asleep.

"No, you mentioned you needed to call him right before you fell asleep, so I gave him a quick ring to let him know you made it safely." Amelia stared at her as though deep in thought. Finally, she placed her hand on top of Jenna's and smiled. "Honey, is there something going on you want to talk about? I know Josh loves you and cares about you deeply. Is there some misunderstanding? Something that he did?"

Tears pricked Jenna's eyes and made it hard to swallow past the lump in her throat. Lately, her emotions seemed beyond her control, and she didn't like it. Not one bit. "No, Josh didn't... we just... I really can't talk about it, Aunt Amelia. Not yet."

"Okay, honey." Amelia patted her hand comfortingly before sitting back in her chair. "But when you're ready, I'm right here for you."

Jenna hung out at the apartment, sleeping and thinking for the rest of the week. She texted Josh once a day just to let him know she was fine and taking her vitamins. She couldn't bring herself to talk to him on the phone or go home for the weekend.

The sound of his deep, baritone voice, laced with pain and hurting, would make her emotional. Seeing him in person would be her undoing. With an abundance of time to think and put her thoughts in order, she realized it was completely unfair to blame her predicament on him. She'd made the choices and now had to face the consequences.

Monday morning, she dragged herself into the office. Jenna had no idea how she would make it through the day. The thought of spending eight hours upright made her head heavy.

As she sat at her desk trying to decide what to do, her friend Barb strolled in and shut the door. Jenna had known the woman as long as she'd worked in the building. Barb was the person who originally hired her, had been a mentor, and was now a good friend and confidante.

"What's going on with you? You look terrible."

Barb's intense stare, coupled with the furrows of worry etched across her friend's forehead, caused Jenna to fight the urge to squirm in her seat.

"It's the new job. My doctor informed me that I'm exhausted and won't be able to keep up with the hours and travel schedule required." Jenna kept her gaze fastened to a pile of paperclips on her desk instead of Barb.

"I could have told you that." Barb sat down in the chair across the desk and laughed derisively. "In fact, I'm pretty sure I tried when you first mentioned applying for the job. I actually managed to last four months in that position when the powers-that-be talked me into taking it. That was a few years before you moved here. The job is grueling, unpleasant, and designed for single men with the stamina of a super hero. Roger was ready to file for divorce after the first two months. I was lucky he stuck it out until I came to my senses and requested my old job back."

"Good grief! Why didn't you tell me?" Jenna asked, staring at Barb. If she'd warned her, maybe she wouldn't be in this current mess.

"I did tell you. I told you repeatedly. I think my exact words were, 'Jenna, don't do this to yourself or Josh. You have no idea what you are getting yourself into.' However, you weren't inclined to listen and had to figure it out for yourself firsthand." Barb leveled a knowing glance her direction. "I might be taking a stab in the dark, but I'd bet money that if you hadn't been plagued with exhaustion and forced to go to the doctor, you'd still be kidding yourself that the job is great and you're learning so much from the challenge, yada-yada-yada. Right?"

Annoyed that Barb knew her so well, Jenna narrowed her gaze at her friend.

Barb grinned. "We need to figure out how to get you out of that job and back into an office job.

You'll most likely take a cut in pay, but it's well worth it to get your life back." Barb tapped an index finger against her chin running through the employee database in her head. "Who is retiring, quitting, or has their head on the chopping block?"

Jenna's mouth lifted in a smile. It was impossible to ignore Barb's humor.

"Oh, I know. There's a position for a human resources specialist opening up in a few weeks. Frietag is transferring to the Salem office because her husband got a new job and they're moving. I just heard that one this morning, so the vultures haven't started circling yet. You should apply for it. It doesn't include the glamour and unlimited power of your fabulous new position, but you get to work consistent hours and sleep in your own bed every night."

"So how do we get me that job?" Hope, like a spring of sweet, cool water, poured refreshingly over Jenna's parched soul. "And when do I drop the bomb that I am all done with the traveling trainer position?"

Barb she sat back in her chair. "Let's make sure we play this right. Your current supervisor likes you, respects your work, and thinks you have ambition and talent to burn. She's your best ally. You need to tell her right away that your marriage and your health can't keep going with the current position but you love your job and working here, blah blah blah. Mention how you really wished there was an opening that would be a good fit for your skills. Let her come up with the idea for you to apply for the vacant position, since it also falls under her supervision. When she does, act interested. Let her talk you into it then she'll make sure you are transferred. Voila! How hard is that?"

"Not hard at all if it goes according to your evil plan." Jenna leaned back in her desk chair and sighed. "The part you forget is that I'm not good at playing games. I tell it like it is and have very limited patience in waiting for people to get to the point."

"If you want this to work, you're going to have to suck it up, girlfriend." Barb rested her hands on her lap as she crossed one leg over the other and swung it in smug satisfaction at her brilliant idea. "Come on, Jenna. You can do this. You are trained to do this. So go do it."

"There is one other teeny little thing that I probably should mention." Uncomfortable sharing all her secrets with Barb, Jenna realized she needed to confide in someone.

"Go on," Barb encouraged when Jenna remained oddly silent. She waved her hand dramatically for emphasis. "The teeny little detail would be?"

"I'm pregnant." Jenna let out a whoosh of air with the confession.

Barb jumped out of her chair and screamed. "You are not! Say it isn't so?" She ran around the desk, yanked Jenna to her feet, and gave her a hug as she bounced around enthusiastically.

A knock sounded at Jenna's office door and it swung open. A coworker looked at the two of them like they'd gone mad. "Everything okay in here?"

"Everything is just fine, Bill." Jenna grabbed

Barb's arm and gave her a small pinch. "Thank you for checking, though."

"Yep, all's well." Barb settled back down to earth and put a serious expression on her face. "I thought there was a spider on Jenna's sleeve, but it was just a piece of lint.

Bill rolled his eyes then shut the door.

The moment the door latched, Barb resumed bouncing on the balls of her feet. "I'm so happy for you. This is great news."

"I'm glad someone's happy, because it wouldn't be me. It is terrible, earth-shattering, life-altering news," Jenna said, sinking back into her chair.

Barb sat down and stared at her so long, Jenna began to fidget. "What am I going to do?"

"How far along are you?"

"Eight weeks."

"That's why you're tired. That's why you have to change jobs, isn't it?"

"Yes. Now help me figure this out," Jenna pleaded.

"You're going to do exactly what I told you to do. Under no circumstances are you going to mention being pregnant. Not to anyone. By the time you start to show, they'll be mesmerized by your talent and competency in the new position and will be more than happy to keep it open for you while you're on maternity leave. I'd hold out for working part-time from home after the baby comes, if I were you. That position could totally be tele-commuter but they won't go for it on a full-time basis. Dazzle them with your talent, girl, and they'll be putty in your hands."

Jenna laughed for the first time in days. "You make it sound like a recipe. Here are the ingredients, stir this, mix that, bake for twenty minutes and the perfect life pops out of the oven."

Barb pointed to Jenna's stomach and smiled. "That is exactly right. A perfect little life will pop out of the oven."

Wistful, Jenna sighed again. "You have no idea what this is doing to me."

"I think I do. You forget that I have three children. I was once in your shoes as the career woman with the perfect job, perfect husband, perfect life. Then a weekend at the beach with Romeo changed my life forever, but it changed in the very best way. Don't fight it, embrace it. Your career is meaningless if you don't have a life. I bet Josh can barely contain his excitement."

"Um... about that." Jenna fiddled with a pen, drawing loops on a notepad on top of her desk instead of making eye contact with Barb. "I may have put a damper on his enthusiasm. I sort of blamed him for ruining my life and ran out on him last week. Aunt Amelia is letting me stay with her for a while. I haven't told her why, just that I needed some time to think."

"Have you lost your mind? Don't shut Josh out, Jenna. You'll be making a mistake you'll regret for a lifetime if you do."

"I know, but I needed a little time to absorb all this. We just found out Tuesday."

"Okay. Fine. Let's rehearse what you are going to say to Mrs. Gordon. You're going to go make nice and get that job. Got it?"

"Got it."

After half-an-hour of role playing and coming up with every possible scenario, Jenna walked to her supervisor's office and knocked softly on the door. Mrs. Gordon looked up from her desk and smiled.

"Jenna, come in. I was hoping to see you today. I've heard nothing but glowing reports about what a fantastic job you're doing. I'm very proud of you."

"Thank you very much. Actually, I wanted to schedule an appointment to speak with you about my position." Jenna stood just inside the door.

"No time like the present. Have a seat." Mrs. Gordon motioned to a chair across from her.

Forty-five minutes later, Mrs. Gordon assured Jenna of her placement in the position that would soon become available. In exchange for that, she promised to leave the following morning for her final road trip. Plagued by exhaustion, she wasn't sure how she would survive more time traveling, but decided she could do anything for two weeks.

On her way back to her office, she gave Barb two thumbs up as she passed her office door.

Desperately wishing she hadn't run away from Josh, she wanted to go home and see him. However, it would save her time and give her more rest if she stayed at Amelia and Phil's.

As soon as she left work, Jenna tried calling Josh's cell but it went straight to his voice mail. She tried three more times throughout the evening, growing more upset each time he failed to answer. After the last call, she left him a lengthy message and asked him to call her back as soon as possible.

Early the next morning, she ate breakfast, took her vitamins, and said goodbye to her aunt and uncle. She stood outside waiting to cross the street to her car when her cell rang.

"Babe, it's me. I just got your message. I'm so sorry. Jake and I went to Clay and Callan's for dinner last night and I forgot my phone in my dirty jeans. I didn't even think to check it when I got home," Josh hurriedly explained. "Are you really leaving this morning for another two weeks?"

The sound of his voice filled her with mixed emotions. Part of her was still angry at him, but part of her longed to be back in his arms, to be surrounded by his love. "Yes, I'm not thrilled about it, but I have some things I want to discuss with you when I get back. I'd like to come home then, if that's okay?" Jenna hoped Josh would be as wonderful and forgiving as always and ignore her bad behavior of the past week.

"More than okay." Josh released a sigh of relief. "I miss you so much, Jenna, and I love you."

"I love you, too, more than anything, even my career." Jenna said, with a shaky laugh. She opened her trunk and struggled to hang onto her phone and set the suitcase inside. After slamming the trunk lid, she climbed behind the wheel and buckled herself in. "I'll call you tonight. Have a good day."

"Be careful driving, Jenna. If you get tired, pull over somewhere and rest. If you ever get to the point where you can't keep driving or you need help, call me. I'd drive all over God's green earth for you, so don't forget it," Josh instructed. His words of caution warmed her heart, reminding her how much he cared about her.

"I won't. Thanks, Josh."

In much better spirits after his call with Jenna that morning, Josh whistled as he loaded hay bales onto a semi-truck trailer with the loader tractor. His cell phone rang as he set the last bale on the load. As he backed the tractor away from the trailer, he glanced at the caller ID. Jake could wait a few minutes for a call back while Josh concluded business with the hay buyer.

A few minutes later, Josh had a check in his pocket and waved to the driver as the truck pulled out onto the road from the stackyard.

He hurried to return Jake's call. It didn't take long for his hired hand to answer. "Hey, Jake, sorry I didn't answer. I was finishing up with a hay buyer. What can I do for you?"

"I just got called in for a job interview at the lab that I've been trying to get into for months. The appointment is at two this afternoon. Do you mind if I take the rest of the day off?" Jake sounded anxious and excited.

Josh knew the interview was important to Jake and his future career plans. "No problem. I hope you nail it. When they hire you, I'll be sorry to lose the best hired hand I've ever had."

Jake laughed. "You mean the only hired hand you've ever had. Thanks. I really appreciate it."

"Knock 'em dead," Josh said as he disconnected the call.

Evidently, Jake took Josh's advice to heart because two days later he accepted an offer for the job as an intern. He would start work a week from the following Monday, leaving Josh very little time to find a replacement for Jake.

As obnoxious as the young man could be on occasion, Josh trusted him, appreciated his ability to take on any task without any complaint, and his knowledge of everything it took to manage a farm. Jake was a good friend and in many ways, like a younger brother. Josh would miss having him around.

To celebrate Jake's new job, Josh grilled steaks and broke out his last few brownies for dinner that night.

"Congratulations, man." Josh thumped Jake on the back as they sat down at the counter in the kitchen to eat. "I'm proud of you."

"Thanks, man. That means a lot to me. I appreciate you giving me a job and a place to live this summer." For a change, Jake sounded serious. "It's been really nice to get to know you and Jenna better."

"I appreciate all your hard work and help this summer. You've done a lot of things that weren't expected of you and I'm grateful for the gentle way you've treated Jenna."

Jake stopped cutting into his steak and looked at Josh. "Other than the snake in my bed and the, um, mistaken identity issue in the kitchen, it's been awesome." He grinned broadly before continuing to slice into the juicy, tender piece of beef. "And no, I still say I didn't see anything."

"Good answer." Josh gave Jake a playful punch on his arm. "Anytime you want to work for me, I'd be happy to have you."

"Thanks. If I ever get tired of the city and decide to move back here to the sticks, I'll let you know."

Josh laughed. "Bright lights can make you bleary-eyed before you know it. I stuck it out through four years of college and eight years at the dealership."

"Do you ever miss it?" Jake asked, curious about Josh's decision to leave behind a high-paying city career to become a farmer. "The excitement and the fast-pace? The money? The sounds? The food? The adventure around every corner?"

"Honestly I don't. I've got about all the excitement I can handle right here and as for adventure, being married to Jenna is better than anything I could have ever imagined."

Jake turned and studied his friend and employer, a warm smile lighting his face. "If you and Clay hadn't snatched up the only two girls fit to marry, then maybe I'd be more inclined to head that direction. Unless or until I find someone as special as them, I plan to enjoy the life of being single and unattached."

"You've got plenty of time to think about settling down." Josh took a bite of his steak, chewing thoughtfully. He was more familiar with how much Jake enjoyed playing the field than his hired hand realized. "Just be careful you don't end up in a situation that forces your hand, if you know what I mean."

Aware that Jake had overnight guests of the female persuasion a few times, Josh also noticed it was never the same girl. Jenna was unaware of the extra-curricular activities taking place in the house down the road, or she would have had a full-blown hissy fit.

Josh figured it really wasn't his business what Jake did in his spare time, but he hated the thought of Jake tripping down the road to parenthood or matrimony before he was ready.

"I know what you mean." Jake stared at his food, avoiding eye contact. "Thanks for being cool about, you know, my guests."

"Yeah. Just don't mention it to my wife. She doesn't have a clue and you wouldn't want to be around if she did." Josh raised an eyebrow at Jake when he looked up from his plate. "I guarantee more than just your ears would smart for a good long while."

Jake gave him a sheepish grin then they returned their attention to their meal, lost in their own thoughts.

Chapter Eleven

Exhausted beyond anything she'd ever experienced, Jenna had no idea how she'd finish the drive home that night. Nearly six hours away from Tenacity, she acknowledged she had a problem.

An hour later, she gave up and sat in a hotel room, crying in frustration. The undercurrents of overwhelming fatigue and fear kept yanking her off balance. Jenna could barely keep her head above the surface of her roiling emotions, let alone focus or function normally.

Finally admitting defeat and her need for help, she phoned Josh.

"Hey, babe!" Josh sounded happy she called. "I'm so excited you'll be home soon. I can't wait to see you."

"I'm glad, Josh. I'm looking forward to seeing you as well," Jenna said, mustering the nerve to ask him for a huge favor.

"You don't sound well, Jenna. Are you sick? What's wrong?" Worry carried through his voice when he spoke. She heard him shut off the tractor as the background noise faded into silence.

"Honestly, I'm done in. I… I'm not going to be

able to drive myself home tonight or even tomorrow. I just can't." Annoyed by the tears once again stinging her eyes, she hesitated. "Do you... what I mean is... do you think you can come get me? I know you're so busy and I hate to ask, but I don't know what else to do."

Josh heard the doubt and anxiety in Jenna's voice. Strong-willed and independent, he assumed she was on the verge of a complete breakdown to ask for his help.

"Do you have anything you need to finish there?" Josh asked, starting to make plans as he climbed on the four-wheeler and headed to the house.

"No. I just want to be home." Jenna sank down onto the hotel bed and brushed away the tears on her cheeks. She hated feeling weak and useless.

"Hang in there, babe. I'm going to find someone to come along with me and leave as soon as possible. We'll be there as quick as we can then we'll all come back tomorrow." Josh thought of the work he'd leave behind at home, but nothing was more important than Jenna. The fact she called and asked him to come made it clear how bad things were for her. It might do lasting damage to his wife's stubborn pride to have to admit she needed help. "I'm almost to the house. Let me get inside then you can give me directions to your hotel and the room number."

Jenna gave him the information then she broke down into tears once more. "I'm so sorry, Josh. I hate this. I hate being a burden to you, especially when you're so over-burdened with farm work. I'm really sorry."

"Jenna, there isn't anything in this world more important to me than you. The whole farm could burn to the ground and it wouldn't matter as long as you're safe. Got it?"

"But I've been so awful to you." Jenna sobbed, bordering on hysteria. "I don't deserve for you to be so good to me."

"I love you. Always have, always will. Now, get some rest and eat something. I'll be there before you know it."

Josh disconnected the call and immediately called Jake. He'd sent him to finish a custom baling job a few miles down the road.

"Hey, man, what's up? I'm just pulling out of the field and should be back in a few minutes." The sound of the tractor nearly drowned out Jake's voice.

"I've got a small emergency. I'll fill you in as soon as you get back. Just pull the tractor in here at the house," Josh said, hanging up. He jerked off his work boots and clothes, ran into the bathroom, and took a quick shower. By the time Jake walked inside the kitchen, he was dressed and pulling on his good boots.

"What's up? Is Jenna okay?" Jake asked, concerned.

"Jenna's too ill to drive home and I need to go get her. Someone needs to come with me so we can get both vehicles home. Would you be willing to go? We'd need to leave right away. It means about a five-hour drive one way, then turning around and heading back in the morning."

SHANNA HATFIELD

"Of course I'll go. Can I run home and take a quick shower?" Jake asked as he backed toward the door.

"Absolutely. I'll throw a few things together while you get ready." Josh plugged his cell phone in to charge as Jake turned and ran out the door then jumped on the four-wheeler. It was almost five. If they got on the road soon, they should arrive around ten. With any luck, they could all get some sleep then hit the road bright and early in the morning.

Jake was back in twenty minutes with a small duffle bag. Josh rushed out the door as he pulled up, also carrying a small bag along with bottles of water, some jerky, and a couple of candy bars.

"Have you ever been to the big city of Burns?" Josh asked as they tossed their bags into the backseat of Josh's pickup and climbed in.

"A few times with the high school rodeo team, and once for a horse sale. Not much to see on the drive there unless you really like sagebrush," Jake commented as they drove out to the road.

"If my GPS is functioning correctly, we should be there in about four and a half hours." Josh pulled onto the highway.

"Great. Hour upon hour of listening to you yammer on," Jake teased, settling back into the seat. "Is this punishment for me taking the job at the lab?"

"You know it." Josh gave Jake a wicked grin. As he leaned his elbow out the window, he turned to look at the young man. "I really appreciate you doing this. You certainly didn't have to, especially since tomorrow is your official last day as my one

172

and only employee."

"No problem. I'm glad I was still here to help. It's not every day you're needed by a damsel in distress."

"I guess when you look at it that way, we're two heroes going to rescue my fair maiden." Josh laughed at an image of Jenna standing like Rapunzel at the top of a tower, waving a handkerchief at them.

The two men fell into the easy camaraderie they shared and the miles flew by. After a few hours of driving, they'd devoured the jerky and candy, and remained hungry. When they stopped to fill the truck with fuel, they ordered burgers and fries before getting back on the road.

A few minutes past ten, they pulled into the hotel parking lot at Jenna's hotel in Burns. Quickly grabbing their bags, they walked to the front desk and secured a room for Jake. The front desk agent called Jenna to get her permission to send Josh up to the room. It took just a few minutes to reach her room. He knocked on the door and she opened it, falling against him, crying.

"I'm so sorry, Josh. I'm such a wuss and this is a complete waste of your time. I don't mean to be such a bother. I'm so sorry," she sobbed into his shirt.

"It's fine, babe." Josh rubbed his hand soothingly across her shoulders as he gently nudged her back into the room.

Jake stood a few doors down the hall, in front of his room, and couldn't help but stare. He'd never seen Jenna be anything but calm, cool, and collected, with the exception of the day she thought he was Josh in the kitchen. He could see why Josh was in such an all-fired hurry to get to her. She obviously wasn't in any shape to drive home.

Josh made eye contact with Jake and nodded his head in thanks as he closed the door.

After dropping his bag on a chair, Josh put both arms around Jenna and let her cry, whispering soothing words as he held her close. When she finally stopped sobbing, he wiped the tears from her cheeks with his palms and kissed her softly on the lips.

"I love you," he said, wrapping her in his arms and breathing in her familiar scent. Her essence seeped into his heart and warmed his soul. "I missed you so much."

"I missed you, too," she whispered, leaning into him and feeling his strength flow into her. "I love you so much, Josh. So very much."

"I'm glad. It makes it mighty convenient that way," he teased, trying to lighten the mood.

She released a shaky laugh and he smiled. "I'm about beat. Let's get some sleep. Morning will be here before we know it and Jake is going to demand a good breakfast. He complained for the last hour that I'm trying to starve him to death."

Jenna smiled as she changed into her pajamas and climbed into bed. "That sounds like Jake. I'm sure going to miss having him around. He's a really great kid."

"Yeah, he is, and he isn't too shabby as a farm hand either. I don't know how we're going to find someone to replace him." Josh slid between the sheets and pulled Jenna close. She laid her head on his chest and released a contented sigh. Sleep soon claimed them both.

The next morning found the three of them at a little café down the street from the hotel. The men ordered meals with bacon, eggs, hash browns, and stacks of pancakes. Jenna requested toast and tea.

She nearly lost what little toast she'd eaten when Jake cut into his sunny-side up eggs and the yolk ran across the plate. She didn't have morning sickness, but certain smells or seeing certain foods made her nauseated in a matter of seconds. Turning her head away, she took several deep breaths then sipped her tea.

"You don't look so good, Jen." Jake noticed the green tinge that suddenly appeared on her face. "Are you okay?"

"Yes and no," she answered cryptically. She looked at Josh, hoping he would sense what it was she tried to convey without saying anything. He caught her eye, smiled, and nodded.

"What does that mean? Yes, you are okay or no, you aren't?" Jake set down his fork and stared at Jenna with real concern. He'd known her since the summer she and Josh started dating and it wasn't like her to dance around something. She generally got straight to the point.

"I'm not well right now but I'll be perfectly fine in a while. In less than seven months," Jenna said, giving him a shy smile.

"Seven months? That's a long time to be sick. Can't your doctor give you something for that?" Jake stared at her, confused.

Jenna laughed then put her hand on top of Jake's and patted it gently. "Jake, we're going to have a baby. That's why I'm not feeling well."

It took a moment for the news to sink in but when it did, Jake's head whipped up and he glanced from Josh's broad grin to Jenna's indulgent smile. "For real? You're not kidding me? That is great news!"

When Josh looked at Jenna instead of answering, she nodded her head. "It is great news, Jake, and we're very much looking forward to meeting this little person. We haven't told anyone yet, so can you keep this under your hat for a few weeks?"

"Sure." Jake's foot jiggled in excitement as he resumed eating his breakfast. "I'll be an almost-uncle, right?"

"Absolutely. If you like, the baby can call you Uncle Jake." Jenna beamed at him, pleased by his response to the news.

Josh watched his wife, thrilled by the enthusiasm Jenna exhibited as she told Jake they were expecting.

"Awesome!" Jake took a few bites of his breakfast then stopped his fork mid-air as a thought struck him. "You mean I know something Clay doesn't know?"

"I told Callan, which means Clay knows, but I made her promise not to tell anyone." Josh smiled at Jenna, relieved to see her nod at him encouragingly. "But you definitely know before anyone else. We haven't told Pop or Jenna's folks yet either."

"This is too cool. When the baby is old enough,

his ol' Uncle Jake will show him how to ride and rope and everything he needs to know about horses and being a cowboy." Jake envisioned how much fun it would be to have a nephew to follow in his footsteps.

"And what makes you think it will be a boy?" Jenna asked with raised eyebrows. "It could very well be a girl."

"Nope, no more girls. We already have Audrey and Emma to fill the girl quota. We need a boy to even things up."

Josh laughed. "Who can argue with that?"

"You two are something else." Jenna shook her head then finished her toast.

They were soon on the road and the trip home proved uneventful. Jenna slept part of the way, but when she was awake, she continued apologizing to Josh for her behavior. She had plenty of time to think about the baby and her attitude and knew she was the one to blame for getting pregnant.

Opening her heart to Josh, she talked to him about getting past her fear of parenthood and embracing the idea of becoming a mother. She also told him about the plans for her to switch jobs and shared some of the feelings brought on by the sudden changes in her life.

Josh tried to be understanding. The books Callan gave him were full of good advice and information. By the time they rolled into the driveway shortly after noon, Jenna had torn down most of the wall she built between them. Josh was glad to be back on even ground with his wife.

Jake pulled in right behind them and Josh asked

him to come inside the house. While Jake helped
Jenna set out the fixings for sandwiches along with
some fruit, Josh went to his office and wrote Jake
his final paycheck, adding a bonus for his hard work
all summer.

When he returned to the kitchen, he slid the
envelope across the counter to Jake. "Your final
paycheck, my friend." Josh thumped Jake on the
back. "We're going to miss having you around here,
so be sure to visit when you have time."

"I will and I already told you, I'll help
weekends when I'm home until you get through
wheat harvest." Jake looked at Josh like he was
getting forgetful in his old age. He walked over to
Jenna and put his arm around her shoulders.
"Besides I've got to keep tabs on the little mama
and my almost-nephew."

"Jake, you are too much." Jenna laughed,
putting her arm around him and giving him a
squeeze. "We're really going to miss you."

Chapter Twelve

Unable to find anyone to fill Jake's shoes let alone the position, Josh did the best he could to keep up with the farm work and still spend time with Jenna. She was home evenings, always tired, but starting to feel better.

Earlier that afternoon, he met her at the doctor's office for her ultrasound. Accompanying her to the room where they did the procedure, he observed the process as they spread gel all around her abdomen.

Jenna hadn't mentioned it, but he couldn't help but notice she sported a little baby bump. He thought it was wonderful. Although, knowing his wife, she probably thought it looked much bigger than it did.

He watched as the technician moved around the device on her belly. In grainy black and white, he spied an image of their baby.

"Oh, my. What do we have here?" The tech sounded amused before turning to look at them. "Can you both see the screen okay?"

"Yes," Jenna answered. Josh had trouble seeing it from the other side of Jenna, but numbly nodded his head. The experience was way outside his comfort zone.

"Well, daddy-to-be, why don't you come over here? You probably can't see much from over there," the tech said, smiling at Josh at she motioned to a spot closer to her.

Josh walked around to stand behind the technician as she pointed to the screen. "See right here is a head, and an arm and a leg, and right there is the other head, and a leg."

"What do you mean other head and leg?" Jenna's voice rose sharply and her eyes widened in panic.

"It looks like you'll be welcoming twins to your family," the tech said, beaming. "Again, congratulations."

"Twins? Twins!" Josh leaned closer to the screen, rubbing his hands together like he tended to do whenever he got excited about something. "Can you show me all that again?"

The technician happily pointed out the outline of each baby and then listened to the two tiny heartbeats that sounded more like flutters of air.

Visibly moved by the experience, Josh needed a moment to gather his composure while Jenna stared unseeing across the room and her face grew pale. When the tech finished, she printed out a copy of the photo and handed it to Josh while Jenna cleaned up.

"This is amazing," Josh said for the eighth time, lost in the fact they were going to have not one but two babies.

"The next time you come, we should be able to

identify the sex of the babies for you. You'll be astonished at how different the photo will look from the one today," the tech said as they prepared to leave.

Josh pumped her hand with a warm handshake then escorted Jenna out the door, practically floating on air in his excitement at the tech's news.

Done with work for the day, Jenna was glad because she'd gone from being traumatized about her pregnancy to shell-shocked. Still not convinced she'd be a fit parent for one child, she struggled to embrace the idea of bringing home two.

"Babe, what's wrong?" Josh asked as he walked her to the parking garage. "Talk to me."

"I'm not sure I can do this," she said, eyes glazed with fear.

Josh laughed, squeezing her hand. "Like it or not, there's no turning back now."

"I know that you dense man! I meant that I'm not exactly the most maternal thing on the planet. I'd almost talked myself into thinking I could bring home one baby and not accidentally do it mortal harm, but two? Josh, I'm afraid I'm not going to be any good at this parenting thing. I'm nothing like Callan."

"What's Callan got to do with our babies?" Josh asked as they stopped beside her car.

"She loves being a mother. She was born to be a mother." Jenna sighed and leaned against the car. "I'm just not like that at all."

"You should talk to Callan about all that sometime soon. I think you might get a different perspective on her being born to be a mother. As for you, don't sell yourself short. You'll be a fantastic mom. You're a wonderful wife, so why wouldn't you be good at mothering as well? It's all about nurturing and loving, right? And you are dynamite at both of those."

"Can't you ever just let me pout and have a pity party without boosting my confidence and making me feel like I can do anything?" Jenna tried to sound annoyed, but the way her eyes lit up gave away her pleasure at his comments.

"No can do." Josh kissed her cheek and pushed a stray lock of hair behind her ear. "You'll be a great mother, Jenna, so don't worry about it. I should know, having been raised by one of the worst mothers in the history of parenthood."

"I'm sorry, Josh. I sometimes forget how hard your mom made life for you and Callan because you both turned out to be such wonderful people."

Josh shoved his hands into his pockets as he looked at his feet. He hated thinking about his mother or talking about her. His mother never wanted him or Callan and made the fact perfectly clear nearly every day of his life. That was why he insisted their baby never know Jenna didn't want it, even if she'd done a complete turnaround in her thinking.

"Josh?" Jenna tipped his chin up with her finger, so he met her gaze. "We'll both be the very best parents we know how to be. Right?"

"Right." A small smile broke through his dismal thoughts as he returned his focus to their twins. "Now that we have an official photo of the babies, can we start telling everyone?"

"You act like it's something that'll be announced on the news at five this evening or trumpeted across the morning paper as a headline." Jenna laughed at the idea.

"I've got time to call the paper before they go to print," Josh teased, giving her a roguish wink. "Seriously, though, why don't we have a barbecue tomorrow and invite over the people we want to share this with the most?"

"Okay. Let's ask Callan and Clay to come over early and she can help me get the food ready since I will quite likely require a nap before everyone arrives."

After driving home in separate vehicles, Josh went back out to work in the fields while Jenna took a rest. He returned to the house late that evening to find Jenna collapsed in the living room. Although she slept, one of the baby books from Callan was open on her lap.

The kitchen was a disaster. It looked like she'd been baking and getting things ready for the barbecue. Chunked potatoes cooled in a bowl and a pan of boiled eggs overflowed with cold water. Dishes filled the sink and the counter bore traces of chocolate.

Hurriedly opening the refrigerator door, Josh spied a chocolate cake and resisted the urge to cut out a huge slice.

Instead, he dumped the water off the eggs and peeled them, placing them in a resealable bag, then put the eggs and potatoes in the fridge. He loaded the dishwasher, wiped down the counters, and rinsed the dishrag as Jenna walked in from the living room and sat down at the bar.

"Josh, I'm sorry. I didn't mean to leave such a mess. I got so tired, I needed to sit down for a minute and fell asleep." Jenna glanced around the clean kitchen in appreciation. "I hate for you to work so hard outside and then have to come inside and help me. I'm really sorry."

"Babe, let's come to an understanding right now." Josh leaned across the counter until his nose and hers nearly touched. He took her hand in his and gave it a comforting squeeze. "I know the babies are sucking your energy and strength right now. I also know you feel terrible about not being able to do all the things you usually do, but it's fine. If that means I need to put in a load of dishes or laundry or scrub the bathroom, I'll take care of it. You may have to point me in the right direction sometimes, but please stop apologizing. I'll do whatever needs to be done that you can't, but I want you to stop being sorry. Your job is to make sure you take good care of you for the sake of the babies. Wow! I just said babies. That makes it seem real somehow, doesn't it?"

"Yes, it does. That and the photo tacked to the fridge for the world to see," Jenna teased as her gaze settled on the grainy ultrasound of their twins. Josh placed it on the refrigerator door as soon as he arrived home from the doctor appointment. When Jenna walked into the kitchen, it greeted her and the sight of those two little babies brought a sense of joy that was slowly overcoming her sense of dread.

"Since I've been so extraordinarily helpful this evening, I don't suppose I could have a piece of cake as a reward. Please?" Josh begged, looking much like he must have as a little boy with a wave of his dark hair falling across his forehead and gray eyes glittering.

"You may not cut into the cake in the fridge." Happy she'd made Josh his own little cake, she grinned at him. "You may, however, have what is sitting under the bowl in the pantry."

Josh hurried to open the pantry door and found a plate sitting under a bowl with an individual chocolate cake. Frosted and ready for him to devour, he slid the plate onto the counter, took out some vanilla ice cream, and dropped a scoop on the cake.

He sat down next to Jenna and savored the first bite, closing his eyes and sighing in pleasure.

Josh smiled gratefully as he dove in for a second bite. "Thank you, Babe. This is really good."

"You're welcome." Jenna wrapped a hand around his arm and gave it a loving squeeze. "Are you going to be a complete pig and not even offer me a bite?"

Josh glanced down at the cake then back at Jenna. He hadn't planned on sharing. It was chocolate, after all. "Do you want some?"

"No, I'm just giving you a bad time, but pass the ice cream. It sounds good."

The next evening, the people who meant the most to them gathered at their house for dinner. Phil and Amelia drove out from the city. Callan, Clay, and their girls were there along with Clay's parents, Jake and his parents, Josh's dad, and Josh's Aunt Julie and Uncle Ralph as well as Laken and Tyler Johnson with their two kids, Alex and Brant.

Jenna removed the ultrasound photo from the refrigerator because she didn't want to give the surprise away, especially when Callan and Clay arrived early to help get ready. Although they knew about her pregnancy, they didn't know she was expecting twins.

Josh took over grill duties and Clay helped set up chairs and tables, ran errands for Jenna and Callan, then directed guests as they arrived to the backyard under the shade trees. Once everyone arrived, Josh asked Clay to give thanks for the meal. When Clay finished, Josh cleared his throat and looked around the group.

"Jenna and I are so happy you all could be here tonight. We not only wanted to enjoy a meal together, we have some news to share." Josh wrapped a protective arm around Jenna at her place by his side. She blushed but offered him an encouraging nod. "We're going to add two new farmhands to our operation next spring and we wanted you all to know."

"Two?" Callan asked with a surprised smile.

"That's right, two." Josh beamed proudly, looking around the faces of family and friends and seeing confusion. He took a deep breath and continued. "We just found out yesterday we're expecting twins."

Amid much hugging and words of

congratulations, dinner sat forgotten on the table. Josh watched his dad wipe a tear from his eye. At eighty, he was still active and spry, but Josh knew the news was something he was overjoyed to hear.

While the men sat around talking about farming after the meal, the women retreated to the kitchen where they made Jenna sit at the table with her feet up and passed around the ultrasound picture.

Callan was nearly in tears as she looked at the babies. She leaned down next to Jenna and squeezed her hand. "I know this isn't what you had planned, but what a blessing, Jen."

Jenna patted Callan's hand where it rested on her shoulder and smiled. "I guess sometimes we have to let go of our plans so we can embrace something better - God's plans. Thanks for supporting Josh. It meant so much to him. I appreciate your help while I was coming to my senses."

"Anytime," Callan said, looking at the picture again. "These two babies are just the sweetest things ever."

Outside, Jake sat next to Clay, discussing his new job. Emma suddenly appeared and climbed on his lap. She stared up at him with her baby blue eyes, an inquisitive look on her face.

"What's up, Sweet Pea?" Jake asked, cuddling the little girl. Despite her adorable appearance, he was leery. No one knew what to expect when she had that curious look on her face.

Emma rested her head against his chest and swung her feet over his leg. She started talking in a singsong voice. "I was just wondering…"

SHANNA HATFIELD

"Wondering what, Sweet Pea?"

"Where do babies come from?"

Jake glanced around as a look of panic swept across his face. Nervously nudging Clay with his elbow, he struggled to pull his thoughts together. "Well, er, I... um... I think your daddy better answer that question."

Clay's neck muscles tensed while his shoulders inched toward his ears and his shirt collar grew too tight. Emma turned her curious blue eyes toward him with a look of expectancy. She was only six. He had no idea how to respond to her question.

"You know, Sweet Pea, I think the person you should go ask is your mama. She can tell you exactly what you need to know." Clay tweaked Emma's nose then pointed to the house.

"Okay." Emma hopped down from Jake's lap and ran inside the kitchen door.

"Man, now there's the way to handle an intense question." Jake offered Clay a sly grin. "Just pass it off to your wife. Coward."

"Watch who you call a coward, chicken. She asked you first." Clay's shoulders returned to their normal position as he congratulated himself on how well he avoided a sticky question. "Besides, it isn't cowardly, it's smart. You might want to take down notes for future reference. If I told her something and Callan didn't like what I said, then I'd get an earful about my response. This way, I keep myself out of trouble and Emma gets to hear exactly what Callan wants her to hear."

"I still say you're a coward." Jake offered an indifferent shrug, softening it with a grin. "A smart coward, but a coward all the same."

In the kitchen, Emma found Callan and tugged on her hand. "Mama, I asked Jake a question, and he told me to ask Daddy then Daddy told me to ask you. So can I please ask my question?"

"Sure, Sweet Pea." Callan picked up the little girl and set her on a barstool. "What is your question?"

"Where do babies come from?"

"Oh, well, they, um…" Callan's brain went into overdrive searching for just the right answer to the question. The other women in the kitchen listened as silence fell over the room and they waited to hear how Callan would respond. Jenna could barely keep from laughing at the pained expression on Callan's face. "Babies, Miss Sweet Pea, come from God. They are tiny little miracles he sends to mommies and daddies. Your Uncle Josh and Aunt Jenna are extra special because He's sending them two babies. Isn't that wonderful?"

"Yep. When will they get here? I want to play with them." Emma swiveled the stool back and forth as she gripped the counter with her little fingers.

"They won't get here for a long time yet, close to Easter time. So first, we have school starting again and then Halloween, Thanksgiving, Christmas, New Year's, and Valentine's Day. Then the babies will come." Callan tried to explain using dates Emma would understand and remember.

"How will they get here?"

"Aunt Jenna and Uncle Josh will go into the city one day and when they come home they will bring the babies with them."

"Why can't they go get them tomorrow?"

"The babies aren't big enough to come home yet. You know how Grammy's puppies have to be big enough they don't need their mama before anyone can take them? Well, the babies have to be big enough to come home before Aunt Jenna can bring them to stay."

"Okay." Emma shrugged her shoulders and jumped off the stool. "I'm going to go play outside now."

"That's fine." Relieved, Callan sank onto a barstool as Emma raced out the door.

Bobbi walked over and gave her a hug. "You did a splendid job of answering her questions, Callan. Well done."

"Thanks, Mom," Callan said gratefully. A spark of irritation flamed in her emerald green eyes as she stared outside at the backyard. "Just wait until I get my hands on Clay. That son of yours is going to get an earful later. The big coward."

As their guests departed, each one offered another round of congratulations for Josh and Jenna's happy news.

After waving a final good bye from the front porch, Josh put his arm around Jenna and walked with her inside the house where welcome coolness provided respite from the sweltering August heat.

"That was a nice evening, if I do say so myself," Josh said, as they walked down the hall toward the family room.

"It was nice, wasn't it?" Jenna sat down on the couch and put her feet up on the ottoman. Josh pulled out the tails of his shirt while Jenna plucked the ponytail holder out of her hair. "Did you hear about Emma's questions?"

Ready to relax, Josh laughed and sat down beside her. He gently repositioned her so he could massage her neck and shoulders while they talked. "Jake and Clay were both quite proud at how fast they passed the buck along to Callan."

"I think Clay may regret that once they get home and the girls are in bed." Jenna laughed, recalling the look on Callan's face. "I just hope I can come up with great answers like she did on the spur of the moment. Everything she said was true, and the answers were simple and easy for Emma to understand."

"After Callan told Emma where babies came from, she marched back out to Clay and Jake. She glared at them both and said, 'Mama said God makes babies. Why didn't you tell me that?' then ran off to play on the tree swing with Brant. It was pretty comical."

"I can imagine." Jenna closed her eyes and enjoyed the massage her husband delivered to her tired muscles. It was as close to anything remotely resembling intimacy they'd shared since she'd found out she was expecting.

Jenna kept waiting for Josh to exhibit some interest in her beyond the babies and so far it hadn't happened. She was starting to show. Maybe the baby bump caused Josh to lose interest in her. She hoped he wouldn't turn into one of those husbands who would spend the next several months viewing her only as a temporary housing unit for his offspring.

As he sat kneading her shoulders and neck, Josh shifted his leg so he bracketed her body with his and she scooted back against him. He found her proximity along with her warmth and perfume nearly intoxicating.

He missed being close with Jenna. Between her not feeling well, being gone, and blaming him for her career aspirations going up in smoke, there hadn't been much opportunity for amorous overtures, but it wasn't due to a lack of desire on his part.

According to the books he read, pregnancy could give a woman a glow. Jenna had it to spare. Her radiant skin appeared soft and inviting with a lovely bloom of pink coloring each cheek. At that moment, he thought she'd never looked more enticing or beautiful.

He worked his hands across her neck and shoulders, surrendering to the urge to nibble on her neck before running his lips along the outline of her ear. Heat coursed through his veins and his gut twisted with longing.

When Jenna placed her hands on his thighs, rubbing the taught muscles through his jeans, he knew he was about to be consumed with his need for her. Every nerve in his body stood at attention and the attention focused solely on his wife.

Josh tipped his head back, attempting to gather his composure. He happened to glance out the window and see a light on at the barn.

Annoyed, he sighed. "Someone's down at the barn or a light got left on. Either way, I better go check." He pulled his leg from behind her and stood.

"Do you have to go?" Her face held such a look of yearning, Josh felt his knees weaken. "Can't it wait until tomorrow?"

He shook his head. "No, babe, I need to go check it out. I'd rather be safe than sorry." He retrieved a pair of slippers and put them on. "I'll just be a minute. I promise."

When be bent down to kiss her cheek, Jenna pulled him into a kiss hot with desire and loaded with temptation. Josh returned her kiss, aching with hunger for her.

He pulled back and he stared into her face, falling into the dark pools in her eyes. "Jenna, I…"

"Josh, do you find me repulsive? Can you not stand the thought of being with me?" Jenna interrupted, shooting off questions in her standard to-the-point fashion.

"What?" Josh took a step back, startled by her words.

"Since I'm starting to show, I thought maybe you're no longer attracted to me. It's been forever since you've shown any interest in… um… in being together," Jenna said.

Josh sank down on the ottoman and took her hands in his. "Babe, you have no idea. I want you so badly, I can hardly see straight. You mean you're open to the idea?" When Jenna nodded her head, he let out a sigh. "I thought with all that's gone on you just weren't interested in…" He shot her a wicked grin. "Maybe ever again."

Jenna laughed. "I'm interested, Josh. I'm

definitely interested. But you can't tease me with massages like that if you don't intend on doing more and taking it to the next level."

Josh leaned over and brushed aside Jenna's hair. His fingers sent tingling sensations racing through her. As he nuzzled her neck again, his breath warm on her ear, his deep voice took on a husky tone that made goose bumps cover her arms. "I intend on doing much, much more, if you don't mind."

"I don't mind at all," Jenna whispered, turning her head to give him a kiss that ignited the passion flickering between them. When she pulled back, she offered a flirtatious smile while her eyes smoldered invitingly. "Have I told you how smokin' hot that goatee makes you look?"

"Babe," Josh growled. He pulled her onto his lap and kissed her deeply. Reluctantly releasing the lips he'd held captive with his own, he touched his forehead to hers. "I still have to run down to the barn and check that darn light, but I'll be right back. Will you hold that thought, please?"

"You can count on it." Jenna squeezed his hand as he set her back on the couch and gave her one more hurried kiss.

Josh ran out the back door, jumped on the four-wheeler and raced to the barn. It looked like Audrey and Emma introduced the barn cat and her kittens to Alex and Brant and forgot to turn off the main light.

Quickly making a pass through the barn to ensure everything was as it should be, he turned off the light, shut the door, and hustled back home. He jogged inside and hurried into the family room, only to find it empty.

"Jenna," he called, noticing their closed bedroom door. He sincerely hoped she hadn't changed her mind. If she had, he would have to take one very long, very cold shower. Steeling himself for what he would find, he turned the knob, surprised by what greeted him when he pushed open the door.

Jenna had been busy while he was at the barn, lighting several candles and putting on some soft music. She reclined across the bed wearing the little black number she bought for their anniversary. Josh didn't know how she could have looked any more alluring. The smile she gave him caused his heart to race. So entranced by the sight of her, he couldn't move or speak as he stood in the doorway, gaping.

"Babe," he finally whispered, walking toward the bed as he peeled off his shirt and kicked off his slippers. "You're so beautiful, you take my breath away."

"Buck." Her voice was low and enticing, making him forget everything but her right at that moment. When she held a hand out to him, he took it in his and slid next to her on the bed, holding her palm to his heart where she could feel it pounding wildly in his chest. Jenna placed her other hand on his cheek. "I've missed you so much, missed being in your arms. You know this is my favorite place to be."

Josh offered a slow, sexy smile, opening his arms to her. "Then what are you waiting for?"

Chapter Thirteen

Josh stepped out in the early morning light, relieved to see the sun cresting the horizon. If the good weather held, he planned to finish his wheat harvest before the day was through. Anxious to start, he'd been promised extra help since it was a Saturday. As Jake pulled into the driveway, Josh waved a hand in greeting and motioned him into the house.

With the one combine and truck he owned, Josh could complete the harvest over the course of several days, as long as the weather held out. To speed things along, Steve and Clay generously offered the use of a combine, along with three trucks to haul the grain into town to the grain elevator. There, it would be weighed and graded before shipping out to wholesalers.

Josh and Steve would each run a combine while Clay, Jake, and Tyler Johnson drove the trucks. Callan planned to help Jenna prepare food for the men who would be starving by the time they took a break for lunch. Bobbi relished the opportunity to keep Audrey and Emma at her house, so they weren't underfoot.

One of Jake's buddies volunteered to drive the fourth truck, but he was unexpectedly called in to work. Desperate for a driver, Josh called his dad and asked if he'd like to drive the truck.

"Boy, would I, Joshie! What a way to spend a day. I haven't driven a grain truck in years. You might have to give me a refresher course, but I'll be there in just a bit," Big Jim said with his characteristic enthusiasm when Josh phoned him that morning. True to his word, he was at their door an hour later, raring to go.

Steve thought they could work in the same field, finish it then move to the next one, so they both started cutting on opposite ends of the field, the trucks falling into line behind the mammoth machines to catch the golden kernels as they spewed out. While one truck filled, the other drove to the grain elevator in town, unloaded and returned.

Mid-morning, Josh's combine broke down and he tinkered with it hoping it would be a quick fix. Wishful thinking got him nowhere as he worked to find the problem.

Finally, Big Jim got out of his truck and asked Josh a few questions before he started poking around. He spent forty years as a farm equipment mechanic and was one of the best during his working years. Retired for the last ten years, the equipment had changed, but the fundamentals were the same.

"Well, Joshie, looks to me like you just need to get these two wires working together." Big Jim was oblivious to the cringe crossing Josh's face when he used the nickname.

His dad had called him Joshie for as long as he could remember and he hated it. Absolutely hated it.

"I assumed that much, Pop, but I can't exactly bring a soldering iron out here." Josh tried to keep the irritation out of his voice. Not only was his dad annoying him, he lost precious daylight with the breakdown. "Let me see what I can find in the toolbox," Josh said, walking around to the other side of the combine and lifting the lid to the toolbox.

Big Jim walked over to his truck and leaned against the side for a few minutes before an idea struck him. He opened the door and pulled out the cigarette lighter. He hustled over to the wires on the combine and fused them together.

"Hah! I knew that would do the trick," he said, admiring his handiwork. He warmed the lighter up again, just to make sure the wires were good and tight. As he stepped out of the truck with it, he stumbled, dropping the lighter.

"Pop, I think I'm going to have to run to the shop," Josh said as he walked back around the combine in time to watch his dad stumble and drop the cigarette lighter in the dry, ripe wheat. It immediately sparked and ignited. So surprised by what happened, Big Jim stood watching the tiny flame grow bigger and bigger instead of getting away from the fire.

Josh ran up and tugged his dad back behind him. "Pop, get back!"

By now, the fire was about the size of a campfire. In the dry wheat, the whole field could be aflame in a matter of minutes. Frantic but trying to hold back his panic, Josh pulled his water jug out of the combine and dumped it on the flames. It sputtered then roared back to life.

Yanking a shovel off the combine, he started digging around the fire for all he was worth, dumping the dirt on the flames and trying to keep it from spreading. Big Jim recovered from his initial shock enough that he jumped in the truck and backed it up then pulled out a shovel and began helping Josh throw dirt on the fire.

When Jake pulled into the field on his return trip from town, he barreled out of the truck, grabbed Big Jim's shovel, and worked with a fury nearly matching Josh's. By the time they had the fire out, a spot about the size of one of the trucks had burned. The smell was awful and made their eyes water.

Gasping for air, Josh leaned on the shovel and mopped at the sweat running down his face with his arm. What could have been a disaster ended much better than he expected. He was thankful Jake showed up when he did.

Jake bent over trying to catch his breath with his hands on his knees.

Josh reached over and clasped Jake's shoulder.

"I can't thank you enough for jumping in to help," Josh said, hoping Jake knew exactly how grateful he was for his efforts.

"You're welcome," Jake said, still waiting for his breathing to return to normal as he grinned up at Josh. "Here you've gone and got your pretty face all dirty."

"Well, you won't be winning any beauty contests today, either," Josh teased.

Josh gave Jake another thump on his back then straightened just as Big Jim collapsed on the step of the truck.

Josh ran over to him, followed closely by Jake. "Pop, are you okay? Pop?"

Big Jim's face looked pale and his skin felt clammy when Josh touched his forehead. Jerking off his ball cap, he fanned it in front of the old man's face, stirring the air and hoping it would help revive his dad.

"Pop, don't you do something dramatic. We've had enough fun already today."

"I won't, Joshie, just need a breather." Big Jim's voice came out in a weak whisper, but he opened his eyes and tried to smile reassuringly at his son.

Josh dug his cell phone out of his pocket and called Callan. "Cal, can you come get Pop? We've had a little excitement and I think he really needs to go back to the house now."

"Sure, Josh, is he okay? Do I need to take him to the doctor?" Callan asked, worried.

"No, I think he just overdid and needs to rest." Josh watched the color return to his dad's face. "If I asked nicely, would you be game for driving a truck for a while?"

"Um... I... well..." Callan stuttered, then released a sigh. "Just give me a minute and we'll be there."

"Bring some water with you, please?" Josh begged before Callan hung up.

Jenna and Callan pulled up in Josh's pickup a few minutes later. Jake and Josh stood beside Big

Jim where he slumped on the truck step. The sight made them both concerned.

"Hey, girls," Big Jim said when they got out of the pickup. "You missed the show."

They stared at the scorched spot in the wheat field and looked at Josh, openly curious as to what transpired.

"I'd say we did, Daddy." Callan held onto her father's arm to help him balance as they walked to the pickup. "You know, I've been wanting to drive this ol' grain truck and the boys are holding out on me. Would you mind if we traded spots for a while? Jenna and I have lunch all planned, but she could still use your help while I play out here. What do you say?"

"That sounds like a deal to me, sweet daughter. I was about ready for a break anyway," Big Jim said as he climbed into the passenger side of the pickup. Callan dug out a couple of water jugs, two wet towels, and some sandwich bags filled with cookies.

Jenna leaned near Josh and whispered, "You can fill me in later." She and Big Jim waved as they took refreshments over to where the rest of the crew worked on the other side of the field before returning to the house.

Jake and Josh both kissed Callan's cheek when she handed them the cold, wet towels. They wiped the refreshing cloths across their faces and necks, removing soot and dirt. They wasted no time in consuming the water and the cookies before observing Callan's outfit.

She'd traded her shorts, tank top, and sandals for a pair of Josh's jeans, one of his shirts, and

Jenna's boots.

Unaware she'd be called into service as a truck driver, Callan dressed to be inside the air-conditioned house. Being a good five inches taller than Jenna and a size or so larger, she couldn't wear her clothes, even though their feet were the same size. There was no way Callan would drive the truck wearing anything less than jeans and a long-sleeved shirt. She'd seen the men in her family itching like mad from the wheat chaff and dust on numerous occasions.

"Aren't you the Miss Farmer of the Year fashion plate?" Jake teased, tugging on Callan's borrowed ball cap.

"Don't you get lippy with me, buster," Callan warned, pushing the hat back up. "You can take me like this or I'll go back to the house." She studied the ground where there had most certainly been a fire and pointed her hand to it. "What happened?"

"Pop." Josh ran a hand through his hair, shaking out some of the dirt and soot covering him from head to toe. "I broke down and was digging in the tool box to see what I could find. When I walked back around the combine, Pop stumbled and dropped the cigarette lighter in the wheat. It literally burst into flame. I dumped my water on it and then started shoveling like crazy. Pop was trying to help. He may have had a heart attack if Jake hadn't jumped in when he did."

The three of them walked over the charred area and found the cigarette lighter. Josh picked it up in his gloved hand and set it on the dash of the truck. He'd worry about fixing it later.

"You know what the best part of the whole thing is, Cal? He fixed the problem." Angry at the destruction of the crop his dad almost caused, Josh also felt pride that Pop managed to make the needed repairs.

"Yep, that's Daddy." Callan tugged her borrowed jeans up and tightened the belt. "This looks like it's going to be a very long day, so if you want me to help, let's get the show on the road. Just so you know, the first load I drive into town, I'm stopping by my house so I can change. Now somebody show me what to do."

Callan rode with Jake while he filled his truck. He gave her detailed instructions on what to do when she got to town before he turned her loose in the truck Big Jim had been driving. She fell in line behind the combine and did just fine. Before she knew it, her truck was full and she drove down the highway toward town.

She stopped on the way to Tenacity to change, unable to make herself appear in public looking like she was dressed for some hillbilly costume party. When she arrived at the grain elevator, the guys working it were surprised to see her instead of Big Jim. After giving them a brief explanation, they helped her unload and soon had her on her way back to Josh's.

She and Jake got into a good rhythm of alternating loads. Just when she thought she might die of heat and thirst, Josh declared it time for the noon break.

They sat around the big farm table in the dining room enjoying the air-conditioned coolness of the

house as well as a lively lunch conversation. Big
Jim was back to his normal jovial self and Jenna
seemed to be holding out well. She would have to
take a nap before thinking about preparing dinner,
though.

Everyone pitched in to do the dishes and Callan
suggested they put a roast in the slow cooker so
Jenna wouldn't have to worry about the main dish.
That left Jenna free to rest for a few hours. Big Jim
sat down in Josh's recliner and fell asleep.

The crew gathered plenty of cold water bottles
and snacks before heading back out. Jenna stood on
the porch giving Josh one last hug when they heard
Jake yell and watched him fly out of his truck,
jumping around excitedly. Clay broke into
uproarious laughter, removing his hat and slapping
it against his leg.

"Got ya!" he hollered at Jake, pointing a finger
his direction.

White as a sheet, Jake glared daggers at Clay.
"That is so not funny, man. Not funny and not
cool," Jake grumbled, growing angrier by the
second.

Josh walked over to Jake's truck and spied the
rubber snake Clay had wound around the gearshift.

"It's a little funny." Unsuccessfully, Josh tried
to hide his snickers. Jenna pinched his arm, making
him laugh aloud.

"Score!" Clay gave Josh a high-five as he
winked at Callan.

"Be warned, you've just started a war." Jake
leaned inside the truck and used a screwdriver to
dislodge the rubber snake. He tossed it Clay's

direction before climbing in the truck and heading back to the field.

Josh picked up the snake and threw it in the garbage. He knew if Jenna came across it later, she'd scream her head off, forgetting that it was a fake.

As Callan walked out to her truck with Clay, Jenna heard her say, "That was so mean, Clay. Funny, but mean. You know he's terrified of snakes."

After everyone left for the fields, Jenna retired to her bedroom for a rest. She awoke from a two-hour nap refreshed and energized. When she wandered out to the kitchen, she spotted Big Jim sitting in the recliner watching television.

"Hi, Pop. Did you get some rest?" she asked, leaning over to kiss his weathered cheek.

"I sure did, honey. Do you need some help in the kitchen? I'm pretty handy at peeling spuds." Big Jim got out of the recliner with a few creaks and cracks in his joints.

"I'd love some help." Jenna hooked her arm through his. She enjoyed spending time with Josh's dad. Although she didn't know Josh's mother well, Margo took joy in making cutting remarks and being unpleasant. The woman passed away not too long after she began dating Josh.

Jenna often wondered how Big Jim stayed married to such an unhappy woman for more than fifty years. He was one of the most sincere, kind people she'd ever encountered and he lived to make someone else's day. However, she did think his name was somewhat misleading. Even with his shoes on, he wasn't quite as tall as her five-foot six-inches. What he lacked in stature, though, he more than made up for in heart.

"If you can tackle the potatoes, I'll work on putting together a salad or two, and whip up some biscuits. How does that sound?" she asked as she got out a large bag of potatoes and a big pot.

"Sounds dandy to me." Big Jim slid onto a barstool and accepted the peeler she handed him.

They kept up a friendly conversation and soon had the meal nearly ready. Big Jim helped her unload the dishwasher from lunch and they set the table for dinner.

"Just think, this time next year, you'll have two high chairs pulled up to the table," Big Jim mused as he laid down silverware at each place setting.

Jenna stopped and stared at him. She hadn't thought that far ahead, but his observation was correct. As she started to look forward to the arrival of the babies, Jenna wondered if they'd be boys for Josh to train in all things farming or girls for her to pamper like princesses. Maybe they'd have one of each. That would be fun.

"You're right. Next year everything will be different, except you'll be right here keeping them entertained while I cook." Jenna smiled at her father-in-law and gently patted him on the back.

"I certainly hope so, honey. I can't wait to meet these two very special babies." Big Jim sounded wistful. "You know, I never expected to be blessed with my sweet daughter and Joshie. They were both wonderful surprises. Then when Clay and Callan couldn't have children, that was a disappointment, but it worked out so well with them adopting Audrey and Emma. Now, you and Joshie are going to give me two more babies to love. I don't think it can get any better than that, can it?"

"Not when you put it like that, Pop." Jenna gave him an impulsive hug, surprised by how frail he seemed. She supposed that was to be expected, considering he was eighty.

"Where is everyone? I'm about ready to belly up to another good meal." Big Jim pushed aside the kitchen curtain so he could look out the window.

"They should be in soon. Josh planned to be done by six so they've got a few minutes yet," Jenna said noticing the clock read a quarter before the hour.

Josh grinned as he watched Jake and Clay pull out of the field to haul the last two loads into town. After climbing down off the combine, he walked over to Steve and shook his hand as he stood next to his own combine.

"I don't know how to repay you for this." Josh waved his arm at the newly harvested field. "It would have taken me all week if not longer to get done what we accomplished today. Thank you so much."

"You're more than welcome, Josh. You help us all the time. The least we can do is give you a day of our time and a few pieces of equipment to use."

"I appreciate it, so much. You'll come have

dinner with us, won't you?"

"You couldn't keep me away. I heard Callan mention berry pie and Jenna said something about chocolate sheet cake. You don't think I'd miss that, do you?"

"Nope." Josh chuckled and turned back to his combine.

By the time they arrived at the house, Callan had washed up, changed her clothes, and helped Jenna put food on the table. Tyler went home since Laken was working the closing shift at her store and he needed to be home with their kids.

Clay and Jake soon arrived and laughed good-naturedly as they strolled in the door. Apparently, hunger chased away the imminent threat of the snake war.

After giving thanks for the meal and the blessings of the day, Josh thanked everyone again for their help. The conversation moved onto the final cutting of hay, school starting, Jake's new job, and, of course, the upcoming arrival of the twins.

"Have you started thinking of names?" Callan asked Jenna.

"I hadn't really got around to it yet." Picking out names hadn't occurred to Jenna. She needed to start a list of things to accomplish before the arrival of the babies.

Jake laughed. "You only need to pick out boy names. I already told you, we're having boys."

Clay slapped Jake on the back and gave him a devilish smile. "We? What's this we business? I'm pretty sure you weren't involved, at all, in any part of these babies coming to be."

Jake turned an annoyed glare at Clay. "Josh and Jenna said the babies could call me Uncle Jake so that makes it my business."

"Oh, I see." Clay attempted to look and sound serious as he considered Jake's statement. "And I suppose you have grand plans of teaching them all about farming and ranching and how to be expert snake handlers."

Jake let out a long-suffering sigh and leaned around Clay, turning a pleading look to Callan. "Tell me again why you wouldn't wait to marry me and instead spend your days having to tolerate this joker? Please, tell me why, Callan?"

When Callan and Clay wed, Jake served as their ring bearer. He thought she was marrying him and his little six-year-old heart was broken when he found out she was, in fact, marrying his cousin Clay. It had been a running joke for years between them that she should have waited for Jake to grow up.

Callan let out a wonderful, warm laugh, and winked at Jake. "I couldn't help myself. This cowboy swept me off my feet and captured my heart completely. What's a girl to do?"

"Wait for me, that's what." Jake feigned an indignant look. He smiled when Callan leaned over and kissed Clay's cheek, gazing at him with her heart in her eyes. He hoped to find someone to love as completely as Clay and Callan loved each other. Until then, he'd keep himself entertained by trading jokes and barbed comments with Clay.

Josh turned his attention to his sister. "So, Cal, if you ever decide you want to give up your event planning business, I'm still looking for a hired hand." Josh raised an eyebrow her direction and nodded his head encouragingly.

"Thanks for the offer, but I'll pass. One day in the trenches is more than plenty to suit me."

"You did a really good job." Josh's admiration carried through in his voice. "I appreciate your help."

"I will deny it if anyone sitting here brings it up again, but it was kind of fun," Callan said with a pleased smile. "For one day."

The group laughed and continued eating their meal flavored with animated conversation.

When the dishes were finished and everything put away, Steve drove the combine back to the ranch followed by Clay, Jake, and Josh, each driving a truck. Callan would drive over her car to pick up the girls and Clay while Jenna would take her car to bring back Jake and Josh.

When the other men drove down the lane, Big Jim gave both Callan and Jenna a kiss ready to return to his retirement center in Tenacity.

"Thanks for a great day, girls. Call anytime you need help or someone to liven up the place," Big Jim teased as he sauntered out to his car.

"Will do, Daddy," Callan called, waving to him.

"Drive safe, Pop," Jenna said, watching as he climbed behind the wheel. "Thanks for keeping me company."

Callan put her arm through Jenna's and they retreated to Jenna's sitting area, decorated in soft blue tones with chocolate accents. Josh called it her girlie room, which was fine with her. It meant all things greasy, smelly, and remotely resembling manly men stuff stayed out of her room.

"We've got a few minutes to sit and rest before we need to head to the ranch. It'll take Steve a while to get the combine there and the trucks will stay with him on the drive over," Callan said as she sat down with two glasses of cold sweet tea.

"I can't believe Pop set the field on fire." Jenna couldn't hide her look of astonishment. "That could have gone so badly. I'm feeling rather blessed, not only by our family and friends, but that things turned out so well."

"I know what you mean. I really think Daddy is starting to show his age. How did he do in here this afternoon?"

"Oh, fine, I think. I slept for a couple hours after lunch and he must have slept most of that time, too. He helped with dinner and was his usual talkative self. When I hugged him, though, he seemed kind of frail." Jenna put her feet up on the couch and held the tea glass against her throat. Sometimes she got so hot she thought she might melt.

Callan held up a magazine and fanned her. "I thought the same thing. I guess we'll have to keep a closer eye on him. He does so well on his own, I forget to pay enough attention to him. It's so easy to get caught up in the rush of our lives."

"You aren't the only one. Maybe we all can take turns checking on him or taking him out to eat, that kind of thing." Jenna closed her eyes and enjoyed the breeze Callan created with the magazine. They were quiet for a few minutes, then Jenna opened her eyes and smiled. "Your arm will fall off if you don't stop and you worked as hard as the men today."

Callan returned the magazine to the coffee table and leaned back with a sigh. "Don't tell the guys, but I wouldn't want to do that every day for anything. I don't think I'm ever going to stop itching, my arms are rubbery from trying to steer that old truck, and my hindquarters feel permanently bruised from bouncing around in the field. Driving the truck was kind of fun, but not enough I'd do it every day."

Jenna laughed. "Cal, you are something else. Josh said you worked just as hard and did as well as any man would have done."

"That is quite a compliment, coming from my little brother," Callan said, unable to hide her pleasure at Josh's praise.

"I don't think there's anything you can't do if you set your mind to it," Jenna said thoughtfully.

"There are one or two things." Callan grew somber and quiet, thinking of the babies she would never have and the one she lost. There were definitely some things she could never do, which is why she didn't let her thoughts linger there and moved on to a different topic. "There are two things I would really like to do for you, if you'd allow me."

"What's that?" Jenna sat up, gazing with curiosity at her friend. Callan had that intense look on her face she got whenever she was in the middle of planning something amazing.

"I'd like to help you decorate a nursery for the babies and I want to host a baby shower." Callan made mental lists of the things they'd need to accomplish before the arrival of the twins.

"Really?" Jenna grabbed Callan's hand in her own, unable to contain her excitement. "You'd really help me decorate the nursery and throw my baby shower?"

"I'd absolutely love to."

"Then yes, please!" Jenna beamed, thrilled with Callan's offers.

"Let me get the girls back in school and then we can start talking about details." Callan stood and gave a hand to Jenna as she got to her feet. They slowly walked to the back door. "Are you going to find out if you are having boys or girls or one of each?"

"We haven't decided yet. On one hand, I want to know. On the other hand, I'd like to be surprised. What do you think?" Jenna asked as she opened her car door.

"I think you and Josh should talk about it and decide together," Callan said with a grin.

"That's a very diplomatic and not at all helpful answer." Jenna rolled her eyes and laughed. "See you at the ranch."

When they arrived at the Matthews' ranch, Jenna and Callan found the men at the house enjoying a glass of cold lemonade. Emma bounced around between Josh, Clay, and Jake while Audrey sat next to Steve, telling him all about her day spent with Grammy.

"Mama!" Emma yelled as Callan stepped out

on the patio, launching herself into her mother's arms. Callan swung her up and gave her a kiss on the cheek. "How's my Sweet Pea? Were you good for Grammy today?"

"Yep, we had a marvelous time." Emma used her favorite new word. Everything for the last two weeks had been marvelous.

Laughing, Callan set her down. "I'm glad to hear it."

After draining their glasses and setting them in the kitchen, Josh and Jake thanked Bobbi for the lemonade and walked out to Jenna's car.

"Babe, I'm beat. Do you mind driving?" Josh asked as he held open the driver's side door for her.

"I guess not. Are you two going to sit in the back and make me be the chauffeur?" Jenna teased as she slid behind the wheel.

"What a great idea!" Jake hopped into the back seat, sitting as regally as possible in his dusty, sweat and soot streaked clothes.

Josh jumped in on the other side then rapped on the back of the front passenger seat with his knuckles. "Home now, if you please, Jamesette." Using an arrogant tone, he tipped his nose in the air with a feigned haughty look out the window.

"Jamesette? What kind of a name is that?" Jenna laughed at their antics.

"We can't very well call you James. Isn't that what they always say in the movies, 'home now, James?' Isn't the chauffeur always named James?" Josh waved airily to Audrey and Emma as Jenna pulled away from the ranch house, making them break out in giggles as they waved goodbye.

"Right you are, my good man." Jake affected a British accent and nodded his head in agreement. "Hurry it up please, Jamesette. I've got an important engagement this evening. If I don't make haste, I'll be unforgivably tardy."

"And this engagement, for which you can't be tardy, is her name Bambi, Roxy, or Trixi?" Jenna teased, glancing at Jake in the rear-view mirror.

"None of the above." Jake's brows furrowed and he glared at Jenna with indignation. Just because he couldn't remember his date's name wasn't important and beside the point. He didn't appreciate Jenna's insinuation about the type of girl he'd be seeing later that evening, even if she'd accurately pegged his date.

"Let me guess - she's blond and petite with a small vocabulary and large... assets." Jenna couldn't help goading Jake. She'd seen him out on dates a few times and it wasn't hard to picture the type of girl he'd take out.

Openly annoyed, Jake wondered how Jenna knew exactly the type of girl he liked to date. It wasn't like he ever brought one of his dates to any family gathering. He refused to let her unsettle him with her taunting. "For your information, she is in her third year of college."

"Oh, that's great. What school is she attending?" Jenna asked, sincerely interested.

"The community college," Jake answered, realizing too late the fodder that provided for Josh and Jenna's tormenting.

Josh laughed aloud. "Three years at a two-year college. That's great Jake. Sounds like a real

Einstein. What'd you say her name is?"

"I… she… never mind," Jake huffed. He squirmed in his seat, anxious to escape both the teasing and the scrutiny of his friends.

Aware of his irritation, Josh nudged him with his elbow and wiggled his eyebrows, getting a small grin out of Jake.

"If you can give me a minute of your time when we get back to the house before your date with Bambi, I'll run in and write you a check for today," Josh said as Jenna turned down their lane.

"No can do, dude." Jake shook his head. "You don't owe me anything for today."

"Jake, we can't let you do that. You worked too hard to not receive adequate compensation. Besides that, if it wasn't for you, I might have lost my entire wheat field with Pop and the fire." Josh didn't know if Jake fully realized how close they came to the field going up in flames.

"Really, Josh, I won't take more of your money. The last check you gave me was more than generous. Seriously, dude. That bonus was incredible." Jake grinned and playfully punched Josh in the arm. "How about if we call it even and the next time I have to run to the rescue, you can pay twice what I'm worth?"

"Deal." Josh shook Jake's hand and gave him a grateful smile as Jenna pulled into the garage.

"You're welcome to come in if you want Jake, but if you hit the ground running for your date, we understand," Jenna said, parking the car then turning around to glance at him.

Jake leaned over the front seat and pecked her

cheek. "Thanks, Jen. I'll stay for a visit next time. You can give me a list of baby names for my nephews then."

Jake jumped out of the car and ran to his pickup, creating a cloud of dust as he tore down the driveway and headed back toward town.

"There goes one great kid," Jenna said as she and Josh watched Jake drive off.

"Yep. One really great kid with terrible taste in women," Josh observed as they walked inside the house. "But then again, not everyone has my excellent taste."

Jenna stood on her tiptoes and surprised Josh with a warm kiss. "You do taste pretty excellent."

He started to pull her into a hug but Jenna twisted free and ran giggling down the hallway, Josh hot on her heels.

"Don't get your itchy, nasty wheat chaff all over me, Josh Carver. You stay away until you've had a shower, or three."

Chapter Fourteen

Jenna settled into her new job and routine with relative ease. In her second trimester, she felt better even though she worried that she was getting too big too soon. Her doctor assured her it was normal considering the fact she carried twins.

She wondered how much longer she could disguise the fact she was expecting before her supervisor said something. Following her friend Barb's advice, she poured herself into her new job, at least during work hours. Once she left the building, she left her work behind and focused on the farm, Josh, and everything they needed to accomplish before the babies arrived.

The previous afternoon, her supervisor gave her a quick sixty-day review and everything she shared was positive. After expressing her pleasure at how well Jenna fulfilled the duties of her position, Mrs. Gordon let her know how much she valued her expertise.

Jenna prayed the woman would continue to value her once she found out she was expecting. She hoped to get through at least another month before she had to break the news around the office.

At the rate her waistline expanded, though, she thought her condition had to be obvious to everyone. She was convinced she looked like she'd stuffed a basketball in her shirt. Josh teasingly assured her it looked more like a football.

As the weather cooled down, she could hide some of her increasing girth with jackets, sweaters, and artfully draped scarves.

Josh planned to finish the last custom haying job that week. He promised when he was done, he'd take an entire day to do anything she wanted. They needed to start looking at baby furniture, just to get some ideas. With the holidays approaching, she knew time would get away from them and the due date for the babies to arrive would be upon them before they had time to blink.

Although she was still frightened and intimidated at the prospect of bringing home two newborns, thoughts of having Josh's babies made Jenna happy. It had taken a lot of prayer and meditation, but she finally arrived at the place of acceptance and anticipation. Anytime she started to feel overwhelmed by it all, she reminded herself they had many family members and good friends they could count on to provide a helping hand. Jenna knew she would be relying heavily on her sister-in-law.

Callan was already doing so much to help her get ready for the arrival of the twins. True to her word, as soon as she had the girls back into the swing of school, she came over one Saturday morning with photos, catalogs, fabric, and paint swatches and they started talking about the nursery.

As they wandered through the upstairs bedrooms, Callan and Jenna agreed the twins would likely share a room for their first few years. After discussing the good and bad points of each room, they finally decided on the bedroom that offered a fabulous view of the backyard, the barn, and a portion of the fields. Big windows let in plenty of light, yet the trees from the backyard provided welcome shade.

When it was time for the twins to have their own rooms, the other two bedrooms upstairs were nearly identical in size and shape. Jenna hoped that would keep any fights from erupting over "my room is bigger than your room." She could then return the nursery to a guest room.

Jenna sighed as they stood at the window and looked down on the farm. "Can you picture them, Callan, looking out the window? Little girls will enjoy the view of the yard and flowers. Little boys can see the barn and the fields."

"And no matter if you have boys or girls, they'll be excited to watch out the window for their daddy," Callan said, putting her arm around Jenna and giving her a gentle squeeze. "It would be a lot easier to decorate if we knew what you're having."

"I know," Jenna said with a smile. "Josh and I agreed the next appointment we want to find out the sex. If it was just one baby, we might wait and be surprised. Two babies definitely require more pre-planning."

"As soon as you know, we can really start making plans for the nursery. When is your next ultrasound?" Callan whipped out a notepad and jotted notes as she walked around the room.

"Two weeks." Jenna absently rubbed a hand across her baby bump. "In two weeks we'll know if Jake's predictions of boys are correct."

"That Jake." Callan laughed and shook her head, amused by the young man's fascination with the arrival of the twins. "You'd think he was a real uncle for as much as he has carried on about these babies. I wonder what he'll be like when he can actually see them."

"Probably a complete wonderful nuisance." Jenna smiled, hoping Jake would truly consider himself an uncle. "Nearly as bad as their Uncle Clay, I'd guess."

"Oh, Jen," Callan said, looking pleased. "Clay is so excited and happy for you. We both are. You can definitely plan on having lots of extra hands to hold the babies if you need them."

Jenna clasped Callan's hand in her own. "You know I will. I just hope I can be as good a mother as you are to Audrey and Emma. I think you were born to be a mom."

Callan let out a derisive laugh, much to Jenna's surprise. "I'd hardly say that. You know I used to be all about my career. Clay used to call me Miss Business all the time. I was focused, determined, and selfish. I didn't have time or want to make time for a baby. Then, when I got pregnant and lost the baby, I felt like a part of me died as well. I can't ever get that part of me back. You know the story, but I felt like God was punishing me. Until I got things figured out, we had a few hard years. I've been so blessed to have the opportunity to raise

Audrey and Emma. I try to be the best mom to them I can be. Clay and I both make mistakes, especially when we jumped into this mid-stream with the girls, but we're learning. I think the most important thing is to love them. Love them all the time, no matter what, with your whole heart. If you do that, you can't veer too far off course."

Jenna released a sigh and squeezed Callan's hand as they walked toward the stairs. "How did you get so smart and wise beyond your years?" Suddenly Jenna gasped and looked at Callan with her eyes round in surprise.

"What is it Jen?" Callan asked, hoping nothing was wrong.

"I think I just felt the babies move." Jenna beamed. The two women stood unmoving, halfway down the stairs, waiting to see if Jenna felt another flutter. "There! There it goes again."

Callan gave her a hug and wiped away a tear. "Oh, little mama, this is going to be marvelous."

By the time the next ultrasound appointment rolled around, everyone was anxious to find out if the two Carver babies were going to be girls, boys, or one of each.

Josh took the day off and drove Jenna into work, met her for lunch, then drove her to the appointment. The technician didn't have to ask if he wanted to come closer. He stood right behind her as she brought up the image of the babies on the screen.

"Just look at these babies. They're growing right on schedule and appear to be doing very well. Do you want to know the sex?"

"Yes," Josh and Jenna said in unison.

The technician laughed and continued moving around the wand, trying to get the very best look at the two babies. They weren't being terribly cooperative, showing off arms and legs but not much else. The technician turned up the sound so they could hear the heartbeats.

"Can you hear them?" the technician asked, smiling at the look of wonder sweeping across both Jenna and Josh's face. Josh held Jenna's hand and rubbed his thumb across her palm as they listened to the faint whooshing sound of their babies' heartbeats. A tear rolled down Jenna's cheek as she sent another prayer heavenward, thanking God for His wisdom and grace, blessing them with the twins.

"That is amazing," Josh whispered, wiping away Jenna's tear with his finger as he smiled down at her.

"Let's see if we can get a better look at these two and figure out who we've got in there." The technician pushed gently on Jenna's belly with the wand and they watched as one baby came into full view.

"That is definitely a boy." The technician laughed, pointing to the screen and outlining body parts with her finger. "All boy, that one. How about baby number two? Come on baby, give us a peek."

They waited and finally their patience paid off. "That definitely looks like a boy as well. Twin boys. That should keep your hands full," the technician teased as she printed off a photo for them while Jenna cleaned up.

"Two boys," Josh said, barely able to think of little else as he stared down at the photo. "Wow, two boys!"

"Thank you," Jenna said as they left and walked down the hallway. "I guess Jake was right."

"Jake? Huh?" Josh functioned on autopilot, intently focused on the idea of having twin baby boys. He'd been hoping for boys. He and Jenna didn't truly care what sex the babies were as long as they were healthy, but he was thrilled at the idea of having two boys to carry on the Carver name. He couldn't wait to tell his dad.

"Jake. Our hired hand, good friend, sometimes like a pesky younger brother. That Jake? The one who said we would be having boys. Remember?" Jenna teased as they stepped off the elevator and entered the parking garage.

Josh came back to reality and grinned. "Yeah, I remember. I can't believe we're having boys. You are okay with boys, aren't you?"

Jenna laughed. "Doesn't really matter if I am or not, it's not like we can exchange them for girls. I truly don't care as long as they're healthy."

Secretly hoping for at least one girl, if not two, Jenna knew Josh would be elated to have two boys. At least now, she and Callan could start plans for the nursery décor.

"Two boys," Josh said again, as he held Jenna's door and then walked to the driver's side of her car. Her appointment was late enough that afternoon that she didn't have to go back to the office, so Josh drove out of town toward home. When he pulled into the garage, he popped the trunk then helped

Jenna out of the car. She walked around to look in the trunk, filled with bags of a variety of sizes.

"I wondered what you did all day while I worked." She picked up a few bags that didn't look too heavy or large.

"I found a few things I thought we might need for the boys." Josh grinned, enjoying the way it sounded to say "the boys."

"Tell me you aren't going to go crazy and buy every baby thing you see," Jenna said as they set the bags on the kitchen table and she kicked off her shoes.

"Of course not." Josh tried to look insulted. He might have been if she wasn't partially right. "Come see what I found."

He didn't have to ask her twice as she looked on with eager anticipation. Josh unpacked storybooks, most of them involving farming or animals. "I thought we could start reading to them now. The books I read on pregnancy say you're supposed to talk and read to them. They should be at the stage where they're starting to hear, right?"

"Right," Jenna said, impressed with the information Josh retained from reading the books Callan gave him. "What else did you get?"

"Just a few stuffed toys. I thought they were cute." He pulled out a stuffed pony and a cow.

"Good thing these two are boys." Jenna ran a hand over the soft toys, thinking little girls would most likely prefer unicorns or kittens.

Josh grinned and pulled out a box with a baby monitor with a full-color screen. "With this, we can hear and see the babies. It'll be really helpful when we move them upstairs, don't you think?"

"It certainly will be helpful." Jenna admired the monitor. They decided for the first few months, the babies would sleep in the master bedroom, saving Josh and Jenna from running up and down the stairs multiple times day and night. Once the babies started sleeping through the night, or at least for several hours at a stretch, they planned to move them to the nursery. The monitor would be a huge help when they moved the boys upstairs.

"I thought these would be fun, for later." Josh lifted two identical bouncing seats out of boxes. Covered in tan fabric dotted with farm animals, Jenna thought the seats were adorable. She got down on her knees and fingered the animals accenting the seats.

"It looks like you just decided how we're going to decorate the nursery." Jenna gazed at the plunder and envisioned how cute a farm animal theme would look in the room upstairs, especially for two little farmers-in-training.

"I did?" Josh glanced at his purchases with a troubled expression. "I didn't mean to. You can take the stuff back for something else, babe."

Laughing, Jenna grabbed Josh's arm as he started to put one of the bouncing seats back in the box. "No, Josh, I love it. I meant that now Callan and I won't have to think of a theme. You already did it for us. It's a good thing."

"Really?" Josh asked, helping her to her feet.

"Really." Jenna kissed the wonderful man she married. Leave it to him to find perfect things for the nursery when she couldn't even think about where to start. "What else did you buy?" A pink gift bag sat unopened on the table.

Josh handed it to her with a shy grin. "It's a little something for the little mama. Go on, open it."

Jenna pulled out the pink tissue paper to find three maternity blouses that she loved along with a very cute and trendy black maternity dress.

"Josh, these are awesome." Jenna held each piece up and admired it. "You didn't need to buy me anything."

"Yes, I did. I know this whole thing is hard on you and now that you're really starting to show, I wanted you to still feel like your usual stylish self." Josh enjoyed the way her eyes lit as she looked at the clothes.

After squeezing him around the neck, she pulled his head down and kissed his cheek. "What did I ever do to deserve you?"

"I'm not sure, but whatever it was, I'm glad you did." Josh's voice grew husky while his eyes glowed from an inner fire. "Put on that dress and I'll take you out for dinner."

Jenna grabbed his hand and gave him a flirty grin. "How about I go try it on and we stay home?"

"Deal." He pulled her close and kissed her passionately until both of their phones began ringing. Frustrated, he rested his forehead against hers. "Let's ignore them."

"We could, but you know they'll just keep calling." Jenna's lips taunted him just a whisper away.

She took a step back and dug her phone out of her purse then answered it. "Yes, Aunt Amelia, we just got home. Guess. Nope. Yes, two boys!"

Josh answered his phone to find Callan on the line. "Hey, Cal, we just got home. It looks like Jake wins again. We're having twin boys."

After hanging up with Callan, Josh called his dad while Jenna called her parents followed by her sisters.

His last call was to Jake. When he got his voice mail, he left a message.

"Hey, Jake, it's Josh. Jenna had a doctor appointment today and I'm sorry to tell you that..." Josh left a long pause for effect. "You were totally right, man! Two boys! We are having twin boys! Talk to you later."

As she stood in front of her supervisor's door, Jenna took a calming breath. She'd been expecting this meeting for weeks, ever since she started showing. Surprised it had taken Mrs. Gordon this long to request a meeting, she hoped she'd still be employed at the end of the day. Barb remained the only coworker who knew about Jenna's pregnancy. It was past time to let her boss know she was expecting.

Quietly tapping on Mrs. Gordon's door, Jenna turned the knob and entered when she heard the woman say, "Come in."

"Good morning, Mrs. Gordon. How are you today?" Jenna asked politely as she stepped into the office.

"I'm fine, Jenna. How are you feeling these days?" Mrs. Gordon looked over the top of her glasses and motioned Jenna to take the seat across from her.

"I'm doing very well. Thank you." Jenna sat demurely in the chair, although she felt like she was about to be tried, judged, and found severely lacking. "I wanted to thank you again for giving me an opportunity in this position."

"You've been doing an outstanding job." Mrs. Gordon removed a file from a drawer behind her, laid it on her desk, and flipped it open. "You've been in that position for what, about three months or so?"

"Yes, ma'am."

"Do you think your position is one you could do from home on a part-time basis?"

Caught off guard by the question, Jenna answered honestly. "Actually, I do. There are very few instances when a face-to-face meeting is necessary. Most of the communication is via phone and email, and there are a lot of online aspects to the position as well."

"I see," Mrs. Gordon said, taking down notes. "Do you think you would be capable of doing it part-time from home? Could you work in a home environment?"

"Yes, I could."

"Unless you've had some sort of health problem or unreasonable weight gain, I assume you're expecting to expand your family sometime in the near future. Would that be correct?"

Jenna fought the urge to squirm in her chair

under Mrs. Gordon's intense stare. Instead, she sat a little taller and looked her supervisor directly in the eye. "Yes, Mrs. Gordon. I am expecting. I'm due in March and we're having twins."

Much to Jenna's surprise, Mrs. Gordon laughed. "Twins? Oh my. You will have your hands full. Boys or girls?"

"Boys," Jenna said, with a wide smile. "My husband can hardly contain his excitement."

"I would imagine."

"Mrs. Gordon, I didn't mean to intentionally hide my pregnancy. Well, maybe I did a little. I just wanted to establish myself in the position before I told you I was expecting. I know I'll need some time off for maternity leave, but I have every intention of continuing in my job if you'll still have me."

"I appreciate your honesty and we wouldn't think of replacing you. Like I said, you're fabulous in this position and we wouldn't want to change that at all. I do think, however, that you could possibly work from home part-time. I assumed you were expecting and I want this to work for you as well. I have four children and understand the demands of being a mother with a career. It isn't easy. That's why I like to look at ways to make things beneficial for all parties. If you could work from home two or three days a week, would you be interested in working at the office the other days?

"Oh, absolutely, Mrs. Gordon, and I appreciate your generosity. I think an arrangement like that will work out wonderfully."

"I like to think it will. We've got about four

months before you'll be on maternity leave?"

"Yes."

"Great. Now, when are you planning to tell everyone you are expecting? There are more than a few bets that you are and even a few that were guessing you are either due soon or you are having more than one."

Relief washed over Jenna and she took a deep breath. "I can send out a memo this afternoon."

"Perfect!"

When Jenna arrived home that evening, she couldn't wait to tell Josh the news. She'd been dreading the day Mrs. Gordon discovered she was pregnant. She expected to be fired immediately or at least told not to come back after the babies were born. The fact that Mrs. Gordon had been so understanding and actually offered to let her work part-time from home was beyond anything she had hoped.

"She was so nice about it, Josh. Everything is falling into place," Jenna said as they sat down to eat dinner at the kitchen counter.

"That is so great, babe." Josh rubbed her back comfortingly. "You know you don't have to work. We'd make out fine if you didn't."

"I know, Josh, but I'm not cut out to be a stay-at-home mom. I need to work for me, to stay involved, and challenge my mind. Unlike your very talented sister, I have no other marketable skills I could turn into a successful career from home. Besides, my job comes with great insurance and benefits. I think I'll be able to work three days a week from home, so I'll only have to find daycare for the boys the other two days."

"I can take care of them, I guess." Josh wasn't sure how babies and farming would go together, trying to picture in his mind how it would work. He couldn't exactly envision a way to strap car seats to the tractor.

Jenna looked at him as if he'd lost his mind. "I don't see that working at all. You can't take them with you and you can't sit around the house two days a week, especially during the summer. We'll figure something out. Aunt Amelia said she wouldn't mind watching them sometimes. Maybe she would be willing to take them one day a week. I wonder if Callan would mind watching them one day a week. What do you think?"

"I think you'll have to ask Callan. My guess is that she'll probably jump all over the opportunity." Josh liked the idea of the boys being with family members rather than strangers. "You know if Amelia and Callan do agree and something comes up, I can take care of them. I plan to be a very hands-on kind of dad, not one who tells people he's 'babysitting' anytime he takes care of his own kids."

Jenna stared thoughtfully at the man she married. Josh turned out to be nothing like she expected but everything she never knew she wanted. "Has anyone ever told you what an amazing and great guy you are?"

Josh stopped eating and looked at her, aware of the sincerity in Jenna's eyes. He placed his hand on hers and gave it an affectionate squeeze. "Thank you, babe. Whatever I am, it's because of you.

Because of who I want to be for you and for our boys."

"I love you."

"I know. I love you, too. Always have, always will. Besides, you couldn't help yourself," Josh said with a devilish gleam in his warm gray eyes. "It's my swashbuckling good looks and undeniable charm, right?"

"Oh, you." Jenna playfully popped his arm and turned her attention back to her dinner.

Chapter Fifteen

"Babe, we're going to be late if you don't get a move on. You look fantastic. Let's roll," Josh yelled from the living room toward the bedroom. He had no idea what Jenna was wearing, but she always looked stylish and put together.

If she didn't hustle, though, they were going to be unforgivably late. It was their turn to pick up Callan and Clay for a night out. The four of them agreed to dinner out in Portland followed by the symphony's holiday performance. Both Jenna and Callan had been talking about it for weeks.

When Jenna hurried into the living room, or as much as a woman six months pregnant with twins can hurry, Josh smiled. Dressed in the black dress he bought her with a pair of low heels, she looked amazing.

The dress did a great job of camouflaging her expanding tummy. With a simple square neckline and elbow-length sleeves, the front featured a wide flowing ruffle that ran from the neck to the hem. Jenna wore a sparkly black necklace and carried her black dress coat. There was no way she could button it, but the cheery red scarf she looped around her neck would help keep her warm.

As he bent to kiss her cheek, Josh breathed in her vanilla scent. "Maybe we should cancel and just stay home. You look so beautiful." Growling the words in her ear, he pressed a moist kiss to her neck and felt a shiver of anticipation race through her.

Jenna blushed and squeezed his arm. "I look like a hippo dressed for a night on the town and you can't tell me I don't. I think I know what a beached whale must feel like and I still have almost three months to go."

"Remind me to buy you a new mirror because the one you looked in obviously isn't functioning correctly. You're a lovely woman with rosy cheeks, gorgeous hair, and great taste in fashion." Josh kissed her cheek then gave her a playful wink. "I'm glad you like your dress."

"I do love it, Josh, and thankfully, there's room for the babies to grow in it." Jenna shoved her arms into the sleeves of her coat while Josh held it for her.

"I've got the car all warmed up, so let's get going. I'm half starved and you know I'll have to fight Clay for the breadbasket as it is."

They arrived right on time at Clay and Callan's. The couple ran out to the car, looking forward to a night out. Bobbi and Steve kept the girls for the weekend, so Clay and Callan planned to enjoy their time as an unfettered couple while it lasted.

An hour later, Josh pulled up at the restaurant and let Jenna and Callan out at the door so they wouldn't have to walk across the parking lot. As they stepped inside, the girls removed their gloves, scarves, and coats while they waited for the men. When Josh and Clay hustled in the door, the hostess escorted their group to a table and they settled into a comfortable conversation.

Callan and Clay planned to host Christmas, as they did every year, and the discussion turned to who would attend. Josh and Jenna spent Thanksgiving with her family in Seattle, so they would be able to attend the annual Matthews family Christmas gathering.

"Please tell me you didn't invite Bob and Donna," Josh said of their older brother.

"I didn't invite them, exactly." Callan exhibited a sudden interest in her breadstick.

"What does that mean?" Josh glared at his sister with narrowed eyes. Bob and Donna managed to make every gathering they attended miserable with their whining, complaining, and nasty commentary.

"I told Daddy if he wanted them to come he had to do the inviting because I wasn't going to this year. I'm tired of them sucking all the fun out of the holidays." Callan raised a defiant gaze to her brother with sparks lighting her green eyes. "I hope they go visit Donna's family for a change. You know how many times they've seen Audrey and Emma since we adopted them? Once, and that was only because we ran into them at the grocery store. Not that I want the girls to spend time with them, but you'd think they'd show even the tiniest bit of interest in them, wouldn't you? They are their grandchildren, after all."

"When has Bob or Donna ever shown an

interest in anything beyond what benefits them personally?" Josh asked, not expecting an answer. "I hope they don't show up. We could enjoy a peaceful, fun Christmas without the two party poopers there."

"It would be nice to celebrate with the people we really care about and who care about us," Jenna added, recalling all the unpleasant occasions they'd had to endure with Josh's brother and his wife.

Clay nodded, taking the last breadstick then breaking it in two before giving half to Josh. "I'm hoping Big Jim either forgets to ask them or they find somewhere else to go. I want Christmas to be special for the girls and I refuse to let those two ruin it for them, or any of the rest of us. It's our home and we should be able to set the rules."

"Go get 'em, Clay!" Josh encouraged with a jaunty grin.

After giving his brother-in-law a nod, Clay decided it was a good time to change the subject. "How are your childbirth classes going? I heard you had some trouble with them, Josh."

Josh and Jenna recently finished attending a six-week class with several other expectant couples. Under the mistaken assumption that the classes would teach Jenna how to breathe during labor, Josh soon realized that was only a small part of what the sessions entailed.

They'd learned about caring for newborns, options for handling her pain during birth, breastfeeding versus a bottle, and much more. Although the books he'd read gave him some idea of what to expect, he was not prepared for the video they watched during the final class of a woman giving birth in shocking up-close and personal detail. Josh went outside for some air, handling the graphic presentation better than some of the other fathers-to-be. One passed out and two others ran to the restroom, violently ill.

"Thank you for reminding me about that nightmare just as we're about to eat." Josh frowned at Clay. "Your timing, as always, is perfect."

"I do what I can." Clay offered him a jesting smirk. "Really, though, did you learn anything helpful in the classes?"

"We did," Jenna spoke up before Josh could answer. She listened to him rant for an hour after they got home from the last class about how unnecessary it was to be that graphic in the curriculum. Jenna noticed most men were quick to forget their involvement in the whole process when it got down to the nitty gritty details of giving birth.

Jenna touched Josh's hand where it rested on his thigh beneath the table. "Don't you think you learned some helpful information in the class, Josh?"

"Yes, I did. Mostly that I'll never put Jenna through this again." Josh tugged at his collar since it suddenly felt too snug. "We did learn about breathing and coaching. I personally think a whistle and a checkered flag would be a big help, but for some reason, Jenna doesn't agree that would be the best thing to have in the delivery room."

They all laughed at his comment and went on to discuss how well the nursery plans were coming together since Josh unknowingly picked the farm animal theme. Callan planned to host a baby shower the second weekend of January and the nursery would be finished by then.

After dinner, they walked from the restaurant to the symphony. They laughed and talked, enjoying the night out. The holiday selections the symphony performed were wonderful and afterward they walked across the street to a cozy little bistro where they indulged in dessert.

On the quiet drive home, Jenna fell asleep as soon as they hit the city limits while Callan snuggled against Clay in the backseat.

"Is Jenna doing okay, Josh?" Callan asked as they drove toward Tenacity.

"I think so," he said, honestly. "She gets tired easily and her blood pressure has been a little high, but the doctor said that's all normal. She has a hard time resting because it seems like those two little guys know the second she is trying to sleep and start fighting in there to beat the band. The other night, she was trying to sleep and they were kicking so hard, the covers actually bounced. I don't know how she isn't bruised black and blue from the inside out, but those two were really going at it. When I put my hand on her stomach, I could feel them kick and push. If that is any indication of their future personalities, I think we might have a couple of scrappers on our hands."

Clay laughed. "If they're that rambunctious, it's a good sign they're healthy and active, right?"

"Right."

Jenna hadn't experienced any complications in her pregnancy, other than exhaustion, and for all appearances the boys grew normally and right on schedule.

Josh couldn't even begin to fathom how heartbreaking and painful it must have been for Callan to miscarry when she was four months pregnant. She hadn't told anyone, including Clay, she'd been expecting until just a few years ago, three years after it had happened. Their marriage hit bottom when he found out the truth, but the struggle made them decide to work things out and start fresh. As he watched them together, it was easy to forget the painful times they'd faced.

"If there's anything we can do to help, let us know." Callan leaned forward and touched Josh's shoulder with gentle hand.

"I think you've done more than your share as it is, Cal. Jenna is thrilled with the nursery and so excited about the baby shower. When you told her you'd be happy to watch the boys one day a week, she cried for an hour about how you're the best sister in the world. With you watching them on Mondays and Amelia keeping them Wednesdays, Jenna can work from home the other three days and everything should be smooth sailing, or as smooth as it will get with twins."

"I was honored she asked me to watch the twins. I'll get two little babies to love and cuddle and fuss over every week but I won't have them often enough that I'll get tired of babysitting. With the girls both in school, I miss having some noise in the house during the day. It will be perfect."

Clay gave Callan a kiss on her cheek, knowing how much she loved to cuddle babies. "If their favorite uncle just happens to take a long lunch or have a free class period, he might run home to spend some time with them, too."

"Since when do you get all loopy over babies, Clay?" Josh laughed at the picture in his head of his burly brother-in-law making funny faces at two little babies.

"Wouldn't you like to know?" Clay ignored the question, giving Josh a look that dared him to interrogate him further.

"Have you gotten around to picking any names?" Callan asked. She and Jenna discussed a long list of names but the ones Jenna liked Josh didn't and the ones he thought were great, Jenna declared completely awful. Callan had to agree, especially when Josh suggested they name the boys Espn and Fox, for the sports television networks.

"Willard and Ashley," Jenna said as she came awake and joined in the conversation. "How about those names, Josh?"

"Absolutely not! Sounds like a couple of sissy-pants poets," Josh said with disgust. The boys would be farm kids, after all. They needed salt of the earth, solid names. "I already picked out two great names and you shot them down without even blinking."

"Espn and Fox are not great names. Even Clay wouldn't suggest names like that, would you?" Jenna turned around and glanced at her brother-in-law in the backseat.

"Well, um…" Clay didn't want involved in this conversation. No matter what he said, he'd end up making one of them mad. "Why don't you name them after both of your dads or some family name?"

"Hmm," Jenna said, growing quiet and thoughtful. "That isn't a bad idea, Clay. Thanks."

Clay could feel Callan patting his leg, which meant she was pleased with him. If he continued to score points with her the rest of the evening, he hoped he would get a reward for his good behavior. When Jenna turned back around, he gently poked Callan in the ribs then blew in her ear. The glare she gave him warned of the thin ice on which he purposely skated.

"Maybe you can help me with some of your family names, Callan." Jenna turned around again and smiled at her sister-in-law. She couldn't think of any names she liked from her own family tree.

"Sure. I'll bring a list when I come this week to work on the nursery." Callan mentally scanned through family names and immediately rejected most of them.

Josh soon pulled into Clay and Callan's driveway, bidding them good night.

"Thanks for another fun evening," Callan said as Clay held her door and offered her a hand on the icy sidewalk. "I hope we can get in a few more outings before the twins arrive."

"Me, too." Unsuccessful in her efforts to stifle a yawn as she spoke, Jenna made them all laugh.

"I think I better get her home," Josh said as he waved to Clay and Callan. Once they were back on the road, he turned his gaze to Jenna. "It's good we're spending more time with them. They're both a lot of fun, aren't they?"

"Yes, they are. I'm so glad we enjoy one

another's company. It's nice you and Callan have each other, considering."

"Considering what?" Josh asked.

"Considering how much you both despise Bob and how you were raised. I just meant it's nice you two are close and enjoy spending time together. And that Clay and I enjoy tagging along."

"Yeah? I'm glad you both enjoy tagging along. In case you didn't know it, I kind of like you."

Jenna grinned. "I kind of like you, too. Now about these baby names…"

Chapter Sixteen

Clay and Callan's home filled to overflowing with guests and holiday joy on Christmas Day. Audrey and Emma rose early, squealing in delight over the gifts from Santa, as well as those from their parents.

Josh and Jenna arrived before the other guests. Jenna couldn't stop bragging about the wonderful rocker Josh gave her that morning for the nursery. The rich navy overstuffed chair rocked and swiveled from side to side. A matching ottoman gave Jenna somewhere to rest her feet. She envisioned tiny little hands holding onto the edge of the cushion, learning to walk around it.

"I can't wait for you to see it," Jenna gushed as she and Callan worked on meal preparations.

By the time everyone arrived, gifts were once again overflowing from beneath the Christmas tree.

"Mama? Who's Willard and Ashley?" Audrey asked, running into the kitchen and tugging on Callan's apron.

"Who?"

"Willard and Ashley? There are some packages under the tree that say they're for Willard and

Ashley." Confused by the look that passed between Jenna and Callan, Audrey waited for a response.

"Does it say who they're from?" Jenna pulled Audrey into a warm hug and brushed unruly golden curls back from her face.

"Nope. Who do you think they're from?"

"I don't know, but I'm sure we'll find out." Callan offered Jenna a rueful smile. "For now, you and Emma leave them alone, though."

"Okay, Mama." Audrey ran off to play with the other children.

Later, as they all crowded into the living room to open gifts, Jenna looked around the room, counting her blessings to be a part of this family. Big Jim, Bobbi and Steve, Jake and his parents, Josh and Callan's Aunt Julie and Uncle Ralph, as well as Laken and Tyler Johnson and their two kids were all there to enjoy the day. Thankfully, Bob and Donna were not in attendance.

When only two packages remained under the tree, addressed to Willard and Ashley, Jake handed one box to Jenna and the other to Josh. Jenna laughed when she pulled out two pairs of the tiniest little Wranglers she had ever seen. Josh's package contained two little John Deere ball caps.

"Oh, Jake, these are awesome!" Jenna motioned for him to come close and gave him a peck on the cheek. "You do know we aren't naming the boys Willard and Ashley."

Jake laughed, returning to his seat. "I know. Since you still haven't picked names and Josh told me how much he liked those particular names, I thought I'd put them on the tag for now."

Josh rolled his eyes at Jake then held up a little ball cap. "I don't think this is quite my size."

"They're for the babies, Uncle Josh, not you," Emma said in exasperation.

"Oh, my mistake." Josh winked at the little girl.

Jake and Clay disappeared and soon returned carrying a huge box, setting it down in front of Jenna.

"This gift is a group effort," Clay said as he and Jake stepped back. "We hope you like it."

Josh helped Jenna untie the bow, pull off the paper and open the box. When he took the top of the box away, it revealed a hand-carved child-sized table with four chairs. Made of oak, the table had rounded corners and sturdy legs. Each chair bore the design of a farm animal, with two horses and two cows completing the set.

Jenna studied one of the horse chairs. The four chair legs looked like horse's legs while the seat resembled the animal's back. The neck comprised the back of the chair and a wonderfully detailed face of the animal covered the outside of the chair's backrest. There was even a mane on the horse chair, made out of yarn.

Holding up one of the chairs, Josh examined the excellent craftsmanship. Gratitude flooded through him while Jenna sniffled to hold back tears. Comfortingly, he rested a hand on her shoulder and glanced at Clay, then Jake. "Who do we need to thank for this amazing gift? It's just unbelievable."

Everyone remained quiet as Josh looked around the room, studying each face. His gaze finally rested on his brother-in-law. "Come on, Clay. Who worked on this project?"

Clay waved his hand around the room. "Uncle Ralph let us use his wood shop and helped quite a bit. Jake put in time when he could and Big Jim, Dad, and Uncle Tom worked on the chairs. Callan and Aunt Julie added the mane. Like I said, it's a group effort."

"Don't let him fool you," Jake said, thumping Clay on the back. "He spent hours carving on those things."

"It's a beautiful gift." Jenna struggled her way out of her chair and waddled over to Clay to give him a hug. "These will be a wonderful keepsake for the boys. Thank you, everyone."

"You're welcome," Clay said, carefully hugging Jenna. As he did, he felt a baby kick. When he leaned back and stared at her stomach, Jenna smiled and grabbed his fingers in hers. She placed his hand on her belly and held it steady. The baby kicked again, making Clay's eyes light with wonder while Jenna grinned.

"Can I feel, too?" Audrey pleaded. Jenna guided her hand to the spot and Audrey giggled as she felt a thump against her hand. Emma insisted on her turn. They finally had to explain to Emma a few weeks ago that Aunt Jenna was not getting fat, but that was where she carried the babies until they were ready to come home. Thankfully, she hadn't demanded more of an explanation than that.

"Okay, that's enough." Clay pulled both girls onto his lap as he sat back down, glad that Jenna and Josh had liked the gift and thrilled at the unexpected opportunity to feel a baby kick.

The day ended on a high note when Jake announced he had already gotten his fill of working in the city and would start a new job in February at the county extension office in Tenacity as a soil and water agent.

"I have to be able to keep my eye on all of you and I can do that better closer to home," Jake offered a lighthearted explanation.

Josh thought Jake's decision probably had a lot more to do with the fact that he had too much country boy in his blood to be happy stuck in an office all day. It could also have something to do with the girl he'd been trying to avoid.

They'd all noticed Jake's cell phone rang several times throughout the day. When Jake checked the caller ID, a look of annoyance crossed his face before he shoved his phone back in his pocket.

After dinner, Josh watched as Jake turned off his phone with an irritated grimace. He hoped the young man wasn't in trouble of any kind, but trusted he would come to him or Clay if there were anything they could do to help.

"I for one will be glad to have you around. If you ever need something to do on the weekends, I can always find some extra work," Josh said, playfully punching Jake on the arm. "If you need somewhere to live, you know the Harold house is available."

"I've lined up a place to stay, Josh, but thanks," Jake said, sincerely grateful for the offer. "Some of my buddies from high school share a house and they have a room opening up right after the holidays. Living in the city and going to college is a whole lot different than living there and working in an office every single day. When you said you didn't miss the city at all, I finally understood what you meant. I got my fill and then some."

"Is everything okay? No problems?"

"Nah, nothing like that." Jake shook his head then released a weary sigh. "There's this one girl who won't leave me alone. I figure moving here will help fix that problem. She has no idea where I'm from and when I'm no longer in the city, she'll have to give up, eventually. I hope. She can't seem to get it through her head that I'm not interested in a relationship of any type with her. Why can't some girls understand that just because you go out once doesn't mean you want to marry her?"

Josh laughed as he remembered a few of the girls he'd dated. "Did I ever tell you about the girl that stalked me? I finally had to get a restraining order against her and that was after only two dates."

"Seriously?" Jake looked at Josh in surprise.

"Seriously." Josh nodded in confirmation as he and Jake cleaned up the gift-wrapping debris. He took a moment to study his young friend. "Jake, thanks again for the jeans and the hats for the twins. As soon as the boys are big enough to wear them, we'll have to take a picture of them with you."

"Cool. I had to get something to start them on the road to farming, you know. Besides, if you're going to give them names like Willard and Ashley, they're going to need all the help they can get."

"They are so not going to have lame names. I can promise you that." Josh grinned, throwing a ball of wadded up wrapping paper at Jake. "I'm still trying to talk Jenna into Espn and Fox. Now those are names you don't forget easily."

Jake laughed and tossed the wrapping paper ball back at him. "Good luck with that."

Jenna gave Callan a hand with the leftovers in the kitchen while the men picked up the mess in the family room. "I can't believe all the wonderful gifts we received today. That table set Clay made is amazing. I had no idea he could carve like that."

"It was definitely a challenge for him, but he loved doing it. You know these babies are going to be extra special to us all, don't you?"

"I do. I'm truly thankful they're going to have so many loving family members around to help them grow up."

"Not all kids are as lucky as ours," Callan said, watching Emma and Audrey give their Grammy and Gramps one last hug before they left. "By the way, thank you for letting Clay and the girls feel the babies kick. Clay hasn't ever had the opportunity before and I think he was pretty awed by it."

"No problem." Jenna was glad she could do something to bring a little joy to Clay. He'd always been so kind to her and done so much for them through the years. "Although I'm a pretty private person, it seems like when your belly precedes you into a room, total strangers feel the need to touch it and comment. I guess I'm getting kind of used to it." Jenna shook her head in disbelief. "Now there's something I never thought I'd say."

Both of them laughed then went to the living room to tell those departing goodbye. Josh and

Jenna were the last to leave. Since they drove Jenna's car, Clay volunteered to deliver the table set sometime during the coming week.

Chapter Seventeen

New Year's Day arrived with Clay, Callan, and the girls at Josh and Jenna's. Callan wanted to finish the nursery before the baby shower the following Saturday. She enlisted Josh and Clay's help in getting everything set up.

The two men grunted as they carried the heavy child's table up the stairs and into the room, placing it in front of a sunny window. After adjusting the placement of the chairs, Callan stood back and smiled. Everything looked perfect.

They refused to let Jenna see the room until it was completely finished. Callan fussed with every little detail until Clay assured her there wasn't anything left to adjust. Josh ran downstairs to let Jenna and the girls know it was time to check out the room before Callan changed her mind.

"You're going to be so surprised, Auntie Jenna. Just wait 'til you see the…" Emma's voice suddenly cut off as they walked up the stairs.

Callan pictured Audrey's hand clapped over her sister's mouth and smiled at Clay.

"Audrey! I told you I don't like that," Emma spluttered as they approached the landing at the top

HEART OF HOPE

of the stairs. "I'll be quiet now."

"You don't know how to be quiet," Audrey stated, running up the last few steps right into her dad.

Startled by his presence, Audrey looked as if she'd been caught with her hand in the cookie jar. "Hi, Daddy."

"Audrey, we talked about putting your hand over Emma's mouth. You know she hates it," Clay said firmly, staring down at Audrey while fighting the urge to smile. Their little Sweet Pea had a terrible time keeping her lips closed let alone sealed. However, her blabbermouth tendencies didn't mean Audrey could continue slapping a hand over her mouth every time Emma said something she shouldn't.

"I know, Daddy, but she was about to spill the beans, again." Audrey studied her feet, swirling a pattern into the carpet with her big toe. "I'm sorry. I'll try to remember not to do it again."

Clay hugged his daughter and gave her an encouraging smile. "That's my girl. Thank you." He picked up Emma and took Audrey's hand in his then followed Jenna into the nursery.

"Isn't it great, Auntie Jenna?" Emma exclaimed, waving both arms in the air. "The babies will love it here."

"I think you're right, Sweet Pea," Jenna said quietly, taking in the wonder of the room. It looked better than anything she'd dared to imagine.

Tan walls surrounded the room with navy and deep cranberry-red stars dancing along a border near the ceiling. Tan valances with navy and red stripes hung at the three windows, providing a colorful accent without blocking any of the glorious light that streamed in during the afternoons.

Jenna's overstuffed navy rocker from Josh sat in one corner by the windows with the table and chairs centered beneath the middle window.

A small oak bookshelf sat beneath the third window, holding storybooks and a few farm-themed toys. A toy chest, painted navy blue with a tan and red stripe sat in the next corner. The stuffed horse and cow Josh had purchased last fall peeked out of the open lid.

Two oak cribs with navy and tan bedding sat against one wall near the rocker. Dangling above each crib was a farm animal mobile. One the wall between the two cribs was a saying, applied in navy vinyl lettering with red stars accenting the words:

Little boys with grubby hands,
Sticky kisses, and pockets full of surprises,
Are God's way of reminding us
Miracles come in all shapes and sizes.

Across the room on the opposite wall sat a tall oak chest of drawers and a sturdy changing table. Two oak shelves above the changing table provided additional space for necessities. Several wooden pegs decorated the wall by the door in a seesaw pattern and the two little John Deere ball caps hung there. The cute bouncing chairs Josh had purchased rested beneath the pegs, waiting to be put into use. A large closet offered plenty of space for additional supplies, clothes, and linens.

"Callan, I don't know what to say," Jenna hugged her sister-in-law and dear friend. She released a contented sigh, wiping at the tears sprinkling her cheeks. "This is beyond wonderful."

"I'm so glad you like it." Callan swiped away her tears and settled an arm around Jenna's shoulders as they walked around the room.

"If you like it, why are you crying?" Emma asked, confused as she looked at both women.

"Sometimes when women cry, it means they really like something," Clay said, giving Emma a reassuring hug. "I think your Aunt Jenna especially likes the nursery."

"Should I cry, too?" Emma asked, prepared to work up a pout.

Josh and Clay laughed. "That won't be necessary, Sweet Pea. Let's go downstairs and get washed up for lunch." Clay suggested as he took the girls and left the room.

"Callan, this is amazing. Now, we'll just have to be patient until we can put the room to use." Josh hugged his sister and kissed the top of her head.

"Those two boys of yours will be here before you know it. You've only got two months left and it will fly by," Callan said, adjusting a picture of farm animals that hung by the door.

"I love the saying on the wall, Callan. It is absolutely fantastic," Jenna said as she walked over to the cribs and stared at the words. "Everything is perfect and I can't thank you enough."

"You already have." Callan stood in the doorway, watching the way Jenna reverently ran her hand along the smooth wood of one crib. "With the room complete, we can focus on your baby shower next weekend."

The two women agreed it would be easier on them both to hold the baby shower at Jenna's. Callan arrived early that morning and got to work with preparations. Jenna found it hard to wait until the guests arrived, excited to show off the nursery to those attending.

For a cold, January day, they couldn't have asked for better weather with clear roads and the sun shining brightly overhead.

Although Jenna's mom and sisters were unable to make the drive for the shower, Jenna carried her laptop into the living room and Skyped them so they could still "attend" the event.

Callan enlisted Bobbi's help to get the food ready and games set out before the guests arrived. Josh helped Jenna clean house the previous evening and everything looked welcoming and nice, especially with the decorations and flowers Callan added.

Although Emma and Audrey begged to attend, Callan knew the girls would be bored long before the shower ended. Instead, Clay took them out for lunch and to a movie. They were thrilled to get some special daddy time.

Josh disappeared when the first carload of women arrived and promised to stay away until all the cars were gone. Jenna assumed he would wander over to the heated shop and hang out for the afternoon.

By the time the last of the guests departed three hours later, Jenna felt exhausted but happy beyond words. The gifts included oodles of diapers and baby clothes, bottles and pacifiers, baby washcloths and towels, cute farm animal toys, and several blankets.

Bobbi and her sister, Maggie, Jake's mom, went together and purchased a twin-sized cradle for the babies to use the first month or so after their arrival. Jenna nearly wept when she saw it. It was so lovely and such a wonderful gift. She kissed both their cheeks and thanked Bobbi and Maggie repeatedly.

Callan helped Josh pack all the goodies up to the nursery and put everything away under Jenna's direction. She sank down into the rocker and held a set of blue sleepers on her lap, thinking about the babies who would soon be dressed in them. It was almost too much to take in.

"You okay, babe?" Josh asked, hunkering down by the chair and gazing into her face. "You're awfully quiet."

"Yes. I'm fine. Just thinking about how these two boys will be here soon and life will be different," Jenna said thoughtfully.

"But different in a good way, right?" Josh asked, hoping Jenna still didn't harbor some deep-seated resentment toward the babies.

"In an absolutely amazing way." Jenna smiled and pressed her hand to his cheek. She set aside the sleepers and held her hands out to him. "If you'll help this walrus up, I want to go downstairs and find a place for that beautiful cradle in our room. I just can't believe Bobbi and Maggie bought that for us."

"Well, why wouldn't they?" Callan turned away from the drawer where she neatly folded tiny little onesies and put them away. "They said they wanted to get you something nice and it was something you needed. They knew how much you loved it, Jenna. Besides, we're all like family, aren't we?"

"Yes, we are, although I don't know what I did to deserve to be a part of this family. You all are so good to me and it's greatly appreciated." Jenna fought down the tears that threatened to spill and focused her attention on the sunlight streaming in the window. "I'm so glad my mom and sisters could see the shower today, even if they couldn't be here in person. Sometimes technology comes in really handy."

"It was a great idea to have them attend virtually," Callan said, walking behind Josh and Jenna as they slowly went down the stairs. As she watched her sister-in-law waddle down the steps, Callan thought she seemed overly big for having two months left before her due date. Between Jenna's flagging energy and her need for rest, Callan hoped the babies didn't get in a hurry to arrive.

Later, when Josh and Jenna sat in their room admiring the cradle from their spots on the bed, Jenna released a happy sigh. Josh placed a hand on her belly anticipating the kicks that would soon begin. He didn't have to wait long before his hand began bouncing from the movement of the babies.

Grinning, he left his hand on Jenna's stomach but moved his head closer. "Hey, don't you know it's bedtime and your mama needs to rest? You two are strong kickers, aren't you? We'll have to get you a football and a soccer ball so you can kick all you want, but not at Mama's windows, right?"

The kicking grew in intensity and Jenna laughed. "I guess they're answering. Keep talking to them. They hear my voice all day, but they get so excited when they hear you."

Josh gave Jenna a smile that warmed her from the inside out and kissed her softly. "Thanks, babe. I really want to be a part of all this, but sometimes I don't know how, exactly."

"You're doing a fantastic job. I don't know too many men who would want to be as involved or take as much interest in their bloated, pregnant wife and the brood she will soon be hatching as you have." Jenna gave Josh a teasing grin. "You're incredible Josh Carver and I love you."

"Love you, too, babe. Always have, always will." Josh kissed her again and turned his attention back to the twins. "And I love you guys. Mama and I just need to figure out what we're going to name you. What names do you like? Axyl? Tron? Skyler? Skeeter? Any of those names ring your bell?"

The babies suddenly stopped kicking. Jenna laughed so hard she could hardly catch her breath. "That'll teach you to throw out names I don't like. Even the babies know they're bad."

Josh shrugged his shoulders and continued

gently rubbing her belly. "Whatever. But we're going to have to figure out what to call these boys soon. Did Callan bring you a list of family names?"

"She did, but there isn't a lot to choose from. Truthfully, there are a lot of names on the list, just not many I like. I seem to have the same problem with the names from my side of the family. Who names their kid Horace?"

Josh turned on his side and studied Jenna. "We'll get it figured out."

When she caught him staring at her, she suddenly felt self-conscious. "What?" She yanked the covers up to her chin.

"You get more beautiful every day," Josh whispered, stroking his thumb across her cheek.

"You're clearly losing your eyesight. I think we better call the doctor for an appointment on Monday."

"My eyesight is perfectly fine." Josh leaned close and kissed Jenna tenderly before turning off the bedside lamp and pulling her close to snuggle into the warmth and comfort of his arms. "Maybe it's never been better."

Chapter Eighteen

At thirty-one weeks pregnant, Jenna frequently found herself short of breath plagued by raging heartburn and fatigue. Her blood pressure ran a little on the high side and twinges of pain in her back made sitting for any length of time uncomfortable.

She awoke that morning feeling unwell, but decided to go to the office.

As she sat at her desk and tried to focus on her work, her stomach suddenly tightened and a horrible cramping sensation ripped through her. Frightened, she took a few deep breaths and waited for the pain to pass. When it did, she convinced herself all was well until another painful cramp hit her a few minutes later, followed by a third.

Contractions? She couldn't be having contractions. It was too early.

Frantic, Jenna picked up the phone and called her friend Barb's office.

"What's up girlfriend?" Barb asked in a friendly tone.

"I think I'm having contractions," Jenna said, panting as another pain hit her. "Can you take me to the hospital?"

"I'll be right there."

Jenna managed to rise from the desk and put on her coat before Barb burst into her office.

"You look terrible. Do you want me to call an ambulance?" Barb wrapped her arm around her as they walked to the door.

"No. You can get me there faster than waiting for an ambulance. Please?"

"Okay. We can do this." Barb motioned to the front office receptionist to walk with Jenna to the door while she ran out to the parking garage and got her car. She braked to a stop in front of the building and opened the passenger door as Jenna walked out leaning heavily on the receptionist.

"Can you please let Mrs. Gordon know we're heading to the hospital," Barb asked the receptionist, as she shut Jenna's door and hurried to the driver's side.

Located about ten blocks away, Barb soon pulled up at the hospital's emergency room door and escorted Jenna inside.

"What do we have here?" a nurse asked as she approached them with a wheelchair.

"She's at thirty-one weeks with twins and thinks she's having contractions," Barb said as helped Jenna into the chair and wheeled her down a hallway.

"Are you a relative?" the nurse asked.

"A friend, but I'll call her husband and let him know to come if you think I should."

"That would be a very good idea. You might want to tell him to hurry."

Barb called Josh and he answered on the

second ring. "Josh, this is Barb. I just drove Jenna to the hospital. She seems to be having contractions. Can you come, please?" Barb attempted to hold her voice level, but couldn't keep her concern for Jenna at bay.

"I'll be there as quick as I can. Thanks, Barb."

Out in the barn when he answered the call, Josh hurried outside and ran to the house. He didn't take time to clean up or change, just grabbed his keys and ran out to his pickup. As he raced down their lane to the road, he uttered the same prayer repeatedly. "Please, God, please, take care of Jenna and the boys."

Forty minutes later, he pulled into the hospital parking area and sprinted through the emergency room doors to the desk located there. A nurse led him past a waiting area where he saw Barb anxiously flipping through a magazine. He lifted a hand in greeting but kept walking, following the nurse into a curtained room.

When the nurse pushed the curtain aside, Josh stepped into the room. Jenna rested on the bed, looking pale and weak. He rushed to her side, picked up her hand, and kissed her cheek.

"Babe?" he asked quietly as she opened her tear-filled eyes.

"The doctor said she'd be right back and then we'd talk. I'm so scared, Josh. It's too early for the babies to come."

He slid his arm around her shoulders and pulled her head to his chest, rubbing her shoulders soothingly. "It'll be okay, Jenna. Everything will be okay."

Dr. Meliah walked in the room a few moments later with a clipboard in her hand. Her usual calm façade was absent, replaced by a concerned look.

"Josh, I'm glad to see you here," she said, pulling up the rolling stool by the bed and taking a deep breath.

"You were smart to come in when you did, Jenna. Those were real contractions and I think we've got them stopped for now. Those boys of yours are getting anxious to meet everyone, but their little lungs aren't developed enough to make a healthy appearance. We could let you deliver now, but I think we're looking at too many health complications for the babies that I just don't want to risk. You and the boys would be better off if we can postpone their delivery a few weeks. If you can go even another three weeks, I'd feel much better about these two making an appearance. I'm also worried about your blood pressure. I hate to tell you this Jenna, but you're going to have to go on bed rest, for your sake and theirs."

"What does bed rest mean?" Josh was concerned about how Jenna would handle the answer.

"Just like it sounds. Complete bed rest. No working. No walking around more than is absolutely necessary. No physical exertion of any type. Nothing. Nada. Bed rest." The doctor intently studied Jenna as she stared at her wide-eyed and afraid. Dr. Meliah then turned to Josh. He nodded in agreement, letting her know he would make sure Jenna followed orders if he had to tie her down to the bed.

"Here's the choice, Jenna. You can get bed rest here at the hospital or we can try it at home. If I let you go home, you have to promise that you won't do anything. I mean it. I know you'll be bored silly, but it's either that or you stay here. Now what'll it be?" Doctor Meliah stood and wrote something on a prescription pad then raised an eyebrow at Jenna.

"I'd prefer to go home, please," Jenna said quietly. "I promise I won't do anything to jeopardize the twins."

"Good. I'm going to give you a prescription to take so we can stall those contractions. One of the side effects is that it lowers your blood pressure. In your case, that's a good thing. I want to see you again next week, preferably in my office and not here. Okay?" The doctor shared a smile with Jenna.

Jenna nodded while Josh took the prescription from Dr. Meliah.

"Josh, why don't you come with me to finish up the paperwork while Jenna gets dressed then I'll have a nurse bring her to the door. If you can pull the car around, you can take her home and get her started on that bed rest."

"Yes, ma'am." Josh followed the doctor out the door. He stopped to speak with Barb and thanked her for driving Jenna to the hospital. He promised to keep her updated and have Jenna call her later.

A nurse helped Jenna out of bed then brought in a wheel chair as she finished dressing. By the time she rolled her to the door, Josh waited with the pickup.

The nurse looked from the truck to Jenna and shook her head. "She can't climb up in there. Are you nuts?"

"Since her car is at the office…" Josh grinned at the nurse. "I've got this. No problem." Josh scooped Jenna out of the wheelchair and gingerly sat her down in the pickup. He pulled the seat belt out and handed it to her then closed the door.

The nurse beamed at him. "I'm glad to see she's married to a thoughtful, He-Man kind of guy. You take good care of her."

"Yes, ma'am. I plan on it." Josh smiled before climbing behind the wheel of his truck. "Babe, I'm taking you home then I'll run into town and get the prescription filled. Will that be okay with you?"

"Yes," Jenna whispered, grasping his hand in both hers. "I'm so sorry, Josh. Thank you for coming to get me."

"You're welcome. I'm just glad you and the boys are okay."

"But Josh, what if I… what if we…" Tears poured down her face. Jenna had been so terrified when the contractions started coming faster and faster. What if the doctor hadn't been able to stop them? What if the babies had arrived this early? She struggled to stay afloat in her sea of "what ifs."

Josh turned her chin so she looked directly at him and smiled, eyes brimming with love. "Jenna, you got to the hospital in time. Nothing happened. We'll deal with this and in a few weeks, when they are big and strong enough, those boys will let us know they're ready to meet us. Everything is going to be just fine. You didn't do anything wrong, Jenna. It just happened."

"But I'm the one who didn't want them in the

first place. I'm the one who keeps pushing myself. I'm the one responsible for them and look what happened."

"Do you want these babies?" Josh asked in a low voice.

"Of course I do. You know that I've wanted them for months," Jenna said, shocked that Josh would even ask her that question.

"Are you deliberately doing anything that could harm them?"

Grieved, she leaned against the door. "Josh, how can you even ask that? You know I wouldn't ever do that."

"Exactly, so why are you beating yourself up for something beyond your control," Josh said, making his point. "Quit fussing and trust God. I prayed all the way to the hospital that you and the boys would be fine, and he answered that prayer. Let's just take one day at a time."

Jenna released the breath she held. Josh could almost see a weight lift off her shoulders. She nodded her head, unable to speak.

When they arrived home, Josh unlocked the back door and opened it then returned to get Jenna from the pickup. Carefully scooping her into his arms, he carried her into the house and down the hall to their bedroom. He helped her remove her coat and suit jacket before she sank onto the bed. Quickly pulling off her shoes, he covered her with a quilt that draped across the foot of their bed.

"Do you need anything? Do you want to change your clothes now or can I get you something to eat or drink?" Josh leaned on the bed with his arm braced against the headboard while concern etched grooves in his forehead.

She placed a hand on each side of his face and stared at him for a minute. "No. I think I'll rest for a while. Maybe you could run into town while I take a nap." She gave him a kiss then settled into the soft comfort of their bed.

Josh pulled the shades down to darken the room and shut the bedroom door. He hurried into Tenacity to the town's one superstore, leaving the prescription at the pharmacy. While he waited for it to be filled, he grabbed a cart and started doing some grocery shopping. If he was going to have to do the cooking, meals needed to be simple.

He selected a stack of magazines and a couple of best-selling novels he thought his wife might enjoy. Jenna would be bored out of her mind if she had to stay in bed for the next six to eight weeks.

Back at the pharmacy, he paid for her prescription then rolled his full cart into the checkout line, right behind Callan.

"Josh, what are you doing here?" She turned around when he said her name, drawing her attention. As she hugged him, she couldn't miss the tension in his shoulders. "Is everything okay?"

"No. Jenna started having contractions this morning and I had to pick her up from the hospital. The doctor ordered bed rest."

"For how long?"

"For as long as we can put off the twins' arrival." Josh absently removed his ball cap and plowed his hand through his thick hair. "I don't know when I've ever been as scared as I was when

Barb called this morning. I feel like I've lost five years off my life."

"Josh, I'm so sorry." Callan placed a comforting hand on his back. "What can we do to help?"

"Maybe you could stop by in a few days for a visit. I think we'll have to take turns keeping Jenna entertained." Josh moved his cart farther ahead in the line while Callan started taking items out of her cart and placing them on the conveyor.

"I'd be happy to help out. Just tell me when to show up and I'm there. Can I bring you meals or do anything else?"

"If you could help out with meals on the days you come over, that would be awesome. I can cook, but I think Jenna will get tired of my limited menu selections in a hurry."

Callan laughed. "Sure. Anything else?"

"No. I just need to figure out a way to get Jenna's car home. It's still in the parking garage at work."

"I could stay with Jenna while you and Clay go pick it up. He finishes his last class today at three. Audrey and Emma get off the bus at three-twenty. The girls and I could stay with Jenna and fix dinner for everyone at your house."

"Sounds like a great idea. I'll let Jenna know as soon as I get home."

Josh set Callan's bags in her cart then paid for his own items and they walked out together.

"You'll come over about three-thirty?" Josh asked as he helped Callan load her groceries in her car.

"Yes. If you think of anything you need in the meantime, just let me know." Callan closed the trunk and turned to study at her brother. "Just remember God knows the plan and everything will be fine."

"I know. Love you, Cal."

"Love you, too. See you in a while."

"Remember, you need to be quiet and not jump on Auntie Jenna's bed or anything," Callan warned again as they got out of the car and walked to Josh and Jenna's back door. Before they could knock, Josh opened it and welcomed them inside.

"Hi, Audrey. Hey, Sweet Pea. How was school today?" Josh asked, hugging both girls then escorting them inside the kitchen.

"Fine," Audrey said, sipping on the juice box Callan handed her when she got off the bus. She slipped off her backpack and left it on the floor by a barstool.

"My day was great!" Emma replied with her typical gusto. "We got to see a movie about baby froggies." She turned to her dad with a questioning look. "What are they called?"

"Tadpoles," Clay supplied.

"Yeah, we saw a movie about tagpoles and frogs and toads. It was awesome." Emma launched her wriggly little body onto a barstool and started swinging her feet.

"It sounds awesome." Josh bent over and

brushed her nose with his, making her giggle.

"Are you two going to help your mama take good care of Auntie Jenna while your daddy and I go get her car?"

"Yep," both girls answered with nods of their heads that made their curls bob.

"Great. We'll be back before you know it." Josh mischievously rubbed a hand over Audrey's curls, sending them into a complete state of disarray. Audrey huffed and reached up to smooth her hair while scowling at her uncle.

Josh grinned then glanced at his sister. "Thanks again, Callan, for all this."

"You're welcome. We're happy to help, aren't we girls?" The girls nodded in agreement, although Audrey had lost a little of her enthusiasm.

"Need anything from the city?" Clay kissed each of the girls on the head then gave Callan a kiss on the cheek. He held her hand as she walked with him and Josh to the door.

"No. I'll have dinner ready when you two get back. Drive carefully."

"We will." Clay wrapped an arm around her, drawing her close for a sweet kiss. He winked then hurried out the door after Josh.

"Mama, we saw you kissing Daddy again," Emma observed in her singsong voice.

"You did?" Callan placed a hand over her heart in mock dismay. "Oh, my goodness. Whatever will I do now? Am I in trouble?"

"Mama." Audrey rolled her eyes and accentuated every letter of the word. "We can't make you be in trouble."

"You can't?" Callan sat down at the counter
and lifted Emma onto her lap. "Who can?"

"Daddy," Emma said, swinging her feet. "But
then he'd be in trouble, too, because he kissed you."

"Oh. I see. So what are we going to do about
it?" Callan asked in all seriousness, glancing from
one girl to the other.

"No more kisses for the rest of the day."
Audrey meted out a harsh punishment.

"None?" Callan feigned a crestfallen look.

"Nope." Emma shook her head.

"Not even to wiggly little girls?" Callan started
planting multiple kisses to Emma's cheeks and
head, making both girls laugh.

"Stop, Mama!" Emma giggled. "You're going
to smofercate me."

"We can't have that, can we?" Callan set
Emma on her feet and stood. She grasped Emma
and Audrey's hands in hers then walked down the
hall to the master bedroom. "Be very quiet and
we'll peek inside to see how Auntie Jenna is doing."

Quietly pushing open the door, Callan grinned
at her sister-in-law. Jenna was propped on her side
in bed, flipping through a magazine.

"Well, hello there." Jenna smiled as the girls
approached the bed and stared at her. "I thought I
heard giggles."

"We came to keep you company." Audrey sat
down next to her aunt. "Mama said we have to be
quiet and can't jump around like a bunch of wild...
What was it you said, Mama?"

"Banshees," Callan supplied. "Do you need
anything, Jenna? Can we get you anything to drink

or eat?"

"I'd love some hot tea," Jenna said. "Maybe the girls can tell me about school today while you make us all some tea."

Callan left Emma talking about "tagpoles" while she made tea and placed cheese and fruit on a plate. The snack would tide everyone over until dinner.

She returned to the room with a big tray and set it on a corner of the bed. She gave the girls half-full cups of not quite hot tea then handed Jenna a full steaming cup. After pulling a chair up closer to the bed, she and Jenna visited until the girls asked to watch cartoons.

Instead, Callan made them sit down with their homework at the kitchen table while she started dinner preparations. The girls had completed their homework and helped set the table by the time Josh and Clay returned with Jenna's car.

Jenna shuffled into the family room where she reclined, propped on her side watching the news. Josh snagged a footstool out of the pantry and placed it beneath the table then helped Jenna stand. Slowly walking with her to the table, he pulled out her chair and made sure her feet found the little stool.

"It is so nice to be upright," Jenna said, looking around the table. "Thank you so much for making dinner, Callan, and for rescuing my car, Clay."

"You're welcome," they both said. Clay leaned toward Callan and started to kiss her cheek, but Emma's giggling interrupted him.

"No more kisses, Daddy. Mama can't have any

more kisses today."

Clay turned and looked at his daughters. "Who says?"

"We did." Audrey offered her father a determined glare. "We saw you kissing before you left. Mama can't have any more today."

"They laid down the law, Clay. There wasn't anything I could do about it." Callan shook her head and stuck out her bottom lip, pretending to pout.

"We'll revisit this later." Clay placed a napkin on his lap and stared across the table at the girls with a look only a father can muster. He turned the conversation in another direction, looking at Jenna with a teasing grin. "So, Jenna, do you have streaming movies?"

"Nope, but we might have to get Netflix." Jenna took a helping of salad and passed it along to Josh. "I finally have time to read all the books I've wanted to read and watch all the movies I keep thinking I'll get around to seeing someday."

"Atta girl. Put a positive spin on this." Clay offered her an encouraging smile. "You'll be so well read and fluent in movie-lore, you'll be able to compete on *Jeopardy*."

Everyone laughed and the meal finished on a lighthearted note. Callan and Audrey did the dishes, while Clay cleared the table. Josh helped Jenna into the family room where he and Emma kept her entertained for a while. When the kitchen was clean and set to rights, Callan picked up the girls' backpacks and suggested they head home for the evening.

Emma and Audrey put on their coats then

leaned over Jenna to give her a kiss and hug.

"Thanks for letting us visit, Auntie Jenna. We'll come back another day," Audrey said as she tugged her backpack over her shoulder and walked out the door.

"Thanks, Auntie Jenna!" Emma waved and ran out to the car that Clay started earlier so it would be warm on the ride home.

Callan hugged both Josh and Jenna then slipped her arms into the coat Clay held for her. Clay thumped Josh on the back then kissed Jenna's cheek after he pulled on his own coat.

"Call if you need anything at all," he said as they walked to the door.

"Thanks, guys," Jenna yelled from her spot on the couch. "I appreciate it."

"Thanks again. You two are the best." Josh walked them to the door. As he watched Clay settle his arm around Callan's shoulders, he laughed as he recalled the dinner conversation. "Just remember, you're on kissing probation."

Callan rolled her eyes and gave his arm a playful slug. "Just wait until you have four little eyes watching your every move and see how funny you think it is."

Josh sauntered back to the living room and sank down beside Jenna then put his arm around her.

"How are you holding up, little mama?"

Jenna turned her head to look at Josh and smiled. "I'm doing okay. You know, you really have the nicest family. Is there anything that sister of yours won't do for you?"

"Nothing I can think of." Josh appeared thoughtful as he quietly considered the relationship he shared with Callan and Clay. "She and Clay have always been there if I needed help. We've been there for them. That's what family does, right?"

"Yes," Jenna said, rubbing her belly. "I just hope our boys grow up to be as close as you and Callan. I always thought my sisters and I were close, but I can't imagine them dropping everything to come help me with a problem the way Clay and Callan do for us. You've done the same for them. It's really a blessing."

"Yep. I know it." Josh placed his hand lightly on her stomach. It seemed to get bigger by the day. "Do you want to sit here awhile or would you like to go back to bed?"

"I'm sick of staring at the bedroom walls. Can we just hang out here for a while?" Jenna snuggled against Josh as he grabbed the remote and flipped through the television to see what they might be interested in watching.

"You bet. Are you in the mood for reality nonsense, something mysterious, or a comedy?"

"Some of those reality shows cover all three don't they?"

Chuckling, Josh agreed. "They sure do."

Chapter Nineteen

Josh and Jenna settled into a new routine. He spent as much time as he could with her and made certain when he left the house, she had everything she needed close at hand. In case she needed him while he was out, he kept her cell phone charged, within her reach.

Family and friends took turns visiting, usually in the afternoons. Many of them brought a meal. Callan arranged for someone to provide dinner every other day. With the abundance of food everyone brought, Josh only had to cook a few times since his sister set up the meal deliveries. Everyone who came brought Jenna bits of news, shared stories, and did their best to take her mind off her confinement for an hour or two.

One Saturday, Barb drove out for a visit and caught her up on all the office news.

"Mrs. Gordon was nearly beside herself the day I took you to the hospital. She says you're the best person she's ever had in that position and she isn't letting anybody mess with it. Whenever you're ready to come back to work, rest assured, your position will be available."

"That's good to know," Jenna said. She worried about leaving work so abruptly, with no warning. She'd been trying to get things ready for her maternity leave, but with so many weeks left before her due date, she didn't have everything done she'd planned to do. Although she'd asked Dr. Meliah's permission to do some work from home, she received a negative response to the request along with the reminder she needed to rest.

Since winter was a slow time for Josh on the farm, he cleaned the house, bought the groceries, and did whatever needed to be done. Jenna reminded him about paying bills and he'd even managed to figure out her filing system. She decided, during her bed rest, to take up crocheting. Maggie Chandler, Jake's mother, came over a few times to help her learn.

Maggie arrived that afternoon bearing a pan of lasagna, yarn, and a pattern for a baby blanket. She and Jenna worked intently for a couple of hours. Two little blankets, one tan and the other navy blue, began taking shape. Josh helped Jenna out to the couch right after lunch and that's where Maggie found her when she arrived.

"You're a quick learner, Jenna," Maggie said as she whipped through another row of stitches, watching Jenna work at a slower pace, but doing a great job.

"I so appreciate you teaching me, Maggie. At least this gives me something to do with my hands and a challenge for my head." Jenna concentrated on the hook flashing back and forth in the yarn, carefully following Maggie's instructions.

"I'm glad we could spend some time together. Bobbi speaks so highly of you and Josh, and that boy of mine thinks the world of you both."

"What is Jake up to these days?" Jenna asked. She hadn't seen him since Christmas and assumed he was busy finishing his work at the bio lab before he transitioned into his new job at the extension office.

"He's been staying out of trouble, working extra hours at the lab. He really did like the work, but said he can't stand being in an office all day. You know him. He's a bit of a wild child. I guess you can take the boy out of the country, but not the country out of the boy." Maggie laughed and looked out the window for a moment before she continued crocheting.

"I'll be glad to have him closer to home, that's for sure. I think he'll enjoy working at the extension office and he'll be able to get out of the office most days, which should keep him from getting so antsy. You should see him when he comes out to the farm after staying in the office and city all week. He acts like he did when he was five and couldn't sit still for a minute. Constant motion, that one."

"We enjoyed having him with us for the summer. He was a huge help to Josh. You raised a fine boy, Maggie."

"Thank you, Jenna." Maggie patted her leg. "He is a good boy. I just wish I could do something about his taste in women. My stars, you should see some of the girls he's dated, not that he ever brings them around for us to meet. Isn't there an old country song about liking women on the trashy side? As much as I hate to say it, that would be our Jake."

Jenna laughed. "Oh, I've seen him out a time or two. Maybe he's going through a phase. You know, sowing his wild oats, and all that. When the right girl comes along, he'll change his ways."

"I certainly hope so." Maggie shot Jenna a hopeful glance. "Look at me going on. You're going to have two boys to handle. I hope they grow up to have much better taste in women than Jake."

The women continued crocheting for a while then Maggie put the lasagna in the oven to warm along with a loaf of crusty bread.

"Thank you for coming, Maggie. I'll keep working on this blanket and maybe have it finished by the next time you come," Jenna said, smiling at the kind woman.

"You're doing just fine with it, Jenna. Keep at it and you'll be done before you know it. It was a treat to visit with you, dear."

"Thanks again, and tell that rascally son of yours the next time he's home to stop by for a visit," Jenna called as Maggie walked out the door.

Jenna finished crocheting the baby blanket, read a dozen books, looked at every magazine in the house at least twice, watched movies until she felt cross-eyed, surfed online until she couldn't think of a thing she hadn't Googled and made lists of dozens of baby names, none of which she and Josh both liked. She napped, rested, lazed around, and felt like a useless blob.

One morning, she awoke to find Josh running around cleaning house before that day's assigned babysitter arrive to sit with her that afternoon.

Jenna felt like such a burden to Josh and their family. She'd love to be able to get up and go for a walk or even make a batch of cookies. Grateful to their friends and family for all their time, meals, and care, she still couldn't help feeling cooped up and confined.

She heard the vacuum turn off and knew Josh would put it away before he picked up the duster and ran it around the family room. He walked into their room and quickly dusted every surface then disappeared in their bathroom. Despite his dislike of the chores, he scrubbed the shower, sink and toilet. After wiping down the counter, he carried the towels to the laundry room and started a load of wash.

At least when he did the laundry, she had something to do. He brought each load, fresh from the dryer, to the bed where she could fold the clothes without exerting any effort. She never thought she'd be excited to fold laundry, but it made her feel useful for a few minutes.

"Tell me again who's coming today?" Jenna yelled as Josh clomped down the stairs.

"I already told you, it's a surprise," Josh called back. He banged around in the kitchen and soon appeared in their room with a steaming cup of tea. After setting it down on the nightstand, he gave her a kiss and a wink. "You'll just have to wait and see."

Jenna ran a hand over her hair and looked down at her clothes. She insisted on taking a shower, fixing her hair, putting on mascara, and getting dressed every day. Josh studied her and smiled.

"You look just fine, little mama." Jenna glanced up at him. She hadn't told him, but every time he called her little mama, a piece of her heart melted into a gooey puddle.

"For a hippo." Jenna rubbed a hand over her ever-expanding middle. "I forget the last time I could see my feet."

Josh laughed and grabbed one foot, gently massaging it before rubbing the other one. "They're still right here, just as cute as ever. I need to head out to take care of a few things. Do you need anything before I go?"

"No, I'm good. How far are you going?"

"I'm running into Tenacity on a few errands. I'll be back in an hour. I've got my phone if you need me. Do you want to stay in here or go out to the family room?"

"The family room would be great." Jenna swung her legs over the bed. Josh hovered over her and she pushed him back. "I really want to walk by myself. Shuffling from here to there will be fine. You can walk with me."

After settling into the cushions of the couch, Josh waited until she let out a weary sigh before returning to the bedroom. He retrieved her mug of tea and warmed it in the microwave before placing it on the end table next to her. He made sure the remote was within her grasp then took a step toward the door. Before he reached it, he turned back.

"Are you sure you don't need anything?"

"I'm fine. Go on. Breathe some fresh air for me."

"Okay. I'll be back soon."

Shortly after Josh left, Jenna heard a knock at the front door. "Come in," she called.

The knocking continued, so she yelled louder. "Come on in."

The door opened and footsteps echoed in the front foyer. She thought she heard shushing then three familiar faces peeked around the corner into the family room. Jenna stared at her mom, dad and oldest sister, Chrissy. Slowly raising herself up, she sat speechless as they hurried to her side.

"Jenna, look at you!" her mom gushed as she engulfed her in a hug. Her dad bent down for a hug followed by Chrissy. Her sister plopped down beside her on the couch while her parents took seats on the loveseat.

"Wow, look at this belly." Chrissy rubbed Jenna's stomach then leaned down with her mouth close to it. "Hello, little nephews. Aunt Chrissy is here."

Jenna laughed, cried and smiled, all at the same time. She had no control over her emotions these days and learned to go with whatever came along. Grabbing a tissue from the ever-present box on the table behind the couch, she dabbed at her cheeks. "What are you doing here? This is the best surprise! Josh said someone special was coming to stay with me today, but wouldn't say whom. Oh, this is just wonderful. Take off your coats and tell me everything."

Jenna's dad gathered their coats, hanging them in the coat closet by the front door. Chrissy found mugs in the kitchen and made a pot of tea. They talked for an hour before Josh walked in carrying hot pizza.

"Anyone hungry for lunch?" he asked as he set the boxes on the kitchen counter.

"Josh, I can't believe you didn't tell me they were coming," Jenna called from the couch. "You're so sneaky!"

"Yep, that's me, the sneak." Josh walked into the room and shook his father-in-law's hand, before hugging his mother-in-law and Chrissy. "Dan, Vivian, I'm so glad you could come. Chrissy, I wasn't sure you'd be able to get away, but I'm thrilled that you could. Where are your kids?"

Chrissy and her husband, Greg, had three little girls, ages three, seven and ten. "They're at their grandmother's house today. Their dad gets full-on duty for the weekend. He'll really appreciate me by the time we get home Sunday evening."

Josh laughed. "How was your drive? You must have gotten an early start."

"We did. Since it's a Thursday, traffic wasn't terrible this morning so we made good time," Dan said, rubbing his chin thoughtfully. "I forget what a nice drive it is from Seattle to Portland and really isn't that far. We'll have to think about making the trip more often."

"We'd love to have you whenever you want to head this direction," Josh said, motioning toward the kitchen. "I brought home some pizza and there's a salad in the fridge. Shall we have some lunch?"

"I'm starving." Chrissy walked into the kitchen and opened the refrigerator, taking out the salad and setting it on the table. Vivian and Dan wandered in and set the pizza and napkins on the table. Josh helped Jenna up and walked with her to the dining table, easing her into a chair with the footstool.

Chrissy, Vivian, and Dan watched, seemingly impressed by Josh's dutiful care of Jenna.

"Wow, Josh. Are you always so helpful with our girl?" Vivian asked. "It's so sweet how much effort you put into caring for my daughter."

Josh blushed, but smiled at Jenna then her mom. "Someone has to keep her on the straight and narrow." He retrieved plates and forks, and placed them on the table.

After Josh gave thanks for the meal, they ate lunch and enjoyed the conversation. Fatigue settled over Jenna at the end of the meal. She struggled to think of a graceful way to excuse herself for a nap when Josh noticed her drooping.

"Well, little mama, isn't it about time for your nap?" Josh scooted his chair back from the table and stood beside her chair.

At her weary nod, he gently helped her up and walked her into their bedroom, waiting as she settled herself on the bed. Josh returned to their company. Jenna would sleep for an hour or so, then be ready for more visiting with her family.

As he stepped into the kitchen, he found Vivian and Chrissy loading the dishwasher and Dan wiping off the table.

"You guys don't need to help. You're our guests this weekend." Josh looked around and couldn't find anything that required his attention.

"Now, Josh, you just get this straight from the get-go. We came to help this weekend so whatever we can do, just point us in the right direction," Chrissy informed him, hands on her hips. "Mom and I will take care of dinner tonight. Anything in particular you'd like to have?"

Somewhat taken aback, Josh shook his head. "No, whatever you make will be fine. Really, I didn't invite you to come so you would work all weekend. I just thought Jenna would enjoy seeing you all."

Vivian put a hand on his arm. "We know that Josh, but we want to be useful while we're here. I didn't realize Jenna is so limited in what she can do. Is she really not even able to walk around much?"

Josh smiled. "The doctor said only when necessary. If I'm here in the house and she needs something, it's no problem to help her. We're really trying to make it to thirty-seven weeks with the babies and we still have a few to go to get there."

Chrissy walked over to him and looped her arm through his. "I think it's sweet the way you take care of her and call her 'little mama.' Frankly, I'm glad I had my kids one at a time. She looks positively miserable." Chrissy tipped her head toward the stairs and gave Josh an engaging smile. "How about you show us the nursery Jenna's been bragging about every time we talk to her?"

Josh gave them the grand tour of the nursery and they made all the appropriate comments. Dan studied the table Clay and his cohorts made for Christmas.

"You say your brother-in-law made this?" Dan rubbed his hand over one of the carved faces on the back of a chair.

"Yes. Clay and some of the relatives worked on it together, but I think he did most of the work."

"It's absolutely amazing. Your boys are pretty lucky, aren't they?"

Josh smiled, warmth lighting his eyes to a shade of silvery gray. "I like to think they're very blessed."

"Did you buy these?" Chrissy asked, snatching up one of the tiny John Deere hats from the peg on the wall.

"Nope, those were a Christmas gift. Aren't they cute? You have to see the little Wranglers," Josh said, pulling open a drawer and taking out the miniature jeans.

Vivian and Chrissy made over the clothes and Dan smiled indulgently. "Suppose you've got boots to go with those, don't you?"

"Yep," Josh admitted. He opened the closet and pulled out two tiny pairs of cowboy boots. "Jenna hasn't seen these yet. It's kind of fun to buy things and hide them in here for her to find later."

Vivian and Chrissy shared a look. Josh was clearly more interested and involved in Jenna's pregnancy than their husbands had ever been.

"That's fantastic. Jenna will be thrilled when she's able to come up here again, unless you plan on packing her up the stairs," Chrissy teased.

"If she begged, I might do it." Josh bent over slightly and rubbed his back. "But that's a lot of steps to go up and down."

They all laughed.

Josh helped them carry up their luggage to the two guest rooms. With Callan's help, he'd changed the sheets on the beds and put fresh towels in the bathroom yesterday. Of course, his sister had to fluff the pillows, arrange the soaps just so, and add a bouquet of fresh flowers to the bathroom counter. The little touches women appreciate and men fail to see.

Vivian turned on the bathroom light and noticed the flowers. She turned to Josh with an inquisitive look. "Did you do all this yourself?"

"Callan helped me yesterday. It made us both hustle trying to get everything finished while Jenna napped in the afternoon." Josh grinned as recalled the mad dash he and Callan had made around the house while Jenna slept.

"Please thank Callan for us for all her help. According to Jenna, she's been a lifesaver."

"She's as good as gold," Josh said with pride, taking a step toward the stairs. "I'll leave you all to freshen up. Just wander downstairs whenever you're ready. Jenna usually sleeps about an hour or so."

"Thanks, Josh. We'll be down shortly," Vivian said, turning back to the guestroom.

Jenna awoke, ready to rejoin her family. Josh helped her back into the family room. She, Chrissy, and her Mom sat talking a mile a minute, so Josh took Dan out to show him the shop and barn. His current project involved repairs and maintenance, using the slow months of winter to service and fine-tune his farm equipment.

After years of watching his dad work on a variety of equipment, Josh was handy as a mechanic and kept everything in prime working condition.

Dan was impressed with not only the assortment of tools Josh owned, but also the tidiness of his shop.

"A place for everything and everything in its place, that's what my dad taught me. Sure is a help. I know exactly where to find the tool I need when I want it." Josh ran a hand along his clean workbench.

"That's working smart," Dan said. As an investment banker, he didn't spend much time outdoors and certainly not in the country or working around equipment. But even he could tell Josh ran a successful farm.

"We're really proud of you and Jenna. You've worked hard and built this farm up from nothing. Now you've got a legacy to give your boys." Dan clapped Josh on the shoulder.

"Thanks, Dan, I appreciate it. We've worked hard, but we both love it here. When I first asked Jenna to marry me, I wasn't sure my city girl would ever adjust to country life, but I don't know what I'd do without her. She makes all the blood and sweat seem worthwhile."

"Glad to hear that, son." Dan nodded his head approvingly. "I always pictured Jenna marrying some muckity-muck with a big stock portfolio and a penthouse. However, the first time I saw you with her, I knew you and Jenna belonged together. I thought you'd lost your mind when you decided to buy the farm, but obviously you had a clearer vision of the big picture than the rest of us."

Josh glanced at his father-in-law and grinned. "I don't know. There are some who would tell you I did lose my mind and still struggle to find it."

Dan laughed and slapped Josh on the back.

The weekend flew by and Jenna fought her tears as she gave her family one last hug and watched them walk out the door. Her mom promised to stay for a week when the babies arrived and Jenna looked forward to it. Bobbi and Maggie were as close to mother figures as she and Josh had nearby, so having her mother with them for a week would be special for them both.

"Just think, babe, before long the boys will be here, your mom will be back for a visit, and you'll be able to move around as much as you want." Josh handed her another tissue as she attempted to dry her tears. "That's great, right?"

"Great. Yes. Can't wait," Jenna said, sniffling. Only a few more weeks of erratic emotions, frequent trips to the bathroom, restless nights, and complete boredom. At least it still gave them time to decide on names for the boys.

Chapter Twenty

By mid-February, Jenna no longer fought against the boredom, having grown used to the idle passing of days.

Her blood pressure was lower, although the doctor diagnosed her with preeclampsia. Aware of how serious it could be, Jenna dutifully followed her doctor's orders. The previous week during her regular checkup, Dr. Meliah said if she could make it one more week, she could deliver the twins any time and everything should be fine.

Josh, of course, gave her a pep talk about how they were going to make it, no problem. They narrowed down the list of baby names neither of them hated to three dozen. Bags were packed and in the car, ready to go. They'd discussed at length the birthing plan, the get-to-the-hospital plan, and the notify-all-relatives plan.

A few days after Valentine's Day, Jenna sat on the couch, watching the news. A knock at the door drew her attention and she smiled as Callan breezed into the room.

Josh wanted to attend a bull sale about an hour and a half away and debated for days whether he should go, since she could have the babies at any time.

She encouraged him to go and he reluctantly agreed, but only if Callan stayed with her for at least part of the time he'd be away.

"Are you sure you don't want me to stay?" Josh asked Jenna for the tenth time that morning.

Laughing, she rolled her eyes and pointed a finger toward the back door. "Go. Get out of here. Do whatever it is you do at a bull sale. I'll be fine. Callan will take great care of me."

"Only if you're sure…" Josh kissed her cheek again and backed toward the door, offering her one last opportunity to ask him to stay.

Jenna waved her hand at him in dismissal and released a relieved sigh when he finally left.

"Good grief, he's like a mother hen with a chick." Callan laughed as Josh pulled out of the driveway and drove down the lane. "Has he been hovering like that for long?"

"Since the last trip to the doctor," Jenna said, trying to find a comfortable spot on the couch. The last few days, she'd been hard-pressed to sit comfortably. Last night, an ache started in her back that seemed to grow worse instead of better.

As she rubbed her hands over her protruding belly, Jenna knew her figure would never be the same. However, stretch marks seemed like the least of her worries.

Her feet and ankles were a bloated mess and if her hands grew any more swollen, she'd have to let Josh cut off her wedding ring. She should have removed it a month ago, but refused. Now, she worried about losing circulation in that finger.

She felt nauseated and twinges had been fluttering in her stomach for hours. If she didn't know better, she'd think she was heading into labor. Even if she were, it would be awhile before anything serious started happening. Briefly considering what she ate the day before, she decided she probably just suffered from indigestion.

When she awoke that morning, she hadn't felt like eating anything despite Josh trying to talk her into toast. She relented and had a few nibbles just to keep him from fussing and get him out of her hair for the day. She appreciated his attentiveness, but she was tired of him treating her like a sister or a child instead of his wife.

He doted on her, encouraged her, fluffed her pillows, and made her tea. In every aspect, he'd been a role model husband and it made her nuts. She wanted him to leave a mess somewhere, to make some sarcastic comment that made her mad, to ignore her so she could pout for a bit about his insensitivity.

Instead, he treated her like a princess.

With a heavy sigh, Jenna admitted her emotions and thoughts ran amuck. She was probably one of the most blessed women on the planet to have a husband who devoted so much time and attention to her care.

Nevertheless, with him gone for the day, she battled resentment that he could actually walk out of the house and enjoy himself while she sat in uncomfortable misery, waiting.

Sniffling, she grabbed a tissue and gave herself

a mental scolding. As Callan walked by to return a mop to the storage closet, she glanced at her.

After putting the mop away and rinsing off her hands in the kitchen, Callan sat down across from Jenna. "Emotions a little hard to control these days?" she asked with a knowing smile.

"Yes, to put it mildly." Jenna released a choppy laugh. "I cry when I should be laughing, laugh when I ought to cry. I'm mad for no reason, cranky, and irrational. This is so far beyond what's normal for me, and way beyond my ability to comprehend."

Callan leaned back with a thoughtful look. "I remember when Laken was expecting Brant she really had a time of it. Tyler walked around on eggshells for the entire nine months. It didn't matter what he did, she would either yell at him or cry pitifully. I don't think anyone was happier than Tyler when Brant arrived and things returned to normal."

Jenna laughed. "So you're telling me I'm not the only one to ever have suffered."

"Something like that."

"I know you don't talk about it, but when you were pregnant did you have morning sickness or any of the typical symptoms?"

Callan took a moment to answer. Jenna realized she shouldn't have asked Callan about her pregnancy, especially considering how painfully it ended. "I'm sorry. Forgive me. I shouldn't..."

"No, it's okay, Jen. I was just remembering. I didn't really have morning sickness, but some days I felt queasy all day. And exhausted all the time. I remember it hurt a lot, like intense cramping, nearly the entire four months. Looking back, I probably should have recognized that as a red flag that something wasn't right," Callan said quietly. She reached out to Jenna and clasped her hand. "I appreciate being able to experience so much of your pregnancy with you. You know whatever you need, Clay and I are here to help."

"Thanks, Cal. It means so much to both of us." Jenna pulled her hand from Callan's and blotted tears from her cheeks. In an effort to lighten the mood, she turned to a topic that Callan enjoyed discussing. "The only thing we need right now is to decide on names for the boys."

"Are you any closer to picking two you agree on?"

"Not really, unless you think Dexter and Angus are good names."

Callan erupted into a fit of laughter. "Tell me Josh did not pick those names."

"He most certainly did. So I had to counter with Quillan and Barney."

"You wouldn't really give the boys those names would you?"

"Absolutely not! Josh can't tell when I'm serious or teasing these days, so I like to have a little fun with it. I need some entertainment, you know."

The two of them studied the list of baby names again. Callan went to Josh's office and returned with a pad of paper and a pen. She started writing out combinations of names they liked and when Jenna saw them on paper, the two she liked the best jumped out at her.

"Oh, Cal, circle those two, right there." Jenna pointed to two names on the list. "I love those names. I think Josh might go for them as well. What do you think?"

"I think they're perfect. Now, we just need to get that hard-headed brother of mine to agree."

By late morning, Jenna's eyes continued drifting shut. She took a nap while Callan did a load of laundry and fixed lunch. An hour later, Jenna awoke, but still didn't feel like eating. Callan made more tea and left her sipping it while she put away laundry then straightened the master bedroom.

"Do you want me to change the sheets on your bed?" Callan called out to the family room where Jenna rested.

"No. Josh just changed them yesterday."

"Okay," Callan said, walking back into the family room. "Anything else I can do for you?"

"I'm fine. I don't need a babysitter every minute. You've got a client appointment you need to leave for soon, don't you?"

"Yes, but I hate to leave you alone. I can reschedule if you want me to stay."

Jenna made a shooing motion with her hand. "I'm fine. Josh said he'd be home by four at the latest and it's almost one now. I think I can take care of myself for an hour or two."

Callan slipped on her coat, uncertain if she should leave or stay. "Are you sure you'll be fine?"

"Yes. I'm going to stay right here on the couch like a big lump and wait for Josh to get home. Thanks for coming. I appreciate it."

"You're welcome. I'll see you day after

tomorrow."

"You bet. I'll be here."

When Callan left, Jenna tossed and turned on the couch, trying to find a comfortable position. She rolled onto her side, but felt even more nauseated. Her back went from an unpleasant ache to sudden, sharp pain.

The twins seemed bent on wiggling nonstop. She wished they would settle down, just for a few minutes, so she could rest. Gently rubbing her stomach, she could tell they had dropped lower, a sure sign they would soon arrive.

Exhausted, she closed her eyes and was nearly asleep when a strong pain ripped through her. From the contractions she'd previously experienced, she sat up. The pain was real, not imagined. Concerned, she glanced at the clock on the wall, waited, and counted. When other contraction hit her followed by another, she took a deep breath. She needed to call someone to take her to the hospital.

Callan would be in her meeting by now and she always turned off her phone when she was with clients. Jenna called and left her a message, hoping the meeting would be brief.

Mentally running through a list of names of who else might be available, she knew Clay was in a class, Maggie and Jake were both working, and Bobbi and Steve were at the bull sale with Josh. Aunt Julie and Uncle Ralph were gone to Florida to visit their oldest son. Jenna grabbed the phone and dialed Josh, hoping he was already heading home.

"Hey, babe, how's it going?" Josh asked, answering his phone on the second ring.

"Josh," Jenna panted as a contraction slammed through her. "I just started having some serious contractions. You coming home sooner rather than later would be a good plan. Right now, if possible."

"Where's Callan?" Josh sounded upset. Jenna heard muffled voices then the sound of something thudding, like he was running.

"She had a client meeting and left a while ago." She gasped through another contraction. "Please say you're on the way."

"I'm on the way. I'll be there as quick as I can. Don't move. See if you can get in touch with Callan or even Laken. I don't want you there by yourself."

An engine revved and tires squealed in the background.

"Josh, drive carefully. I don't need anything happening to you."

"I will and I'll be praying the whole way."

Josh waited throughout the entire sale for the bull he'd been eying to be reach the auction block. He'd just engaged in a good-natured bidding war with an acquaintance from Sublimity when his cell phone rang.

As soon as Jenna said the word contraction, he handed his auction paddle to Steve and took off running. He peeled out of the parking lot, grateful the roads were clear and dry. A little more than an hour later, he whipped off the highway, glad he hadn't received a speeding ticket as he shaved twenty minutes off the normal travel time.

He jumped out of his pickup, hurried into the garage, and started Jenna's car. She'd be much more comfortable making the hour-long trip to the hospital in it.

When he ran into the house, he found Jenna on the couch, holding her stomach. Fear filled her eyes while her face held little color.

"Babe, it's going to be okay. Everything will be fine." Josh dropped to his knees on the floor in front of her and brushing the hair off her face. "Are you ready to go now?"

"Yes." Jenna breathed through another contraction. "I just need to go the bathroom again before we leave." Josh helped her to the guest bathroom and waited. He heard her gasp then all was quiet.

"Babe, everything okay?"

"Just a give me a minute."

Her voice sounded panicked and he wiggled the doorknob that she'd locked. "Do you need some help?"

"No!" Jenna yelled. The one thing she was going to do if it killed her was maintain what little dignity she had left with Josh. That meant he would not be emptying any bedpans, he would not assist her in the bathroom, and he most certainly was not getting a view of anything south of her equator.

"Just bring me a set of clean clothes, including socks and shoes, please." She'd barely closed the bathroom door when her water broke, soaking her clothes and puddling on the bathroom floor.

Josh turned and ran into their bedroom, quickly returning with a set of clothes for her. She cracked the door and took them from him before shutting the door again.

"Are you sure you don't need some help?"

"I'm sure." Jenna changed her clothes and threw towels over the mess on the floor.

When she finally opened the door, she looked determined yet frightened. "I think we better get a move on. My water just broke."

Josh blanched before grabbing her coat from a hook by the back door. Quickly helping her into it, he walked her to the car and helped her slide onto the passenger seat. He ran around to the driver's side and they made a fast trip to the hospital.

Jenna called her doctor to let her know they were on their way. Callan called back after receiving Jenna's message and said she would meet them at the hospital as soon as the girls got home from school and would spread the news that Jenna was in labor.

Through his mind-numbing fear, Josh struggled to remember everything they learned in birthing class. What if she went into full labor before they got to the hospital? He certainly couldn't deliver the boys, especially not in the car. Thoughts of everything that could go wrong spurred him to drive faster and send up urgent prayers that everything would be fine.

"You were in labor this morning when you shooed me out the door, weren't you?" Josh asked, looking at Jenna as she held onto the door in a death grip.

"Quite probably," she said as she worked through another contraction. "I thought I had indigestion. I haven't been able to get comfortable for a couple of days, so I really didn't think much of it. I honestly had no idea we'd be racing to the hospital this afternoon."

When they pulled up at the hospital door, Josh helped Jenna out of the car. They barely stepped inside when a nurse approached them with wheelchair.

"We're going to take your wife up and do an exam to see where we're at in this process. Once you're parked, one of the other nurses will bring you in. Okay?"

Josh nodded his head.

He ran back out and parked the car, grabbed Jenna's bag, then hurried inside. A nurse escorted him down a hallway to an elevator and through a series of corridors to the maternity ward. He arrived in the birthing room as Jenna struggled to breathe through another contraction. When she saw him, relief flooded over her face and she held out a hand to him.

Dr. Meliah whisked into the room and smiled at them both. "Everything looks good so far. You made it to thirty-seven weeks, Jenna. That is so awesome! I'm going to keep a close eye on you and let your labor progress naturally. We really want to keep on top of the preeclampsia, but you are doing splendidly. I'll check on you periodically, but if you need something, push the nurse call button or Josh can run out to the nurses' station." The doctor left the room with a promise to check back soon.

Josh sat down on a chair beside the bed, held Jenna's hand, and smiled. "We made it all the way here, babe. Can you believe it? We'll be saying hello to those two boys soon."

Jenna glared at Josh, panting through another

contraction. "I can believe it. It seems exceedingly real right at this moment."

"Oh," he mumbled, rubbing the back of her hand softly with his thumb. As he recalled what they learned in class, Josh spent the next few hours coaching and encouraging Jenna. She welcomed anything that would relieve her intense pain, so she was more than glad when the doctor offered an epidural. The needle caused Josh to wince and turn his head away. He could vaccinate cattle like nobody's business, but watching the doctor insert that huge needle into his wife was something else altogether.

Although she was exhausted, they continued working through her contractions. Josh thought the color of her face looked off, not just pale or flushed.

"Josh, something isn't right," Jenna said as panted through another contraction. "Please, Josh, go get someone. Something isn't right."

He ran out of the room and flagged down a nurse who hurried back, took one look at the monitors, and called for the doctor.

Dr. Meliah rushed into the room and watched the monitors. She nodded to one of the nurses, sending her scurrying from the room. The doctor turned to Jenna. "How does your head feel?"

"Like it will explode any minute." Jenna gasped as another contraction hit her.

"I was afraid of that. It looks like your blood pressure is getting higher instead of stabilizing. One of the babies looks to be under some stress as well. For your sake and his, I want to do an emergency C-section. We'll get a clear operating room and wheel you in as fast as we can. Since you already had the epidural, you'll be able to stay awake during the procedure. Do you want to watch it?"

"No," Jenna panted, clinging to Josh's hand. "Will the babies be okay?"

"I hope so, Jenna. We'll get them out here ready to meet you as soon as we can. Just hang in there a little while longer." Dr. Meliah turned and left the room.

In a matter of minutes, a nurse wheeled Jenna to an operating room while another took Josh to scrub. Once they were in the operating room, he sat next to Jenna's head, holding her hand while a screen above her stomach kept her from seeing what happened on the other side.

Terrified as he watched Jenna's face turn ghastly white during the last few contractions, Josh fought paralyzing fear. He continued to send up prayers for the safety of the babies and his wife. If something happened to Jenna, he didn't know how he could face another day.

While he prayed, Jenna had all she could do not to completely break down. If something happened to the twins, she'd never forgive herself for not wanting them in the first place. She wanted them so desperately now, she'd give up everything she had just to make sure they were healthy and safe.

As she turned her head to look at Josh, she stared into his warm gray eyes and found reassurance in his presence. "Josh," she whispered as he leaned closer. "Pray for them, Josh. Please pray for them."

Josh bent close to her ear and whispered the

heart-felt pleas he'd been uttering silently for the last hour. He recited one of Jenna's favorite Psalms and her eyes lost their look of desperation. Scooting as close as he could, he put one arm around her shoulders while the other grasped her hand.

"Here we go," Dr. Meliah said, glancing at them before focusing her attention on the delivery. "Are you sure you don't want to watch, Josh?"

"Positive." The sight of them giving Jenna an epidural made him queasy. He sure wasn't going to be able to watch them go through the surgery.

In no time at all, the doctor lifted the first baby and handed him to a nurse. He screamed with a loud, lusty cry and everyone smiled. He appeared to be a picture of health as the nurse cleaned him.

"He's a fine, healthy boy at six pounds, two ounces," the nurse said with a smile in her voice.

The second baby struggled with the umbilical cord wrapped around his neck. Dr. Meliah carefully untangled it and rushed the limp, quiet baby away from the surgery table. Time stood still until Josh and Jenna heard the cry of their second child. It wasn't a strong sound, but a mewling whimper. Uncertain as to what happened or what to do, Josh continued to hold Jenna's hand and whisper comforting words in her ear.

"They are both going to be just fine, Jenna. Just fine," Dr. Meliah reassured them over her shoulder.

Soon, two nurses stood next to them, each holding a crying baby boy. "Here are your boys," they said, handing the quiet baby to Josh and the first-born to Jenna.

"This tough guy is a little smaller," the nurse

said, touching the tiny bundle in Josh's arms. "He weighs five pounds, fifteen ounces, but he's going to give his brother a run for the money."

Josh smiled and kissed the baby's head, breathing in the scent of heaven. He thought his heart might burst with the love and joy filling it right at that moment.

Jenna looked at the precious baby in her arms and marveled at the miracle God had made, identical twin miracles. Head covered in dark hair, this baby with the strong set of lungs quieted when she began softly talking to him.

"Hey, baby, it's Mama. Welcome to the world. We love you so much." Jenna kissed his head and didn't try to stem the tears running down her cheeks. She looked over at Josh, holding their other son. The baby was a perfect match to the one in her arms. He also had a head of dark hair and seemed soothed to hear his daddy's voice. When Josh glanced at Jenna, his eyes sparkled with unshed tears.

"Thank you, Jenna, for this amazing gift." He leaned over and kissed her forehead as she reached out a hand to touch the baby. "Don't they seem like two living, breathing miracles?"

"Oh, Josh, they're so wonderful, so beautiful, aren't they?"

"They certainly are." He smiled down at her. "They look just like you."

Jenna grinned weakly. "You obviously still need to get your eyesight checked. They look exactly like you."

"You think so?" Josh asked, beaming in

pleasure. He suddenly remembered their inability to settle on names for the twins. "We never got around to picking out names. What are we going to call these two? We can't keep calling them 'the boys.' They need their own names."

"Your sister and I worked on that this morning." Jenna shared with Josh the names she and Callan liked the best. Josh immediately agreed they were the perfect names for their sons.

A short while later, Josh walked out to the waiting area where Callan and Clay sat along with Big Jim, Bobbie and Steve, Jake, Vivian and Dan, as well as Aunt Amelia and Uncle Phil.

When he stepped into the room, they all stood, anxious to hear any news. He grinned broadly as he looked at all the loved ones gathered to support them. "We've got two healthy baby boys and one mama who will be just fine."

Amid the cheers, hugs, back slapping and congratulations, Jake finally asked, "What did you name them?"

"Thanks to some help from Callan, the boys are going to be known as Jaret Cole and Jace Keaton, named after both our families." Cole was Josh's own middle name, his dad's middle name, and his grandmother's maiden name. Keaton, of course, was Jenna's maiden name. Jarct and Jace were two names they both liked.

"Those are perfect names, Josh," Vivian said as she gave him another hug. "Now, when can we see the babies and Jenna?"

Before Josh could answer, a nurse ran into the room. "Mr. Carver, we need you to come, quickly.

It's Jenna."

Josh turned his gaze to their gathered family and caught Callan's eye. "We'll pray," she said. He nodded before he hurried out of the room behind the nurse.

He reached Jenna's side. She was so pale her skin appeared translucent. An oxygen mask covered her nose and mouth, and her eyes were closed. As he took her hand in his, he looked at the doctor with fear in his eyes.

"We're doing everything we can, Josh, but her organs are starting to shut down and she had a seizure. On rare occasions, that happens with preeclampsia no matter how hard we try to stop it."

The doctor continued working while Josh continued praying. All of the sudden, a monitor started beeping.

"We're losing her!" A nurse looked at Dr. Meliah. "Come on. Don't give up now, Jenna."

The medical team worked frantically to keep Jenna alive. "Josh, maybe you better step back now." Dr. Meliah said.

Josh shook his head, and held Jenna's hand tightly in his own as he put his lips near her ear. "Jenna, don't you dare leave me now. We have two beautiful boys just waiting for us to take them home. I need you with me. I love you, babe. Always have, always will. Please don't give up. Please, Jenna."

"No pulse. She's flatlining!"

"Jenna, don't leave me!" Josh cried out. "Jenna, no!"

Epilogue

Four years later

Josh smiled at the tire store receptionist as she handed him an invoice to sign. Quickly writing his name and the date, he turned the paperwork back around to her and slid it across the counter.

"Those boys of yours are growing like weeds," the receptionist said, handing Josh his copy of the receipt as she looked over the counter at the twins, standing one on each side of their dad.

"They sure are," he said in agreement. He couldn't believe the boys were already past their fourth birthday.

The twins were identical in appearance except for their skin color. While Jaret had Josh's dark olive-toned skin, Jace's fair skin with a sprinkling of freckles across his nose came from his mother. They both had Josh's dark hair, gray eyes, and dimples in their left cheeks.

Jace, born with the cord wrapped around his neck at birth, was a little smaller and weaker than his twin. Jaret was protective of his brother, seeming to know he was the stronger of the two.

When they were tiny babies, they often wouldn't go to sleep unless Jaret had his arm or hand touching Jace.

Josh glanced down at the boys and smiled. Expectantly, they gazed up at him.

"Would you like some popcorn?" he asked, already knowing the answer. The tire store usually had fresh popcorn for their customers and the boys anticipated the treat whenever they stopped by.

"Yes, please," Jaret replied while Jace nodded.

Josh partially filled two small bags with the warm popcorn and handed them to the boys.

"Thank you," they both said as they dug their little hands into the bags and took a bite.

"You two ready to roll?" Josh herded them out the door with a wave to the receptionist.

"Yep, Daddy." Jaret vigorously nodded his head. "Let's roll."

Josh helped the boys into their car seats. His pickup would soon smell like popcorn, but he didn't mind. When he snitched a few kernels from Jace's bag, the little boy wrinkled his nose. It reminded Josh so much of their mother, it made his chest tighten with emotion. Both of his sons looked like him, but so many of their mannerisms reminded him of his beloved Jenna. "Daddy, that's mine."

"It is? I better even things up then." Josh stole a few pieces from Jaret's bag.

"Daddy!"

The boys started to giggle when Josh made a funny face at them.

"What do you think we should have for dinner tonight?" Josh asked as they drove home. In the rear-view mirror, he watched the twins devour their popcorn. They were sweet boys with nice manners, especially for four year olds. Josh was so proud of them, some days he thought he might burst.

"Burgers, please," Jace said, munching his popcorn.

"Yeah, burgers," Jaret agreed. "With a pickle."

"With a pickle? Who likes pickles?" Josh asked as they pulled into the driveway and he parked by the back door.

"I do! I do!" the boys yelled in unison.

"Why don't you two go play in the backyard for a while?" Josh set them down on the ground then carried a bag of groceries into the house.

Jace and Jaret ran into the backyard and hurried toward the tire swing hanging from a big oak tree. They reached out for it when a familiar voice called out to them.

"Where's my love, you two?"

The boys spun around and ran onto the back porch, into Jenna's open arms. "Hi, Mama!"

Both boys climbed onto her lap and gave her salty kisses before scrambling down and bouncing off one foot to the other.

"Mama, we got to help Auntie Callan plant flowers today and Uncle Clay had lunch with us and gave us horsey rides." Jace rested his hand on Jenna's leg as he looked at her excitedly, recalling their day spent at Callan and Clay's house.

"Auntie Callan said we are big boys and good helpers," Jaret added, leaning against his mother's other leg.

Jenna grabbed them both in a warm hug and

kissed them again. "Your Auntie Callan is correct. You are good helpers and big boys, and I love you very much."

"Love you, Mama," they said before running back out to their swing and jumping on it together. Jaret turned around and grinned, looking like a miniature of his father. "Daddy said we could have burgers with a pickle for dinner."

"Oh, he did, did he?" Jenna laughed when both boys nodded their heads so enthusiastically they nearly knocked off their little John Deere ball caps.

Jenna had been sitting in the backyard enjoying the warm April afternoon, waiting for her men to come home. As she leaned back against her anniversary bench, she ran a hand over the smooth wood and released a deep, contented sigh. Life was so good. She could hear the pivots cha-chinking as they watered the hay fields while the baby calves chased each other in the pasture behind the house. Watching them frolic and play reminded her of Jace and Jaret's antics.

Jenna worked two days a week in the office and spent the rest of her time working from home. Despite her initial reservations about how it would work, she discovered it was possible to have a successful and rewarding career while fulfilling her most important roles as a mother and wife.

Jace and Jaret had been miracles for which she daily gave thanks, along with her own spared life. Those two little boys, the babies she at one time vehemently wished would just disappear, meant everything to her, along with their daddy.

Josh had to be one of the best fathers. He'd

never shied from changing a diaper, sitting up when the boys were colicky, or rocking them to sleep. Now that they were bigger, he often took the twins with him so Jenna could have some peace and quiet while she worked. Callan kept the boys on Mondays while they spent Wednesdays in Portland with Aunt Amelia, having any number of adventures.

Jenna watched Josh walk out the back door with two glasses of iced tea and smiled.

"Hey, babe, I thought you might like a cold drink." He handed her a glass as he settled beside her. After placing his arm around her shoulders, he pulled her close and kissed her cheek.

"How did your day go?" he asked, taking a deep drink of the tea.

"Great. I was able to leave the office early. It was such a beautiful day, I just had to sit out here to enjoy the warmth and sunshine. How did the boys do with Callan?"

"Good. You know how much she and Clay enjoy having them."

"Almost as much as we do," Jenna said with a knowing smile.

Suddenly serious, she looked at Josh with love and warmth while he fell into the gorgeous depths of her eyes. "If I haven't mentioned it before, I am so grateful to you for giving me all this." Jenna waved her hand around for emphasis.

"All this?" Josh raised a questioning eyebrow at his wife. "All what?"

"You know what I mean." Jenna playfully smacked his leg when he shot her a cocky grin. "Thank you for giving me this beautiful farm, the peace of country life, our sons, and most of all, your love. You took on this city girl and turned her into a country lover. I can't imagine my life any other way."

"I can't imagine life without you in it, Jenna. When I think how close we came to losing you, it just makes me want to fall on my knees and thank God for leaving you here with me and the boys." Josh set down his empty tea glass and wrapped Jenna in his arms. "Thank you for loving this country boy enough to follow along with my dreams and make new ones together. I love you so much. Always have, always will."

"I love you, too." Jenna turned in Josh's arms to give him a kiss. Before their lips connected, she heard a little voice whispering loudly from behind the bench.

"I told you they were doing it again," Jaret said.

"Yep. They sure are," Jace agreed. He stood on his tiptoes and peeked over the back of the bench. "Mama, don't you get tired of kissing Daddy?"

"Never, Jace. Never, ever."

"That makes two of us." Josh bent his head so his lips hovered above hers. "Close your eyes, boys, or you'll see me kiss Mama again."

"Ewww!" The twins covered their eyes with their hands.

Josh and Jenna laughed, knowing in each other's arms, with their boys beside them, was the best place they could ever be.

Chocolate Bundt Cake

My husband's grandmother shared this recipe with me years ago. It's one I've made many, many times and it always turns out moist and delicious - guaranteed to make chocolate fans smile!

Chocolate Bundt Cake
1 box chocolate fudge cake mix
1 small box instant chocolate pudding
1 cup sour cream
½ cup water
½ cup oil
3 eggs
½ cup semi-sweet chocolate chips or chocolate squares chopped into chunks
½ cup chocolate frosting
Powdered sugar

Preheat oven to 350 degrees.

Combine cake mix, pudding, sour cream, water, oil and eggs in a large mixing bowl, beating on medium speed with a mixer until well blended. The batter will be really thick – but that is how you want it.

Stir in chips and spoon mix into a greased bundt pan.

Bake for an hour or until cake pulls away from edges of pan and toothpick inserted in the center comes out clean.

Let cool completely before turning onto a platter or cake stand.

In a microwave-safe pourable container (I use a cream pitcher) warm the frosting on high for about 10-12 seconds. Pour over the cake then dust with powdered sugar and serve.

Depending on how many chocolate lovers are around when you make this, you should get about 8-10 servings.

Want more *Women of Tenacity*?

Keep reading to see what happens when Jake Chandler finally meets the girl who captures his heart in *Heart of Love.*

Thank you for reading *Heart of Hope*. Oh, my goodness! It took a bit of work for Josh and Jenna to get their happily ever after, but I'm so excited for them with those two adorable little boys! If you enjoyed the story, would you please consider writing **a review**? I would truly appreciate it. Reviews are a wonderful way readers discover new books. Thank you.

If you haven't yet read them, I hope you'll check out the entire *Women of Tenacity* series!

Also, if you haven't yet signed up for my newsletter, won't you consider subscribing? I send it out when I have new releases, sales, or news of freebies to share. Each month, you can enter a contest, get a new recipe to try, and discover details about upcoming events. When you sign up, you'll receive a free digital book. Don't wait. Sign up today!

Shanna's Newsletter

And if newsletters aren't your thing, please follow me on *BookBub*. You'll receive notifications on pre-orders, new releases, and sale books!

Love is about to leave one charming cowboy thrown for a loop. . .

Heart of Love (Book 3) — Due to a birth defect that left her mostly deaf, Anna Zimmerman has spent her entire life lingering in the shadows. When a cowboy too handsome for his own good unexpectedly bumps into her, the encounter forces her to realize she needs a change. Determined to begin living the life she's always dreamed about, she grabs onto her courage and faces Jake head on.

Known as a good-time cowboy, Jake Chandler has left a string of broken hearts in his wake. Convinced there isn't a woman alive he can't tease or please into doing his will, he hits a wall when it comes to the shy librarian who works across the street. She's nothing like the women he typically dates, but she might just be the girl who can finally capture his heart.

Uplifting, amusing, and heartwarming, _Heart of Love_ captures the spectacular magic of first love, instant attraction, and sweet, sweet romance.

Continue reading for an excerpt from Jake and Anna's story.

Heart of Love

"There's one for you, Jake, ol' boy," Dave Roberts teased as he stared out the window of their shared office at the brilliant early spring afternoon.

"One what, Davey?" Jake Chandler asked his coworker and friend, not bothering to lift his gaze from the irrigation map he studied on the computer.

"What do you think, you knucklehead?" Dave tipped his head toward the window. "A girl, of course."

Jake glanced up from his work and looked out the window. A tall girl leaned against the brick wall of the county library building. She stood in the shadows, wearing outdated glasses, a baggy beige sweater, and a long skirt. A severe bun at the back of her head gave her the appearance of a stereotypical librarian. Immersed in reading a book, she remained unaware of the speculative stares cast her direction from the county extension office's soil and water department across the street.

"She's just your type." Dave smirked then leaned back in his desk chair with his fingers laced behind his red head.

"Idiot," Jake mumbled, returning his gaze to

the computer and his thoughts to the evening ahead. The date he'd soon be meeting was a beautiful, vivacious blonde who oozed confidence, along with a few other things.

Too bad he couldn't remember her name. *Vicki? Mickey? Rikki?* It would come to him before he picked her up at seven for dinner.

The girls he dated were shallow, often fickle, and not the type someone would take home to meet their mother, particularly his mother. However, as long as the girls were attractive, fun, and unattached, Jake didn't require much else.

He made it clear from the start that his sole interest was in having a good time. Jake thought it was only fair for the girls he dated to know he planned to stay free and unfettered.

No serious relationships.

No commitments.

None of those unnecessary things that sucked the excitement right out of life.

A few girls decided they could change his mind and failed. For the most part, though, his dating game plan worked out well. He enjoyed himself, the girls had a good time, and no one had any hurt feelings or unrealistic expectations.

Jake thought of his cousin, Clay, eighteen years his senior. With no siblings, Jake often looked to him as a role model, mentor, and older brother. Clay was married to the most incredible, wonderful, perfect woman in the world, at least in Jake's opinion. Jake had loved Callan since he was six years old and she treated him as she might have a little brother or son.

When Jake finally fell for a girl, he wouldn't settle for a love any less passionate, with any less depth or devotion than what Clay and Callan shared. Even after all these years together, it was blatantly obvious they were more in love with each other than ever.

Jake was smart enough to realize a love like that didn't come along every day. Until he found someone who completely captivated his heart, mind, body, and soul, he planned to keep on having a good time.

And good times didn't exist with shy librarians afraid of their own shadow.

Jake glanced out the window again and ran a hand through his thick, dark brown hair. The girl outside of the library appeared mousy. Timid and mousy.

A grotesque deformity could lurk beneath that oversized dirt-colored outfit big enough to house a linebacker. Not that he really cared. There was no way in the world he'd ever have an interest in dating her.

He turned to Dave and flashed a white-toothed grin. "You better run over there, Davey, and ask her out. She seems more like your type than mine." Jake saved his work, switched off his computer, stuffed papers into his briefcase, and settled a black Stetson on his head.

Dave chuckled as he gathered up his paperwork and prepared to leave for the day. "Nah, man. She's all yours."

Jake strolled out of the office and paused briefly to wait for a passing car before walking across the street. The county library, extension office, and the education service district shared an employee parking lot located behind the library.

For the past four years, Jake had enjoyed his work as a county soil and water specialist. After graduating from college, he worked at a biology lab in Portland, thinking he'd never move back to the small town where he grew up.

Six months later, he'd had enough of the bright lights and big city to last him a lifetime. Since he'd never fully leave behind his rural roots, he instead decided to embrace them.

His dad heard the county extension office was hiring and Jake immediately applied for the position.

At twenty-five, he and Dave were the two youngest employees at the office. They learned something new every day, but still managed to have a lot of fun. The receptionist, Millie, who'd been there for forty years, kept them all in line.

Briskly walking down the sidewalk, Jake whistled a tune and watched the traffic drive by. Completely forgetting about the girl leaning against the wall, he bumped into her and almost knocked her off her feet.

"I'm so sorry, miss," he said, grabbing her elbow to keep her from falling. His fingers tingled from the contact and he experienced the craziest urge to wrap both arms around her and hold her close. Disturbed by the sensation, he tried not to let it show. "I didn't see you there."

Startled, she gasped and pushed her glasses back up her nose. A very cute freckled nose, Jake noted from his position mere inches away from her.

He looked into her eyes and nearly lost himself in their violet depths. The unusual color astonished him but the way her eyes seemed to see beyond the surface into his very heart left him unsettled yet enthralled.

"Are you okay?" He released her elbow and stepped back. "I really am sorry."

"I'm fine. Thank you." She bent down to pick up the book he'd knocked from her hands.

"Here, let me get that." Jake retrieved the book and glanced at the cover. Much to his surprise, it wasn't a romance novel as he'd suspected, but a book about turf management he'd read for one of his college courses. "Interesting reading," he said, handing her the book. "I liked chapter six the best."

Meekly, she accepted the book and nodded her head in agreement, not making eye contact with him.

"Again, my apologies." Jake tipped his hat and continued down the sidewalk. Before he stepped around the corner into the parking lot, he stopped and looked back at the girl.

Dejected, she slumped against the wall, as if she'd lost her last friend.

At least he knew she wasn't deformed under that hideous get-up, although he still had no idea about her figure. She was taller than he expected — different from what he expected.

For reasons he couldn't explain, Jake started to walk to her, not sure why or what he would say. He stopped when a pickup pulled up to the curb. She rushed over to it and climbed in. As timid as she was, he was surprised she moved with such agility and grace.

Jake turned back toward the parking lot, hurried to his pickup, and slid behind the wheel. Polished and shined, the dark blue pickup was a source of pride for him. He liked things to look finished and detailed.

He kept his hair combed to perfection, his jeans neatly pressed, and his shirts precisely ironed. Over six feet tall barefooted, Jake stood out in a crowd, so he made sure he always dressed with care.

Girls paid attention to a man who put a little effort into his appearance. Most days, Jake put in a considerable amount.

His meticulous attention to his personal grooming had been a topic of Clay's jokes on more occasions than he wanted to remember.

Jake wasn't opposed to getting dirty. Anytime his job required fieldwork, he could guarantee he'd come home filthy. He also raised registered quarter horses, helped his parents with their small farm, and worked at his aunt and uncle's ranch whenever he had the time.

He had yet to find a way to keep neat and clean doing any of the tasks required by farm or ranch work, and that was fine by him. As long as he had time to clean up before he met a date, life was good.

Like the date he was meeting tonight. She was a knockout.

Jake smiled to himself as he pulled out of the parking lot and headed to his place to take a shower and shave before picking up Nicki. Ha! He did remember her name. Unfortunately, instead of seeing her heart-shaped face framed by wispy blond hair, he pictured a pair of soulful violet eyes.

Anna Zimmerman wanted to die and it couldn't happen too soon. As soon as her dad pulled up to the curb at the library, she jumped into his pickup, anxious to be home where she could be herself and relax.

"Hey, Sugar. How'd your day go?" her dad asked with his customary cheerfulness.

"Peachy, Dad. Just peachy." Anna stared glumly out the window.

She couldn't believe it when Jake Chandler bumped into her, knocking the book from her hands and all sense from her head. Even if he had no clue she existed, Anna recognized Jake as the handsome extension agent from across the street.

Convinced she couldn't have looked any worse if she'd tried, today had to be the day he'd accidentally bump into her.

She'd broken her glasses the previous week. Until her new glasses were ready, she had to wear an old pair that made her feel like a complete geek. Her unruly, wavy hair had been so unmanageable that morning, she'd simply pulled it back into a tight bun, lacking the time to battle it into submission. Between weight loss and a career change, her limited wardrobe included outdated castoffs from her high school days or baggy suits in neutral tones from her last job. Neither option did anything to accentuate her figure or bolster her confidence.

Although she'd toyed with the idea of purchasing a new wardrobe, she'd put it off mostly because she hated to go shopping. Instead of treating herself to new clothes, her recent wages from the library went into a car that was once again at the shop. And if the stupid car hadn't been broken down, she would have left the library via the back door, escaping the possibility of a chance encounter with Jake.

Embarrassed by her appearance, as well as her inability to speak coherently in his presence, she wished he hadn't bumped into her. It highlighted the extent of her miserable, lonely existence.

Certain she'd die an old maid living in a tiny apartment full of cats, Anna really wasn't very fond of house cats and hated the thought of spending her life alone and unloved.

It wasn't that she was unattractive. Anna was tall, with an hourglass figure, an abundance of wavy brown hair streaked with gold, and the most unusual violet eyes. Her problem attracting men stemmed from the fact she was bone-deep, to-the-core shy.

Four years of college and two years of employment in downtown Portland hadn't knocked it out of her. She wasn't sure, at this point in her life, anything would.

Her limited dating experience included three boys she'd been fixed up with by well-meaning relatives and friends. She hadn't made it past a second date with two of the guys, especially when she found it hard to speak to them and her stomach ached with nervous trepidation.

The third boy showed decided interest in her, but he bored her to tears. She spent part of her senior year of college hiding out from him before he finally got the message she didn't want to date him.

Years ago, her mother gave up trying to get her to "let her light shine." Anna had always preferred her lamp stay hidden in a corner with a heavy shade covering the top of it.

Lately, though, she'd experienced a growing urge to step out of the shadows and live a little.

The people who took the time to know the real Anna discovered someone intellectual, funny, and sweet with an underlying current of restlessness.

She possessed a sense of adventure and a streak of pure, wild passion. Anna had no idea how to deal with either, so she trapped those inclinations far beneath the surface where she could forget they existed.

The run-in with Jake made her idea of changing, of forcing herself out of her comfort zone, seem crazy.

"What's wrong, Sugar?" her dad questioned, giving her a sidelong glance. "Things not go well at work?"

"Work's fine, Daddy." Anna sighed. "It's just me. That's all."

Ken Zimmerman looked at his daughter with concern. He loved Anna and wanted to see her happy. She struggled with so many things, especially confidence. If he could buy it for her, she'd have more than she would ever need.

Unfortunately, what she needed was something

only she could give herself. Anna was a lovely girl, inside and out, but she tended to shy away from people, avoid relationships, and remain aloof. He supposed he and his wife, Sue, were partially to blame.

Anna was born deaf in her right ear with extremely limited hearing in her left. Over the years, they shielded her as much as they could from the cruelty of the world. Anna's shy nature seemed to have compounded the problem. Around strangers, she was very quiet, withdrawn, and unsure. If people took the time to get to know her, they'd have a loyal friend for life.

Disheartened, Ken wished more people took the time to get past the protective shell she tended to show the world. He reached over and gave her shoulder a reassuring squeeze.

Anna sighed again, but turned to offer her dad a sincere smile. "Thanks for picking me up, Daddy. I know you were busy today. Did you make any sales?"

"You bet I did!" Ken grinned. "I love spring when everyone gets excited for something new." He sold farm equipment for the local John Deere dealer and ranked as one of the top salesmen in the region.

"That's great, Daddy." Anna mustered some enthusiasm for her father's successes.

The further they drove out of town, the more she dropped her defenses and relaxed. She would be the first to admit she put up walls around herself. She developed the habit when the kids at preschool taunted her about her inability to hear as well as the way she talked.

Phonics were a nightmare that Anna didn't think she'd ever completely overcome, another reason she tended to be quiet around strangers. To compensate for her lack of verbal communication, she studied everything she could get her hands on. As a result, she was bright, intelligent, and well read. Her slight mispronunciation of some words was the price paid when a deaf girl learned to talk.

After failing to utter one intelligent word to Jake Chandler, he most likely thought she was a complete bumbling idiot. It would have been bad enough if the situation had happened with anyone else, but it had to be Jake.

Anna developed a crush on him the first week she'd started working at the library a couple of months ago.

There wasn't a female working within a four-block radius of the extension office that hadn't noticed the tall, handsome cowboy with the summer-sky blue eyes, chiseled jaw, and model-perfect physique. A girl would have to be blind or comatose to overlook him.

Despite her attraction to him, or maybe because of it, she hoped he'd forget he'd seen her.

As her Dad turned down the lane that led to their farm, Anna took a deep, cleansing breath. It was good to be home.

When they walked inside the kitchen together, she smiled as her dad kissed her mom on the cheek.

"How was your day, Susie-Q?" Ken used the nickname he'd bestowed on his wife nearly thirty years ago.

"Just fine. It feels good to be back to work full-time," Sue said as she started setting out the makings for tacos.

Last fall, Sue had been riding with their son, Sam, in his car when an impatient driver decided to pass another car in a deep fog and hit them head on.

Sue spent months recovering from a broken arm, shattered collarbone, and cracked pelvis. Recently, she returned to full-time work as the office manager at an investment firm in Tenacity.

Sam wasn't quite as fortunate as Sue, suffering partial paralysis from the waist down. He worked to recover from the collision both physically and emotionally.

Before the accident, he was a fun-loving cocky guy with the world on his string. He was engaged to a lovely girl, had his own apartment over the barn, and ran the farm while Ken worked at the equipment sales job.

Now, Sam was quiet, withdrawn, and grappling to find a way to get past his bitterness while overcoming his physical challenges.

"Let me change and I'll help you finish dinner, Mom," Anna said as she hurried to her bedroom. At twenty-four, living at home with her parents, it seemed like she'd taken huge steps backward in her life. After the accident, she quit her job in Portland and returned to the farm. Her family needed her more than she needed her independence.

She finished braiding her hair and secured the end with an elastic hair band as she walked into the kitchen. Anna felt confident and strong at home, where no one would make fun of the way she spoke or act offended if she didn't hear what they said.

Home was her comfort zone, fortress, and refuge.

"Hey, Sam!" Anna smiled at her brother when he rolled into the kitchen in his monster-truck version of a wheelchair that allowed him to get around on farm with relative ease. "How's it going?"

"Just dandy, for a cripple," Sam responded. She caught a wry grin as he turned his wheelchair around to face the dining table.

Anna rolled her eyes and faced her mom. One of these days, the Sam they used to know would resurface. She was sure of it. Little bits had started to emerge in the last month. The warmer weather helped his attitude and outlook.

Immediately after the accident, Sam was so angry. He struck out at everyone and everything. His fiancée, Lisa, was beside herself when he called off their engagement and told her he never wanted to see her again. It was a good thing Lisa ignored his protests and continued to be a solid support during his months of recovery. Although their wedding plans lingered in limbo, Anna held a surety that they would find a way to make a life together. They loved each other too much not to try.

Sam, who treasured every stem of hay, blade of grass, and stalk of wheat that grew on the farm, battled to adjust to the fact that he could no longer do what he loved — farm.

Despondent and ready to give up, Sam reluctantly agreed to see a new therapist Sue located in Portland. Mel came to the house four times a week and put Sam through hours of grueling exercises and massages. After a month of work, the family could see real progress. Despite many doctors predicting a life bound to his wheelchair, Sam had a glimmer of hope something more might be in store for his future.

Since his initial sessions went so well, Sam now visited Mel three times at week at his facility in Portland. There, he had access to unlimited equipment and a therapy pool. With the settlement from the accident, Sam had purchased a hand-controlled car. A simple thing like driving himself to his appointments gave him a returned sense of freedom he'd missed since the accident.

As she helped her mom finish preparing the meal, Anna handed the plates and cutlery to Sam so he could set the table. Her dad hurried out to feed the livestock and returned as they placed the last dish on the table.

"Perfect timing, as usual." Ken grinned while he washed up at the sink. Once he sat down at the table, they all bowed their heads and he said grace.

The conversation around the table held a lively tone until Sue asked Anna about her day.

"It was fine, Mom." Anna toyed with the taco on her plate.

"It doesn't sound like it was fine. What happened?" Sue knew she'd have to dig before Anna would confess what bothered her.

Anna continued moving salsa around on her plate. "I made a complete fool of myself today."

"You do that every day," Sam teased, as only a brother can.

Anna looked up long enough to shoot him an icy glare. He didn't notice, since he was already receiving a warning look from his mother.

"What happened, Sugar?" Ken asked. Curious, he wanted to know what disaster Anna thought had befallen her this time. For some reason, things that wouldn't bother most people deeply affected his daughter. Maybe it had to do with her self-confidence or her general fear of people. Whatever caused it, he wished he knew a cure for it.

"I was waiting for Daddy outside the library, reading a book and not paying attention. The next thing I knew, Jake Chandler bumped into me and the book went flying. I was so embarrassed." Heat warmed her cheeks as she recalled the incident and Anna refused to make eye contact with anyone at the table.

"And?" Sue asked, confused. "Surely, there has to be more to the story for you to be so upset."

"He handed me the book and went on his merry way." Anna huffed in frustration. How could her family not understand the magnitude of this chance encounter?

Baffled, Sue looked at Ken while Sam reached for another taco, wisely keeping his thoughts to himself.

"How did that make you look foolish?" Sue placed a gentle hand on Anna's arm. "I think you left out something."

"Because I'm a big klutz and dropped my book and I couldn't have looked any worse today if I'd tried," Anna said, exasperated.

Abruptly, Sue turned to Sam and asked him

about his therapy session.

Anna finished her dinner with her temper on a high boil. Obviously, no one cared that she'd been humiliated. Or that the one guy she had any interest in happened to be the one who bumped into her on a day when she looked like a fashion disaster.

Jake would never give her a second glance. The impact of that, the importance of that, was beyond her family's ability to comprehend. As soon as the dishes were finished, Anna started out the back door but her mom stopped her before she could escape.

"Anna, do you have a crush on this Jake Chandler? Is that the problem?" Sue tamped down a smile as she held Anna by the shoulders, forcing her to look into her face.

"Mother!" Anna drew out each letter until it sounded like a six-syllable word. "Please!"

"Please what?" Sue squeezed Anna around her shoulders as they stood at the door. "I think you like this Jake person and that's what has you so upset. You didn't do anything to look foolish. He bumped into you. Was he rude? Did he say something to upset you?"

Anna released a long sigh. "No. He was very polite and apologized. He picked up the book and handed it to me and commented about what chapter he liked best, then apologized again and left."

Sue couldn't stop the smile that bloomed on her face. "He sounds like a very nice young man, Anna. He probably didn't think a thing of it. You shouldn't either. You have to try not to be so sensitive, sweetie. Someday, someone will come along who appreciates all you have to offer and recognizes you as a beautiful, intelligent, hard-working girl."

"That is never going to happen, Mom."

Available now!

About the Author

PHOTO BY SHANA BAILEY PHOTOGRAPHY

USA Today bestselling author Shanna Hatfield is a farm girl who loves to write. Her sweet historical and contemporary romances are filled with sarcasm, humor, hope, and hunky heroes.

When Shanna isn't dreaming up unforgettable characters, twisting plots, or covertly seeking dark, decadent chocolate, she hangs out with her beloved husband, Captain Cavedweller, at their home in the Pacific Northwest.

Shanna loves to hear from readers. Connect with her online:

Blog: shannahatfield.com
Facebook: Shanna Hatfield's Page
Shanna Hatfield's Hopeless Romantics Group
Pinterest: Shanna Hatfield
Email: shanna@shannahatfield.com

CPSIA information can be obtained
at www.ICGtesting.com
Printed in the USA
BVHW040913150820
586519BV00014B/728